CHARLOTTE

Carol Leyland

Copyright © 2023 by Carol Leyland.

All rights reserved. No part of this book may be used or reproduced in any form whatsoever without written permission except in the case of brief quotations in critical articles or reviews.

This book is a work of fiction. Names, characters, businesses, organizations, places, events and incidents either are the product of the author's imagination or are used fictitiously. Any resemblance to actual persons, living or dead, events, or locales is entirely coincidental.

Printed in the United Kingdom.

For more information contact :

carolleyland73@gmail.com

Book design by Josie Hammond Stone

Cover design by Heather MacPherson

ISBN: 9798397145978

First Edition: October 2023

To Pam with love and gratitude xx

Acknowledgments

There are many people I'd like to thank for their support and wishes over the past year whilst writing this book. The biggest thanks go to my children Damian, Rowan and Eleanor, love you all to the moon and back.

To all the Julie's, the two Lou's, my bestie Debs, Katie, Maggie, Jemima, Susan and Jo (the Muffs) thank you for your encouragement through this. To Jill and Adele big thanks for proof reading and for listening to my brain unravel this past 9 months.

To Amanda for the encouragement to keep going when I wanted to quit, Suzanne for early morning coaching and Mable and Molly for late night cuddles. And to Jules for reading it on train journeys and your feedback and kindness.

Special thanks to Heather McPherson and Josie Hammond-Stones for the cover photo work and the graphic design.

I can't thank you all enough for your love, care and support.

And to all the late bloomers, it's a scary path to take, but when taken with baby steps and the support of some fabulous friends, anything is possible. You've got this.

1
New Beginnings

Alice stood in the doorway of her cottage, eyes full of tears, looking at the remnants of her marriage being loaded onto the removal lorry. Her so-called happy life she'd lived for the past ten years with her supposed soulmate Sally, blown apart. Her long blonde hair draped around her face, shielded her tears from passers-by in the street. She retreated into the house to pack the remainder of her clothes into her suitcases, and a multitude of books into boxes the removals company had left for her.

The chocolate box cottage in Terrington was situated near Castle Howard, an affluent area which claimed many doctors, solicitors, and business owners as its occupants. They'd all been shocked at the sudden sale of the house which had been remodelled within an inch of its life. The same house which had provided the backdrop to many lively BBQ's and parties. Where caterers and designers had been frequent visitors.

Alice had come out late in life, falling in love with Sally at the age of 40, leaving her husband of twenty years for the lesbian life she had craved since the age of 18. She'd romantically believed that it was forever and had been living the dream until the Sally had broken her heart. Their life together had been a fresh start for Alice, no one knowing her past, and feeling free within herself, more than she had ever done.

Over the years, prior to coming out, Alice had many lesbian friends she had confided in, but had never dared to make the leap until she was swept off her feet by Sally at a party. What had followed was months of turmoil of being desperate to be with Sally but not wanting to break her husband Harry's heart. But the heartbreak had been inevitable. Harry and his family, who had become Alice's too, disowned her.

Alice felt alone in her misery and had piled on weight since the breakup with Sally. She felt utterly unlovable, rejected and ugly.

The divorce to Sally had been swift, she'd rolled over and not fought anything, her heart too broken, going against what all her friends advised. Sally's legal brain had so much more time to organise her side of things, as she'd been planning to leave for at least a year.

She'd come out with what she'd put into the cottage five years ago, with Sally taking the lions share. She'd always earned more money than Alice's university history lecturer salary. So, in her panic of needing a place to live, she'd scoured the internet for months to find somewhere, settling on a house in need of a lot of work because it was all she could afford. Alice initially thought it would give her something to think about, other than her anger and broken heart, but now moving day was here, she was having second and third thoughts. Its attraction had been its character and that it was close to work without too much of a commute, and it meant she could socialise with her friends without having to drive miles home.

The removers passed her in the living room with the large pink sofa, squeezing it expertly out of the small cottage doors. Most of the furniture had been claimed by her ex-wife Sally, things that they had chosen together, things that Alice had bought for Sally, pieces of her life and heart disappearing before her eyes. Following them to the front door she stood and watched as the removals man waved as he closed the back doors of the lorry and climbed into the cab next to his workmates.

The removal truck pulled away, just as Jen her best friend arrived in her works van, which contained a donated divan bed and assorted kitchen items her friends had pulled together for her. They all knew the pain of a lesbian drama and subsequent breakup, and they'd all supported her as best they could. Jen jumped down from the van, she was wearing oversized dungarees and sauntered up to Alice with an exaggerated swagger.

'What on earth are you wearing?' asked Alice, her tears subsiding and a smile appearing on her tired face. 'And what have you done to your hair?'

'It's a lesbian toolbelt darling, what every handy girl needs! Don't you like the shaved look? It's great for the summer' she giggled, roughing her hand over the top of her head. 'How are you doing? Bearing up?'

'Just about, I've stacked my boxes in the kitchen' said Alice, walking through the lovingly created kitchen with a large white island and white marble tops. 'You're like a chameleon Jen, just as I get used to one hair style you turn up with another'.

'Like to keep Holly on her toes, she likes a bit of variety' said Jen with a cheeky grin and a wink.

Alice smiled but then a wave of sadness hit her.

'Just look at the Aga, isn't it just the most beautiful one you've ever seen? I can't believe someone else is going to get to use and love it.' Her face crumpling as the tears flowed down her face. Jen pulled her into a big hug, handing her a tissue, pulled from one of her many pockets.

'Come on, let's say goodbye to the house. It's a shit thing to happen, but you'll be ok, we've all got your back' said Jen as she started taking boxes effortlessly to the van. 'How many fucking books? Are you making your own sodding library?'

'I've an addiction to books' Alice said with a wry smile. 'A girl's allowed her guilty pleasures in a time of crisis.'

Jen loaded the van as Alice did a final check around the house, closing and locking the door and posting her key through the letterbox.

She stood back and took one last look at the detached house with four windows and a door in the centre, just like the house in Playschool, with the quintessential English roses around the door, it looked at the peak of its beauty.

'Goodbye country idyll' said Alice sadly, the feeling of loss gripped her chest, making her breathless. 'Let's go before I break back in and claim squatters' rights. You go first, I'll follow.'

The drive down to York was swift, and seeing the luscious green hedges and fields dissipate to be replaced by concrete, traffic and the waft of pollution, only added to the sense of grief. The sun had gone to be replaced by dark clouds, looming ominously down from the sky.

Jen pulled up in front of a row of houses, the grey day echoing the mood of Alice, as she parked her car on the drive, and looked up at the flaking façade.

'I've got this,' said Alice, 'I'VE got this' taking the bunch of keys from her jeans pocket.

'Come on Alice, it's going to be ok, YOU HAVE got this,' interjected Jen, 'It's going to be ok, and look at what you bought, it's gorgeous, or it will be.'

'Ok let's see if its miraculously updated itself since I last saw it.' Alice slid the key into the lock and cautiously opened the door, which opened into a long narrow hall, with dark old carpets, the walls were orange with peeling anaglypta wallpaper. 'Well, it looks like I've work to do doesn't it! The skip comes tomorrow so that'll keep me busy won't it.'

The two friends walked around the house, the living room with the same walls and carpet, a theme that flowed into the dining room with a step down into the kitchen which wouldn't have been out of place in a 1950's drama.

'Fuck my actual life, this should be in a museum, are you keeping it?' said Jen, opening and closing Formica drawers and cupboards.

'No, all the backs are rotten, it needs taking back to the brick and treated so it must go, shame though. Let's have a look upstairs.' said Alice leading the way.

The spindle staircase was original, and would once have been very impressive, however it had been painted and over painted many times, and now was a shade of nicotine.

The bathroom was out of the ark, with a large cast iron bath with ancient toilet and basin. Alice flushed the toilet and ran the taps. 'Well at least they work, one less thing to worry about,' laughed Alice.

Jen, eager to see more, bounded into the front bedroom, 'Bloody hell, look at this fireplace, now this is a gem.' Jen stroked the mantlepiece top, peering up the chimney, swiping away cobwebs and long dead spiders with her hand.

The back bedroom was half the size of the one at the front but had a similar fireplace and mantel.

'I was thinking of renting out this room, what do you think?' asked Alice. 'It's still a decent size and will be nice and quiet'. Alice walked over to the fireplace intending to repeat what Jen had done in the other room, leaning forward and balancing on one leg, when the floorboard moved, so she toppled and fell hard onto the floor.

'Ouch, oh shit don't tell me the floorboards are rotten!' Alice looked down at the floor, covered in the same dark carpet, full of dust and fluff, the floorboards rocking under her hands as she pushed down. Jen and Alice pulled at the edges of carpet around the hearth and heaved them back. Underneath was another carpet.

'I'm going to need my Stanley knife to get these up. Better unload the van and I can worry about that tomorrow, better put my bed in the dining room so I can look at the floor when the skips here, what do you think?' asked Alice.

'Sounds like a bloody good plan' said Jen, 'Better get cracking, I'm taking Holly out for dinner for her birthday tonight.'

'Yes mistress, god forbid I get in the way of your love life' laughed Alice with a hint of jealousy.

Jen and Holly had been together since they were teenagers, blissfully happy, living a drama free lesbian life, which seemed such a rarity these days. Sally and Alice had met years later resulting in her coming out, so they'd shared the ups and downs of relationships, commitment and buying and selling houses. However, since Sally had her head turned by a woman twelve years her junior, Jen and Holly had been her rock.

Sally had thankfully moved away to start her own law practice, which removed the fear of bumping into her, but the feeling of anger and loss lay heavy on Alice's heart. She felt the tears welling in her eyes, wiping them away with her hand.

'Alright, let's get the van emptied so you can get your glad rags on! Just think of me sat here surrounded by boxes with my takeaway pizza' Alice said pulling herself together. She'd cried enough tears over that woman.

After Jen had left Alice felt anxiety rise within her, the silence in the house was more than she thought she could bear. She'd struggled with it her whole life, but it had become increasingly worse since the divorce. Just as Alice began to feel the panic rise, there was a gentle knock at the door.

Alice peered through the peep hole to see a tall, dark-haired woman stood on the doorstep. Opening the door cautiously, she was greeted by the biggest, widest smile.

'Hey, sorry to disturb you on moving day. I'm Charlie, I live next door, welcome to the neighbourhood' she said handing over a large arrangement of roses and gerberas in a glass vase. 'I thought you wouldn't have had time to unpack, so I improvised.'

'Wow, hi, thank you. I'm Alice. Come through to the kitchen' she said walking down the hall.

'Blimey, you've got your work cut out here. It's like a time capsule' said Charlie looking around. 'The agent told me today was the day, so I kept my eye out. You'll love the street; we're a lovely bunch.'

Charlie was wearing a smart navy jacket and trousers and a white shirt with cufflinks, which contrasted with her spiked hair, nose ring and silver labret piercing. Alice drifted off, distracted by the cufflinks and the piercings, she realised that Charlie was still talking, reeling off a list of names and professions of her neighbours, Alice stared blankly at her.

'Sorry too much information, I'm a bit like Tigger, sorry! Do you need a hand with anything?' Charlie had the kind of smile where her eyes sparkled brightly, Alice felt mesmerised. 'Was that your friend? Girlfriend?'

Pulling herself together swiftly she responded 'No, that spitfire of energy was my best friend Jen, she's been a super star helping me move. Did you know the previous owner?'

'Yeah, a lovely woman called Eliza. She was in her eighties when she died but was as fit as a fiddle, so it was a bit of a shock'.

'Bless her. Oh, I think the name on the deeds was Eliza. It's such a lovely house but it needs a lot of work doing to it, so I apologise in advance for the noise', said Alice grimacing.

'Don't worry it's cool. I'm out all day so it won't bother me. Moving's a nightmare isn't it' said Charlie stretching her long arms above her head and yawning.

Alice caught sight of the edge of a tattoo on Charlie's arm and felt her stomach flip.

'It's making me feel tired at the thought! You and your mate look familiar, did you used to go to Valentine's?' asked Charlie.

Valentines was York's only gay café which reverted to a bar in the evenings.

'Yes, but not for a couple of years I don't think.' replied Alice frowning at Charlie, wondering why she'd randomly asked her that.

'Ah that's probably where I recognise you from. I've just taken it on,' said Charlie casually. 'It's closed at the minute for a full refurb. Grand reopening's the 1st of July, fingers crossed. You won't recognise the place'.

'Sounds fantastic' Alice said, 'I'll tell Jen and Holly tomorrow when I see them'.

'Great, ok well I'll leave you to it, unless you want a hand with anything?' asked Charlie.

'No, it's ok thanks, once I'm more organised, I'll invite you round for coffee, when I've found the cups!' laughed Alice, realising that she was beginning to feel more comfortable in her new surroundings than she could have hoped for, and her anxiety had gone.

'Enjoy the unpacking' said Charlie leaving, closing the door behind her.

After Charlie left, Alice walked around the house looking at the piles of boxes and began unpacking the basics, finally going into where her bed was set up in the dining room. The tall sash window was overlooked by the neighbours behind, so Alice began opening more boxes in search of her bedding and a blanket to hook over the curtain pole until she could get herself sorted with blinds.

Once made, her bed looked so inviting that she stripped off and crawled under the duvet. The thoughts of pizza and unpacking long forgotten.

2

The Tale of Two Carpets

Despite the blanket at the window, the early morning summer sun streamed into the dining room waking Alice. As much as she tried to return to sleep, she couldn't, her brain was already on overdrive with all the things that she'd to do that day. Alice picked up her phone to see the time, only to find it had died in the night.

Spying her suitcase on the floor she found a pair of pyjamas and her phone charger and headed to the kitchen. Jen had put the kitchen boxes in there already and upon opening, Alice found her donated toaster, kettle, cutlery, and a bag of food with tea, coffee, bread and two jars of her favourites, peanut butter and marmalade. She smiled, plugging in her phone, and putting two slices into the toaster, suddenly realising she was starving.

After eating, her phone started beeping with notifications of messages, emails, and WhatsApp's. Most were from friends, but there was also a diary reminder of the skip delivery which spurred Alice into action. There were still a couple of hours before it arrived, so she set about unpacking the kitchen items then went for a shower. Once dressed in her faithful, comfy old black jeans, and a T shirt bearing the name of her favourite band The Chameleons, she felt set up for the day and ready for whatever it might bring. Sitting cross legged on her bed she set about looking on the internet for furniture. With all the house renovations costs, Alice knew she had to cut back on her expenses so had already decided to opt for second hand furniture. Surprisingly finding there was a shop nearby called Lavender Interiors that sold upcycled furniture which had a selling page. Before long she'd selected two armchairs, a big sofa, and a farmhouse style table and chairs with painted legs and oak top. They even offered local delivery so she fired off an email to the shop asking if they would hold the items until the house was finished. Alice thought how amazing it was to just click, click, click, and you had all you could need, without leaving the comfort of your bed.

Suddenly, Alice heard the beeping sound of a reversing lorry announcing the arrival of the skip. Alice grabbed her car keys and ran out of the house to move her car so that the skip could go onto the driveway, waving her hands frantically as she ran.

'Wait, wait, let me move my car!' rushing into the driver's seat of her car, reversing into the road and parking at the side as the lorry dropped the skip with a loud thump.

'Have you paid?' asked the lorry driver unhooking the chains from the big yellow skip, then dropped the front down for ease of putting things into the skip.

'Yes, I paid on the phone when I booked' doubting herself as she said it in that guilt way you get when your brain is not functioning at full capacity.

'Let me just ring the office and check' he said gruffly climbing up to his cab and slamming his door. Obviously, he wasn't a morning person, and Alice's reply hadn't convinced him at all.

Standing on the pavement at the front of her house Alice was very aware of the racket that her household was bringing to the street at such an early hour on a Saturday. Just then, adding to the noise, her phone rang so she hastily pulled it out from her pocket and answered it.

'Morning Alice how was your first night?' asked Holly 'Jen and I wondered if you fancied some company and some extra hands.'

'That'd be lovely. How was your birthday? Thought you'd still be in bed recovering'.

'Long story, we'll bring lunch, see you about 12,' said Holly ringing off.

The lorry driver was back in his cab and waved goodbye as he accelerated down the street, the bill obviously had been paid.

Alice looked around to see if there was sign of life in the street, but all was quiet, with a lot of curtains still closed. All except Charlie's next door whose shutters were opened.

Alice was just walking into the house when Charlie came out.

'Hey neighbour, how was your first night?' asked Charlie, who today was wearing black jeans, boots and a white T Shirt which revealed two full arm sleeve tattoos. She looked like a walking work of art.

'Very well thanks, sorry if the skip disturbed you' apologised Alice, feeling another flutter in her stomach which confused her.

'Nah, not at all, I'm just heading to the deli for some fresh bread, I can highly recommend it, can I get you anything?' said Charlie smiling. 'I'm a carb girl'.

'Me too,' said Alice smiling. 'I don't suppose you've a couple of minutes to hold the other end of a tape measure for me. I need to buy some curtains and order the blinds; I made do with a blanket over a pole last night'.

'Ingenious' replied Charlie raising an eyebrow. 'Sure, happy to help, I could see if I've some curtains you could borrow if you like?'

'That'd be amazing, thanks' answered Alice smiling. This really was a lovely road thought Alice.

'Great, let's sort the measuring and I will come round later with some, which room are you sleeping in?'

They both went indoors, and Alice pointed out her temporary bedroom in the dining room. Alice explained what had happened and Charlie laughed at the suggestion of rotten floorboards.

'These houses are really well built, it's probably just loose,' said Charlie reassuringly.

They set about measuring, which was so much easier with two people. Charlie told Alice about her plans for Valentine's, and Alice told Charlie about what she wanted to do with the house.

'Would you like a cup of tea? I've found some cups. Or do you have to get going?' asked Alice making the final notes of measurements on her phone.

'Sadly not, rain check? Busy day for me, and I need my carbs before then,' replied Charlie heading for the front door. 'I'll pop in with the curtains later, if you're out I'll leave them on the doorstep, they'll be safe there'.

'Thanks. Ok, well if you're free sometime just give me a knock if you see the light on' replied Alice smiling.

With that Charlie left. Alice spent a pleasant hour online looking at a multitude of blind and curtain fabrics, bookmarking them for when the work was over.

The fact that she was distracting herself with house stuff wasn't lost on Alice, the silence in the house was, as is often said deafening, but outside there was a definite hum of the city going about its business, people going to work, shopping and of course with it being York, towards a hive of tourist attractions. Although Alice had lived in the York area all her life, she rarely visited the inner city itself because of the traffic and crowded streets, all clambering to see the sights, or to grab a bargain in one of the many shops. In the 1990's two large out of town shopping centres were built to accommodate the bigger superstores and it was there that Alice needed to visit to sort out a fridge-freezer and cooker. It felt a waste to have to buy them for such a short period of time, as once the new kitchen was fitted, she wouldn't need them anymore, but she couldn't manage without them before that.

Alice headed off in the car, the internet, although incredibly good in many ways, sometimes it was better to just go in person. Luckily the traffic was light and soon she was wandering around the shop full of all things white and gleaming. They all seemed to do the same thing, but the prices were so varied. Alice stood shaking her head in bemusement, there seemed far too much choice, the assistant's voice became inaudible, and the lights and the walls of the vast hanger of a building began closing in. Everything seemed so overwhelming.

Oh god, oh god thought Alice the anxiety building. She just wanted to run back to the comfort of her old country cottage where everything had seemed safe. Her legs didn't seem to want to hold her up, so she leaned heavily on the nearest cooker, the large lights were too bright, and the floor felt like it was moving up towards her. Alice quickly made her apologies to the assistant, then stumbled out of the shop to her car, her breath catching in her throat, her heart pounding. She reached for her phone and called Jen.

'Omg Jen, I don't feel well. Is Holly there?' Alice spoke in a whisper.

'Yes, yes, she's here, Holly, come help Alice, she's having a do!' shouted down the phone.

'Ouch!' said Alice pulling the phone away from her ear.

'Hi Alice, what's happening? Your old friend anxiety has returned?' said Holly in her soft best bedside manner. 'Have you started your breathing?'

'No, my brain is mush, I can't remember what to do,' said Alice.

'Ok, put me on speaker phone and put the phone on the seat, sit with your head back and close your eyes' instructed Holly.

'Ok' responded Alice, doing as she was told to.

'Now breathe in for five, hold for five and then breathe out for five, you've got this, promise. Let's do it together,' said Holly.

They spent a couple of minutes breathing over the phone, Holly interjecting with kind words of reassurance.

'Where are you?' Asked Jen.

'I'm at Clifton Moor trying to buy electricals' replied Alice, her breathing returning to its normal rhythm, and her head starting to focus.

'Do you want us to come and get you, or can you get home if we stay on the phone?' said Jen,

'I can drive now I think if you stay on the phone' said Alice putting her key in the ignition.

'Great, we'll set off now and meet you there, big hugs,' said Holly.

The three of them chatted as they all made their journeys across York to Alice's house. Alice arrived first and found a bag with some curtains from Charlie on the doorstep, which she put on her bed ready to put up later. She'd just put the kettle on when there was a knock at the door and Jen and Holly came in carrying three garden chairs, toolbox and a hessian bag with packets bulging out of the top. Holly, put down the bag and came towards Alice with her arms outstretched. This show of affection melted her, and she felt the release of months of stress escaping out of her, with large fat tears drenching Hollys curly hair and down her back. It was one of those hugs where you know that you're totally safe, and all is well. *Everyone needs a friend who hugs like that* thought Alice.

'It'll be ok you know. The worst bit's over. Let's go sit in the front room and talk it through if you want to?' said Holly rubbing Alice's back soothingly.

Alice shook her head and replied 'No, I feel better after a good cry, sorry to drag you here on a rescue mission'.

'Don't be daft. We were coming anyway remember. Come on, show me round your lovely house, it looks a brilliant project.' Holly said, linking her arm through Alice's as they took a tour around the house, finishing in the back bedroom where she'd taken a tumble the previous day.

'And this is where I tried to break the house' said Alice stepping onto the wobbly floorboard near the fireplace. 'Charlie my neighbour thinks it's probably just loose. Have you got your Stanley Knife with you Jen'.

'Of course I have you daft bugger, I'm a proper lesbian, always have the right tools at hand' said Jen winking at Holly who promptly blushed. Jen got the cutter out of her toolbox. 'Do you want me to do the honours?'

'No let me, it's got me intrigued' said Alice, taking the Stanley Knife, and getting onto her knees she set about cutting long lengths of the carpet, peeling back old dusty carpet revealing another much older carpet underneath. The three of them folded the strips and moved them onto the landing. Alice was about to start on the older carpet, which had a very 1960's pattern of browns and orange circles which she thought belonged in a museum, it was in immaculate condition despite its age.

'That's a cool carpet Alice, a good clean and it'll be grand' said Jen, forever practical and cost cutting. 'You could have a themed room?'

'Mmm not sure, what do you think Holly?' asked Alice.

'I think you should keep it, a good deep clean and it'll be amazing, and it'd save you money, it's good quality' she said running her fingers along the edge, pulling it back. 'Let's roll it up for now so you can get to your floorboards.'

The three of them rolled, then folded the carpet and dragged it to the corner of the room, then turned to look down at the floorboards, which although old and dusty were in remarkable shape, having been polished and varnished at one time, the outline of where a large rug had once laid, stood out on the surface of it.

'Wow, this floor is lovely too, I wasn't expecting this, that gives me more options. Ok let's have a look at what's going on here' said Alice wobbling the floorboard, which wasn't nailed down as the others were, a short board that abutted the fireplace hearth.

'Thank heavens it's just a loose floorboard' said Alice as she prised the board up with her fingers, revealing a cavity below which hadn't seen the light of day for a very long time. Sitting on the ceiling below, along with a multitude of cobwebs, was a large metal cash box. It was black with red and gold rectangular inlay, with a gold metal handle on top, much larger than the ones that Alice had seen before.

'Oh, my word!' exclaimed Holly, as the three women stood staring down into the hole. 'Can you get it out?'

Alice reached down into the hole and manoeuvred the cash box out. It was heavy and rattled a little when gently shaken but was locked.

'Any sign of a key down there? Can you get your torch out Jen?' asked Alice.

'You really aren't of this century are you, Alice?' laughed Jen. 'Use your phone light!'

'Oh yes, forgot about that' said Alice giggling, finding the function on her phone and pointed it towards the gap in the floor, only to find cobwebs, mountains of dust and a few cross spiders. 'Nope, nothing at all, how intriguing.'

Alice inspected the cash box, it was in remarkable condition for its age, the lid was firmly shut but rattling it she felt something moving inside. Jen knelt down before her, screwdriver in hand, Alice cradled the box in her arms moving it out of Jen's eager approach.

'No! it'll damage it, it's a beautiful example, my colleague Jack collects them, maybe he has a key that will fit?' Alice felt suddenly very protective towards the box and its contents, and she placed it pride of place on top of the fireplace. 'What a lovely thing to find, and at least there isn't woodworm! God I'm filthy, anyone else need the loo before I go clean up?' Alice stood up brushing down her jeans.

'No, I'm good. Shall we have some lunch and then crack on a bit more, I'm starving' said Jen moving towards the door and down the stairs.

'I guess so' laughed Holly 'We do love Jen and her hollow legs, you wouldn't believe that she troughed a massive breakfast a couple of hours ago.'

Alice could hear Jen continue complaining as she closed the toilet door.

'Hey, I'm a busy woman, what can I say, I get hungry'.

Shortly after, Alice walked into the living room, Jen and Holly had unfolded the garden chairs and arranged them in the bare living room, then Jen divided out the goodies from the bag from the deli.

'Got your favourite, brie, and grape, welcome back to civilisation honey!' said Jen, throwing a bag over to Alice.

'You two are amazing, thank you!' replied Alice, putting her nose into the paper bag, inhaling the fresh aroma of baked bread and brie. 'Smells delicious, mmmm, bloody hell I've missed this.'

The three of them ate, the room filled with happy eating noises, until all that was left were empty bags and full stomachs.

'God that's just what I needed, thanks. So, what happened last night? Did you both have a nice time?' asked Alice.' Did you get my card?'

'Yes thanks, it was a bit eventful as it always is when we go out, as you know only too well. The restaurant was double booked, and we ended up with a wrap from the Yorkshire pudding place. York is nuts on a night, I've never seen the sights we saw last night before, mad stag and hen parties with inflatable unmentionables, I swear I blushed!' Holly covered her face in embarrassment. 'We tried Valentine's, but it was closed.'

'Ah that reminds me, my neighbour Charlie owns Valentine's. She said it's closed for a refurb. We could go when it reopens?' Alice asked, packing the rubbish away back into the hessian bag and taking it out to the recycling.

'That'd be brilliant, we were saying the other day, weren't we Jen, that there's nowhere to go that feels safe and fun, I don't enjoy loud pubs anymore, I'm getting old.' said Holly.

'No we're young at heart. Personally I don't want to go out then not be able to hear a word that anyone is saying. God I sound like my mother.' said Alice with a grimace.

'That sounds like all of our mothers, well if they were speaking to us!' said Jen.

'Well, mine has a good excuse' said Alice, 'She's dead.'

'Sorry Alice, I forgot,' said Jen.

'No, it's ok don't worry, it's been a long time' replied Alice.

It was one of the reasons the three women had been drawn to each other. They'd met at the York Women's Centre when Jen and Holly were both ex communicated by their families when they came out. Alice had gone there to try and get some clarity into how she felt about women but hadn't had the guts to come out in the end but had maintained her friendship with them both. York didn't have many places to go after it closed, which is why the idea of Valentine's opening again felt refreshing.

'Well, we'll have to become bar flies and hang out there, what do ya think?' said Jen.

'As long as I'm in bed by 10' Alice laughed. 'You know how I can't do late nights anymore.'

'Omg maybe you are old' laughed Holly, 'Better get you fitted for your Zimmer frame now!'

The three women laughed long and hard.

'Come on let's get these carpets up and in the skip, time's ticking on and Miss Alice needs her early night' giggled Jen.

The carpets came up quickly and easily, and there were no other wobbly floorboards, nor any carpets hidden beneath others. The house now echoed every time they walked upstairs or spoke, but their hard work had revealed lots of interesting floors that would be lovely left bare, including stunning parquet flooring in the living room, and original tiles under the one in the hallway.

'You've bought a really lovely time capsule Alice, those floors will polish up lovely, just need a bit of a clean and fresh varnish, gorgeous,' said Jen. 'Maybe I need to do ours, what do ya think Holly?'

'Look what you've started now Alice' laughed Holly, 'Our house is one long project. Want to come over to ours for dinner? We can do the electrical ordering online if you want?'

'That'd be lovely if you haven't had enough of me for one day,' said Alice. 'I'll just have a quick bath and meet you at yours about 7?'

'Great idea, see you soon' said Jen and Holly, walking past the half full skip. 'We've made a good start today. See you later'.

Alice closed the door, the noise echoed around the hallway. She made her way upstairs and into the back bedroom and stood and looked at the cash box on the mantlepiece.

'I wonder' pondered Alice with a shiver down her spine. 'What a mystery you are.'

3

The Past Revisited

Therapy's a funny thing. You sit and plan what you want to talk about in your session, only to find that as the story unfolds, you end up in a different place entirely. All a bit exhausting really.

Joyce was a marvel; she could drag information out of you with only the minimum number of words. She would sit there on the screen, calm and guiding, and it was these sessions that had been a life saver to Alice for the past year. A smiling face across the internet with words of wisdom that gave peace in the face of the war raging within her personal life. The main topics of course had been the finding out about Sally's infidelity. Her first sessions had been a flurry of tears, snot and rambling, Joyce managing by the end of the hour to ground Alice in a safe place where things looked a little clearer.

A lot of the therapy had gone over her crappy relationship with her mother and the fact that she had hidden herself within a heterosexual marriage for so long. However today Alice knew that even over the screen, there was no escape from avoiding talking about the worst day of her life.

'Today Alice I think that it's time to talk through what happened with Sally. Can you tell me what happened?' asked Joyce, firmly but gently.

This was the hardest thing to discuss, how it had all gone wrong. How to the outside world, and often to Alice herself, all seemed calm and serene. They'd appeared to work well as a couple, hosting dinner parties, attending work events at Sally's firm and any other thing they were invited to. The joke amongst their friends was that Sally would have gone to the opening of an envelope if it benefitted her in some shape or form.

Alice took a deep breath, gathering her thoughts. 'It happened at a drinks party in aid of the local hospice. Sally's firm had bought a table and I was invited along but I thought I'd have to work late so would miss it but at the last minute my meeting was cancelled so decided to surprise her. I missed so many of them because of my workload. I arrived at the party an hour or so late the speeches had started, and I couldn't see Sally anywhere in the function room, so I went through to the bar.' Alice reached forward onto her table and took a sip of water and looked around for her hankie.

'Take your time, remember to breathe slowly, you're in a safe place' Joyce said in a soft but encouraging voice.

'I went through to the bar, which was empty apart from the bar staff, and then I heard a voice coming from outside and I noticed that the French doors were open and could see two women kissing on the patio. I knew it was Sally instantly. My feet wouldn't move. I wanted to turn and run but found I couldn't. Then Sally's boss came in and shouted 'Sally, can you put Emily down it's time for your speech'.

Alice took a very deep breathe 'Then it all happened at once, Sally turned around and saw me, there was a lot of shouting, she said some really hurtful things, but I guess that was because she knew she'd been caught out. She'd broken all her promises to me. Emily just stood there smiling as my world fell apart, she looked like she was enjoying it'.

The tears flowed down Alice's face, as she sat in a stunned silence, washed out by all she'd relived. 'I'd been so full on at work, maybe I neglected her and that's why she found Emily'.

'It's kind that you're trying to justify her words, but she'd been caught out, don't be taking on the burden of blame' Joyce said calmly.

'I know deep down you're right, but the things she said were so cruel. That I was clingy and pathetic, that she'd supported me through my degrees and owed her a lot of money, that she didn't find me attractive anymore and that Emily was who she wanted'. Alice sobbed. 'I'm a failure, I tried so hard, and yes, I did go through uni, but I paid my way, I paid my share of the bills, I never asked anything from her. All I wanted from her was to be loved. I thought we would grow old together, that she was my One. I thought I was her One. I'm so lost. What do I do now?'

'You mustn't be so hard on yourself. Sally's feelings and affections were transferred to Emily, she was a coward in blaming you for it all. You can't make someone face up to their actions, nor stay with you when they want to move on. The best you can do is let them go. Let her go Alice. You've lots of lovely friends you can lean on, and I know that they're taking care of you, either in person or over the phone. It's a matter of taking one breathe at a time, one hour at a time, and slowly you'll get through this'. Joyce's look of concern came through the screen and in that moment, Alice knew she'd be alright in time.

And Joyce had been right. She was ok. The therapy sessions had carried on over that year, almost every week on a Wednesday. At first, they had been a prop to lean on, a focus for the week, but as the months ticked by, the house sold, then the divorce came through and Alice found her doer upper house. In a way Sally had made it easier on them both by moving out instantly, their only communication via solicitors.

And now, here she was back in York feeling in a much better place emotionally, but physically not so great. It'd been incredibly hard and exhausting.

The year and a half since that horrible evening had gone by so fast, and here she was now, single, trying to be strong and independent, wondering what to do next. She was in her 50's, things didn't work as they used to, her body creaked, her back ached and the weight had piled on as she comfort ate her way through the divorce. She felt unlovable, ugly, and unsure of herself. The house was beginning to look lovely and a place where she could be happy, but would she be happy alone for the rest of her life, and if not, how did you go about meeting someone new at her age?

Alice wasn't convinced that Tinder or online dating was for her, she'd seen her colleagues swiping this way and that in their lunch breaks, and it all seemed a scary way to meet someone. How could you gauge if someone was genuine from a picture halfway up a mountain looking puffed out, or windsurfing somewhere off the coast of Cornwall? Her therapist Joyce had said she thought Alice should get out there again, push her boundaries and join some new groups, perhaps she was right. But what did Joyce know, she'd only seen Alice from the shoulders up over Zoom calls, she didn't know the car crash that lay below the screen.

Alice's personal life was a mess; however, her work life was brilliant, and her new tenure as a lecturer had been her academic dream since she'd gone to uni late in life. She'd never dreamt that she would ever achieve her goal, but here she was with a lovely new house, fabulous supportive friends and a job that she loved. Alice knew that she was very lucky that her work colleagues were so understanding, as she'd really struggled to keep her home and work life separate. She felt blessed to be able to take a month off work after the end of the exam season madness, which usually meant a flurry of stressed-out students and pressures of marking endless papers. The break meant that she would be able to focus all her attention on the house, and her plans to get it all done although ambitious, were achievable if the work went to plan, and there were no hitches.

The first few weeks in her new house flew by in a flurry of workmen and women revamping the house alongside Alice's basic DIY abilities. The house hadn't thrown up any unexpected surprises and the planned full rewire, new boiler and central heating system, happened swiftly, whilst Alice sanded, chose flooring, and stripped walls.

Remarkably her old kitchen and bathroom had sold on eBay, so Alice had been staying at Jen and Holly's after the kitchen and bathroom had been removed, awaiting the new one being fitted the following week. She went over to the house every day to check on progress and was on her way there today for the collection of the old units. As she pulled up outside her house, Ted the joiner's van was in the driveway. He had been an amazing find, who knew so much about the area and was a font of knowledge and ideas of what could be achieved in the house. He had fixed the wobbly floorboard in the bedroom and was fascinated by the box found beneath it. Alice had decided to move into that room when the house was finished as it felt like home after the floor had been sanded and varnished and the new blind was fitted. She'd painted the walls a muted duck egg and her new metal bedstead and mattress sat proudly in place, just waiting to be made and slept in. It did feel like an indulgence decorating her bedroom first, but once the floors were sanded and the new radiator were installed, painting was the one thing she could do to save on costs.

'Hi Ted, sorry to disturb, I'm just here as the bathroom and kitchen are being collected, I'll be out of your way soon' shouted Alice above the sound of 80's classics that were always playing on his phone.

'No worries, just finishing off rehanging the doors, they came up really nice haven't they' said Ted, opening and closing the oak door, which now it had been stripped of years of paint looked amazing and full of character.

'Wow Ted, it looks so good, have they all come back from the strippers?' asked Alice.

'Yep, the others are in the dining room now you aren't sleeping in there, will probably be done with hanging them by the end of tomorrow. Are you sure you don't want me to smash open that box for you, it would only take a second? The suspense is killing me'. Ted nodded his head towards the metal box which was still sat on the mantelpiece. This was Ted's regular comment when he saw Alice, after telling him about finding the box, he had been as intrigued as she'd been.

'No, it's ok, it won't be long now before Jack is back at work, I don't want to ruin the box, I'm always the archaeologist,' laughed Alice.

She was as intrigued everyone else had been, but she didn't want to break the box in case it damaged the contents, and the box was so lovely. She'd hoped that when they ripped the house apart the key might have been found but no such luck. She'd sent an email to her colleague Jack to see if he might have a key that fitted the cash box, but she'd got his out of office stating that he wasn't back in the department until the beginning of August. Patience had never been Alice's strong point.

Suddenly there was a knock at the door. 'Ah the eBay people' said Alice turning and running downstairs.

'Hey, sorry we're a bit early, we've come for the bathroom and kitchen' said a woman who was knelt on one knee tying her shoelace.

'Hi, come in, it's through here' said Alice opening the door wider seeing a second person on her doorstep too. The woman stood up, her eyes meeting Alice's for the first time.

'Alice!' said the woman in a thrilled voice.

'Oh, my goodness Lou! I haven't seen you since school. Come in, come in' said Alice happily. Lou and Alice had been the best of friends at school but had lost touch when Lou moved away when she was 17 as her father got a better job in London.

'This is Henry my husband, we moved back to York a few months ago, wow, how've you been? You look really well' said Lou.

They exchanged greetings then Henry, Lou and Alice walked through to the kitchen which had been stripped out and replastered, the old units and bathroom stood in the middle looking very sad for itself.

'Wow this is amazing, I can't believe it's you. Crikey I can't even offer you a drink, as you can see it's a bit basic here at the minute'.

Alice was completely blown away to see Lou after all these years, they had been so close at school, sharing all their secrets. Well not all the secrets, she hadn't told Lou that she thought she might be gay. That was the one thing she couldn't tell anyone back then.

'Hi' said Henry. 'I bet Alice could tell some tales about Lou'.

'Sorry to disappoint but we were exemplary students weren't we Alice' explained Lou.

'Yes, we were little angels,' laughed Alice. 'Where are you living?'

'In Askham Bryan just down the road from where we grew up, my aunt Agnes left me the house, she died last year.' Lou said solemnly.

She and Alice had spent a lot of time at the house in their childhoods. Alice had been lucky enough to have her own pony Misty as a teenager, working as a chamber maid to pay for his livery. Lou had kept her pony at Aunt Agnes' yard and Alice rode the two miles there regularly so they could hack out together. Lou's aunt, who she'd always called Miss Hunter, was an amazing baker and always had buns and biscuits for them. Back then of course they burnt off everything they ate as they were always going somewhere on their ponies or bikes. The house had been an escape for them both from horrible mothers. One of the other bonuses had been the horses that grazed in the fields of locals who liveried there, and they'd both spent many hours larking around in the yard, chatting to the owners and going to gymkhanas in the summer. It was there that Alice had first realised she liked girls rather than boys, developing an enormous crush on a slightly older girl called Harriet. Lou had never realised of course; Alice was very good at hiding her feelings back then.

Alice was pulled out of her reverie to Lou talking still. 'My aunt never married and was very fond of me, so she left everything to me. My mother's fuming, but she's always fuming, do you remember Alice?'

'Absolutely, she was just like my mother never happy unless she was making someone else unhappy. I'm so sorry to hear Miss Hunter has died. She was a lovely woman' replied Alice.

'Thank you, Alice, I know she was fond of you too' said Lou, her eyes welling up, quickly changing the subject. 'I looked for you on Facebook, but I couldn't find you'.

'Ah I've an odd name on it because of working at the uni so the darling students don't try and add me or snoop. I'm a lecturer at York, what are you doing these days? Did you go to art college?' asked Alice. Lou had been an amazing painter at school and wrote some amazing poetry.

'No sadly not, although I still dabble which is why I bought the kitchen to put in the studio as needed something that it doesn't matter gets messy but looking at it, it looks so cute! I've done a bit of everything, but mostly work as a PA in the City. That's how I met Henry, he worked at a bank there for years, but we've decided to sell up and move up here for a quieter life. I can't believe I've found you! This is brilliant!' Lou hugged Alice tightly. 'Are you married? Did you and John ever get it together?'

Alice laughed 'Not exactly no, we've so much to catch up on'.

'We do, why don't you come over for lunch tomorrow? Bring your husband, boyfriend, partner with you?' asked Lou.

'No, it's just me, and lunch would be lovely, what time do you want me?' laughed Alice nervously, feeling now wasn't the time to spill all her secrets.

'Come for twelve, to eat at one. I want to hear all your adventures. Sorry we've to go, we've got a plumber coming in an hour' said Lou looking at her watch. 'We better get this kitchen and bathroom loaded onto the van, sorry to cut this short, I'm so pleased I clicked Buy it Now!'

'Me too, let me give you both a hand' offered Alice.

'Great' said Henry. 'I look forward to all the tales tomorrow'.

After the van was loaded and Alice had waved off her old friend, she stood in the middle of the street remembering, her hand still waving even though they were long gone.

'You trying to hail a taxi? said a voice which made Alice jump.

'Oh, hi Charlie, no sorry, I was miles away, or years away. How are you?' said Alice returning to the pavement. Charlie was outside her gate, dressed in a very sharp suit and shiny shoes. 'Going somewhere nice?'

'Yeah, I've a date with a woman I met last weekend at Tod disco, have you ever been?' asked Charlie.

Todmorden Women's Disco was legendary amongst lesbians in the North of England, close to Hebden Bridge which was allegedly the lesbian capital of Great Britain.

'Not for many years no, did you have fun? Obviously, you did if you met someone' Alice asked with a big smile.

'It was absolutely heaving, since Covid so many women have come out and wanted to experience the delights of Tod. You'll have to come, we hire a minibus, it's fun, give it a go' said Charlie unlocking her car, and with a wave drove off, not waiting to hear if Alice said yes or no.

Ted was just leaving the house as she turned around.

'I'm just going off to get something from Screwfix, shall I lock up?' asked Ted.

'No, it's ok Ted, I've some calls to make, the kitchen and bathroom fitters are coming on Monday and I just want to check everything's still ok with the plumbers as they wouldn't commit to a time. Thanks Ted, the doors look amazing' said Alice closing the door behind her, leaning on it in a daze. *Fancy finding Lou again after all these years.*

4

When the Past meets the Present

Despite Alice's concerns about the work going to plan, all the trades had confirmed that they were starting the following day. The plumbers had also saved her a fortune on tiles, showing her sites online where she could get discounts.

The difficult bit was deciding what to wear for lunch with Lou and Henry, opting eventually for a cornflower blue midi dress and her new converse trainers. So with a happy heart Alice left Jen and Holly's house.

It had been years since she'd last been there. Thirty plus years in fact, and Alice wondered if the village or house had changed much in that time. The biggest change was driving there on the A1237 that had been created to provide York with a route outside the city, intending to declutter the place from cars, however it just provided York with a slow-moving car park during high peaks of the day. However today, with it being Sunday, the road was reasonably quiet as Alice turned off the outer ring road, onto the country lane which snaked its way downhill towards the village, a road she'd ridden her bike and her pony Misty many times.

The village, thankfully, hadn't changed much at all. The pond was still there, and the pretty church and all the chocolate box cottages, which reminded Alice of her lost house with the roses around the front door. She turned off halfway down the village onto a small lane between two grand Manor Houses and headed down towards the large, detached house she remembered from her childhood, with the stable block on the left and the fields ahead. Other than being quite overgrown in parts it hadn't really changed a bit thought Alice. Lou came out to greet her wearing country clothes of checked shirt and tweed trousers with an apron over the top. She greeted Alice warmly.

'You're still as punctual as ever I see; do you like my country attire?' Lou said giggling. 'We're trying to fit in with the locals. Come through to the garden. It's so lovely to see you again' said Lou giving her a big hug of welcome and led her to the back of the house with its far-ranging views. 'What can I get you to drink?'

'Just water for me please. I've brought a bottle of mineral water with me, hope that isn't too odd, and a bottle of white wine for you both, I get tiddly at the sniff of a cork these days,' laughed Alice.

'Forever still organised I see! Let me get you a glass. Ice?' asked Lou.

'Yes, please, where's Henry?' Alice asked looking around.

'He's at the church cutting the grass, he'll be back in half an hour or so, gives us time to catch up' said Lou heading in through the French doors and into a large kitchen beyond. She returned with a jug of ice which Alice poured her bottle of water into and then into a glass on the table.

The two women sat down and soon found that the years had slipped away, and it was almost as though they were sixteen again, gossiping and sharing stories. 'So, if you didn't get it together with John, who did you marry?' Lou had always been straight to the point, no messing about with her!

'No, it never happened with John, as lovely as he was. He looked so much like Gary Numan do you remember?'

Lou nodded taking a sip of wine.

'I met my husband Harry at college and got married when I was 18. But I realised' Alice paused and took a big slug of water, the chill hitting her throat making her cough. 'Ok this will come as a shock. I realised I was gay when I was about 11 but I never said anything to you or anyone for years. But it became impossible to live the lie anymore, so I came out in my mid 30's. Sorry if that is a shock?' Alice took another sip and continued. 'I met Sally, someone who I thought would be my forever person, but we divorced last year, so it's the life of singledom for me I'm afraid' said Alice, looking continuously at her hands, not wanting to meet the eyes of her friend, she'd seen too often in the past the look of disappointment and disgust when you told people you were a lesbian.

'Bloody hell Alice, I'd no idea! That's really brave of you to come out at all. I'm not surprised you didn't come out back then, the 80's was a horrible decade, Maggie's lot were just vile weren't they to any sort of difference,' said Lou. 'So, do you think you'll get back out there again and meet someone new? Or have you been scared off?'

'I never say never, but the opportunities these days for a woman in her 50's aren't that fruitful, I don't think dating apps are for me, and everyone I know is happily coupled up. But you never know, therapy has helped' said Alice, 'Sorry too much information'.

'No not at all, by the time we get to our age so much crap has come our way we need to unburden ourselves somehow. Henry and I are in couples counselling. He's a workaholic and I hardly ever saw him in London. Some days all we could manage was breakfast together, and that was pretty much it. It's part of the reason we decided to come up here for a fresh start and to get him away from the job that I think is slowly killing him. The money's amazing in The City, but what's the point if you die young because of all the stress?'

Lou's eyes were fixed on the scenery ahead of her, and Alice knew that if Lou had blinked her strong façade would be broken and she would cry. 'So, we've moved here and we're trying to build our marriage again, it's been a rocky road, sorry, bloody menopause, hormones are all over the place!' said Lou, wiping her eyes.

'Bless you, that's so hard for you both, I hope that the move helps you,' said Alice. 'And I'm totally with you on the menopause, how did our grandmothers cope without HRT?'

'Mine was perpetually cross, now I understand why. The hot flushes, the mood swings and the weird anxiety that jumps up and bites you when you least expect' said Lou, dramatically mopping her brow whilst whisking a batter mix and checking the pans bubbling away on the AGA. She then took the joint of beef out of the oven which was cooked to perfection.

'I've been having anxiety attacks out of the blue; I thought it was because of the divorce but now I'm beginning to think it's the menopause. Do you remember us at school longing for our periods to start, now I want mine back again, I knew where I was with them,' said Alice.

'Oh my god I do too, we were both late bloomers weren't we and so desperate to be grown-ups, wish we could go back some days, don't you' said Lou.

'Sometimes yes, but not to relive the horror of my mother!' laughed Alice. 'Anyway, you're back home again, and this is a beautiful village, quite a change from London I would imagine.

'Absolutely. We lived in Chiswick, which is quite leafy and vibrant, and close to theatres, so this village is a polar opposite, really quiet, with black night skies, I think it's just the tonic we need'.

'Hope so Lou, and that the therapy helps' said Alice seriously.

'You're still a worrier I see, no change there then!' laughed Lou.

'No, definitely no change there' laughed Alice.

Lou poured Yorkshire pudding batter mix into the individual sections of the tray and put it onto the lower shelf of the AGA, the top shelf Alice could see lovely golden roast potatoes, her stomach growled in appreciation.

Just then Henry came into the kitchen, his country outfit of salmon pink trousers and checked shirt covered in grass cuttings.

'Hey, sorry I missed you arriving, I've been cutting grass at the church' said Henry leaning down to hug Alice and kissed Lou on the cheek.

'Yes, Lou told me, that's a nice thing to do' asked Alice thinking how large the graveyard was.

'Nice bit of exercise but I'm a bit stinky so I'll just jump in the shower and be with you, how long until lunch Lou?' asked Henry unlacing his boots.

'Twenty minutes love, you go and get changed' said Lou following Henry into the kitchen. 'Come see the house Alice whilst the Yorkshire's are cooking and see what's changed or hasn't as the case may be!'

The two women wandered around the house, the rooms and furniture had hardly changed in the passing years, but the wallpaper that had once been pristine was now peeling from the walls, and the paintwork, just like at Alice's house, had become yellowed with age. Photographs hanging on the walls hadn't changed, showing aged pony club gymkhanas, family weddings, christenings and picnics lined the hallway. A bygone era that took Alice back to the days of horse riding and memories of her childhood crush on Harriet. Confusing but happy days, when every day seemed to be sunny. *What rose tinted glasses I wore back then* thought Alice.

'It's hardly changed at all has it. What are your plans? I'm dying to see your studio as well; can we have a look after lunch?' asked Alice.

'Of course, I'll take you over after lunch and show you the plans if you like? It just needs bringing into the 21st century, but I don't want to lose the charm.' said Lou.

'I can understand that' agreed Alice, then seeing that Lou was stood sweating and wiping her brow realised her friend was struggling. 'Can I help with anything?' asked Alice, and with that the two women set about serving up dinner out of the AGA until the large farmhouse table was ladened with plates and trays of food. Far too much food for the three of them.

'Ah, Lou has cooked for the whole village by the look of it, we'll be eating it for the next week' said Henry coming into the kitchen and he began to help out with gravy boats and tureens of vegetables.

The food and the company were lovely, the conversation flowed about their adventurous holidays, their life in London, and the parties that they had been to with famous actors. Alice didn't feel like they were boasting, just sharing their past lives.

However, it soon became clear that there was a sadness beneath the surface, which as their wine flowed, they both began talking about their deep desire for children, but that they had many failed IVF trials, until they ran out of time and energy and became resigned to being childless.

Harry and Alice hadn't wanted children, and neither did Sally, so it had never been an issue. She knew that Jen and Holly had tried a couple of times, but they hadn't been successful. The pain it had caused them was far reaching, and she knew that they both struggled when they saw families with children. Adopting a baby was out of the question due to their ages by the time they had given up trying for one of their own.

'I'm sorry to hear about the IVF, must have been so hard, with the drugs and everything,' said Alice, she could see that Henry was struggling with what Lou had said.

'It's ok, there was only so much that we could take, the drugs sent me loopy and the monthly periods arriving just made life too hard. We're ok now, we have our bad days, but like I said earlier, therapy helps' Lou said, looking for reassurance from Henry who reached over for her hand, his thumb caressing the back of her hand.

'It just wasn't meant to be for us, we can just get a lot of dogs now we live in the countryside, we need the Labrador accessory' said Henry smiling, 'Only kidding, but it would be nice to rescue a dog maybe.'

'Sounds good to me, let's see what happens once the works been done. Right Alice, let me show you the studio before Henry fills the house with dogs and I ask for a horse. Are you ok to clear the table?' asked Lou.

'Sure, I'll leave out some leftovers for you Alice, or we'll be eating the same meal until next Sunday at this rate' Henry said laughing.

Lou took Alice from the back of the house over the lane into the stable yard. It was totally silent, the stable doors all closed and bolted, old name plaques were still mounted on the doors, the paint peeling everywhere. It made for a sad sight from what was once a vibrant yard with lots of chatter and the sounds of horses eating. Lou opened the door of what was once the feed store, and saw her old kitchen piled up in the middle, the old feed bins were gone, and new shelving was stood against the walls ready to go up. Blank canvases, and some that were partially completed, stood on easels in the corner, the beginnings of a studio that Alice was sure that Lou would create some amazing paintings from.

'Isn't it lovely, the yard's been empty for a long time, and I'm still not sure what to do with it all' said Lou leaning on the half stable door looking out to the yard beyond. 'We've 20 acres as well, and the old cross-country course, maybe we could rent the yard out to someone? I'm not sure if we want the hassle of running a yard, I wouldn't know where to start. It seems a shame for it to stand empty though, and I know that aunty really didn't want the stables converted, I think I agree with that'.

'Yes, I think I agree too, it would be lost heritage Lou, there's few of these Victorian stables left. I'm sure you would find someone to rent it to. We had such fun here didn't we, playing horses and chatting with people, happy days, maybe you could get some of that back again?' said Alice, 'Sorry I went all archaeologist on you'.

'That's funny, you sounded just like Aunt Agnes. You know we often wondered if she might be gay, she never married and for years she'd a companion who lived in, but spinsters did that back then didn't they?' questioned Lou.

'I think a lot of lesbians lived like that and called them romantic friendships. Sounds lovely, but really it just meant they had to hide their relationships and couldn't marry. And if one of them died, the family would swoop in and that would be it, she was out on her ear,' said Alice passionately gesticulating with her hands expressively.

'I never thought of it like that,' said Lou. 'We've a trunk full of correspondence that was in one of the lofts that we've yet to go through, feel like we are intruding though.'

Alice then told Lou all about the box that she'd found and how she felt intrigued, but equally that she was going to be opening up a part of someone's life. Although of course there might just be a pile of bills in the box and a lot of dust.

'Maybe you could go through them with me?' asked Lou.

'That would be interesting, just say when you'd like to do it, weekends are best for me as will be back at uni teaching again soon'. Replied Alice 'But I understand if you want to wait a while'.

'Brilliant, once we've got the plans from the architect and go for planning, I'll have more head space I think,' said Lou.

'Lovely, sounds great. I'll make tracks now if that's ok unless you want me to help with anything?' Alice said. She was feeling weary and knew she would have to be on full speed the following day. 'Thank you so much for a wonderful lunch and company, it's been so good to catch up. You look so happy here.'

'Don't forget your leftovers' said Lou heading back into the house to retrieve them. There was no sign of Henry but there were two Tupperware boxes with lovely food in them on the worktop.

'Say goodbye to Henry for me, it's been a gorgeous afternoon' said Alice walking back to her car.

'I will do, I can almost guarantee he will be fast asleep on the sofa listening to the radio by now. It's been lovely to see you, good luck with the fitters and I look forward to hearing all about the work. Drive safely' said Lou giving Alice a big hug.

Alice got into her car and set off back to York. It had been such a lovely trip down memory lane. She hoped that the work at her house would go as smoothly as the fitters had promised. She was really starting to like the house and it was beginning to feel like home.

It was a relief to think that in a week or two's time, all of the major work would be finished, and she could set about painting, she felt a decorating party coming on! Now that would be something else to look forward to. Life really was beginning to look rosy again.

She let herself into Jen and Holly's, they were both out as the cars weren't there, so she put away the Tupperware food, which she knew Jen would devour happily, and went up to her bedroom and turned on her laptop. A couple of emails pinged into her inbox, one was Hobbycraft offering her a discount on paints, and the other, at long last, was from Jack offering to come and look at the box. Yippee thought Alice, progress!

5

What Lies Within

Despite all of the hard work that Alice had done over summer she was itching to get back to her desk and her research, although she felt like her ideas had dried up in the last year with all the stress. At long last Jack had emailed her about the box. He'd looked at the photo Alice had sent him, and he seemed hopeful that he'd be able to help. Alice had invited him round for dinner but didn't tell anyone, mainly because so many people had taken such an interest in the box she wanted to surprise them once she'd an answer. Alice was so excited and had prepared a salad and quiche, with a bottle of red breathing on the side in the kitchen ready for his arrival at 7pm.

Her new kitchen was a triumph, it was in a country cottage, shaker style, with solid wood doors painted cream with cup handles, and oak tops. Alice loved it. There was of course no need for an AGA, but she'd found a small range cooker which fitted in just as nicely, and it made her smile whenever she walked into the kitchen. Her almost new fridge freezer and cooker had been donated to a local charity, and Charlie had taken the old carpet for a project she was working on so all felt good with the world.

The back garden was of course another work in progress, but it had a small patio and seating area and would be perfect for lovely warm evenings if she wanted to entertain outside, which is what she intended to do that evening. She was looking forward to catching up with Jack to see what he'd been up to over summer, and of course to see if he could help with the box. She'd bought a cheap table and chairs from Argos which although weren't as pretty as the wicker set from her old cottage, they were serviceable and practical until she could afford to upgrade them.

The doorbell rang, and Alice jumped. She was very surprised that Jack had arrived on time because he was so often very late. Time keeping wasn't his strong point. Alice answered the door.

'Hey, come on in. It's so lovely to see you'.

'Sorry it's taken me so long to get back to you, wow, this house it's so different to your last one, sorry I shouldn't have said that'.

'No, it's fine don't worry, I'm settling in nicely now, but it's been a heck of a year, but this feels like home now the work has been done. Have you been anywhere nice?'

'Yes, I went on an excavation to Orkney, I was lucky to get a spot on a team at Ness of Brodgar for a month, it was gorgeous but I'm glad to be back,' said Jack. 'You'll soon ground yourself and be back into York routines again Alice, and you'll have to get used to the traffic again of course, it's still a nightmare! So, tell me about this box and where you found it.'

Alice relayed the story of how she'd found the box under the floorboards in the back bedroom. 'I know I could have smashed the box to pieces, but you know me Jack, I like to preserve things, it's my job'.

She retrieved the box from the kitchen worktop and put it on the garden table in front of Jack.

'Ah it's a Chad Valley cash box, dates to the late 19th century, so very much your era Alice. Do you want to try and open it now before dinner, or would you like to do after?' asked Jack.

'No, let's do it now, let's do it now' said Alice enthusiastically clapping her hands together.

Jack produced a bunch of keys from his rucksack, there were an assortment of small keys that looked like they'd fit a multitude of ancient boxes and chests.

'Where on earth did you get them?' asked Alice 'You look like a jailor'.

Jack laughed. 'Er, some on eBay, or antique shops. I've written a paper on old cash boxes, trunks and keys, I'm hoping to publish it later this year'.

Jack looked at the keyhole and the keys in his hand and he started testing them out one by one. Some slipped straight in but didn't move the lock.

Alice's heart was beating out of her chest, she was so excited and desperate to get into the box and find what was in it. Alice went into the kitchen and poured two glasses of red and brought them out into the garden. Jack looked so funny as he worked, with a frown etched on his forehead, and his tongue sticking out of the side of his mouth in firm concentration, trying his hardest to open the box. He came to one of the keys which had a pretty red ribbon hanging from it, Jack's face again was set in firm concentration as he inserted it into the lock, and then with a very audible click, the lock released, and the lid popped up. Jack passed the box to Alice and they both sat looking at the box, neither saying a word.

'Shit I never actually thought any of these would fit, I thought it was a bit of a pipe dream, are you going to open it and look?'.

'God I'm so nervous!' said Alice slowly lifted the lid of the box. Inside was a rich burgundy velvet parcel, which Alice lifted out, laid onto the table and slowly unfolded the fabric. Within it was a large bundle of letters in pristine condition. Alice lifted the letters from the fabric and placed them on the table in front of her. Some of the envelopes were white, some cream, some pale blue, all tied together with a red ribbon, the same colour and thickness as the ribbon that was on the key in the lock.

Alice gently undid the ribbon, forever the archaeologist treating the paper with reverence and patience, her hands deftly flicking through the envelopes.

The name on some of the letters, in the most beautiful handwriting, was Charlotte Hope and others were addressed to Hester Harmson at Alice's address.

'Wow, this is amazing, although I really shouldn't be surprised that they were to someone living here. Charlotte Hope, what a gorgeous name' said Alice, continuing to flick through the letters. 'Some of the letters are to an address in The Crescent, Bath, and some to an address in Knightsbridge. And look at this, some also to Hester at 2 St Leonards Place in York, just around the corner from Kings Manor. I walk past it all the time when I'm going into town. Some have stamps and some are hand delivered, this one is franked 1928'.

Alice handed over the top letter which had a stamp and was franked.

'Yes, that's a King George V stamp, I collect stamps too,' said Jack sheepishly.

'You're as bad a hoarder as me Jack,' laughed Alice. 'I'm almost too excited to open them, is it odd after all this time that I feel like I'm intruding? The researcher in me is begging me to get on with it. Ok I'm going in'.

Alice took the pages from out of the one of the envelopes addressed to Hester Harmson, 2 St Leonards Place, which looked like it had been opened with a letter opener with its sharp edges making a clean cut, not like today where you rip off fingernails trying to open very sealed parcels and packages thought Alice. There were two sheets of paper, again with immaculate handwriting in very straight lines. Alice unfolded the sheets and started to read out loud.

15 St Stephen's Road

Bootham

York

18th September 1929

My Dearest Hester

Well, we are now almost settled at the new house. Mother has taken to her bed and father just sits in the garden with his cigarettes and a decanter he refused to sell. The rooms are so small, and the ceilings are so low compared to Newington Villa, and I don't know if you heard but we've had to sell so much of our furniture. Everything was listed in the Herald, even down to the servant's beds, and of course it included my lovely hand carved bed that I loved. I've one of the small wooden ones that were in the nursery now. The auction was at the house, but we didn't go as we were too embarrassed. All mother is worried about is how Amelia and I will ever marry, but believe me Hester, I can't think of this at all for so many reasons.

There was very little left after the creditors had been paid, enough to buy this house and we were able to keep some of the basic parlour furniture in case we have visitors, but I can't see anyone wanting to come and see us from our old life. Father is looking for work but so many of his old friends have closed their doors to him as they lost money too because of his advice.

Life has changed so much for us, I'm learning how to cook from the Mrs Beaton that we had in the old kitchen which I salvaged, and although we can't afford the best cuts of meat anymore, I haven't killed any of us with my attempts. And of course, there are no more groceries being delivered, and we have to go to the local shops which is not too bad to be honest. It's a side to life that I've never seen before and there are some true Yorkshire characters in the street where we are. I'm developing callouses on my hands which is hysterical after all the time I spent preening myself in my old life. All that seems so unimportant now. I know we are not totally poor, and that there are so many in a worse position than us, but this new life is so tiring, and to be honest I'm making it up as I go along because mother is no help and father has never read a paper that was not ironed before he touched it, so it has been quite a journey for us all.

We both know that from when we helped at the orphanage the horror stories that the girls have lived through, so I'm grateful that we have a roof over our heads and that I have nice clothes to wear, although they really are not practical for everyday life now. The other day, and please don't tell anyone, but I wore fathers old smoking trousers to do the housework, it was so much more freeing than my dresses, and some days I do not put on my corset, I can highly recommend it!

I do apologise for going on about the new house and I do hope that you'll visit us one day, but I understand that you may not be able to.

It feels so long since we were alone together. My mother is being impossible and refusing my pleas to go into town and instead is making me sit with my little sister to keep me occupied and out of mischief she says. She is finding it so hard since we had to let the governess go and is relying on me to teach Amelia. How could that possibly be a good thing? I have so little patience, and my French, as you know is very limited because our teacher Geraldine was so in love with our butler that she spent more time with him than us. I know you fared better with your tutor and actually went to Paris to put it into practice.

I've heard that the Lavender Café has a poetry reading next Thursday with Penelope Aston who we both loved the last time she was here, do you think you could meet me there? It would be divine if you could. I could take Amelia too, but I would rather be alone with you to hear all your news. We have a new daily girl called Anna who was at the St Stephen's Orphanage. Because of all the help that we gave to them, and the money we donated or raised over the years, the matron has let her come to us as part of her training. Mother has asked her to chaperone us as well as part of her duties. It seems such a long time since we met at the garden fete at the orphanage when we were both equals. I'm not sure what the future holds for me now, please tell me that you won't abandon me my dear Hester.

Anna has said that she will bring this to your house on her way back to the orphanage and I hope that you're in York as know you thought you might be going to London sometime soon.

I'll sign off now sending you all my love.

Charlotte x

'Oh my word! What a letter Jack. Poor Charlotte and to think that all this was going on in this house!' said Alice. 'I'm going to have to look into this more. Where did you say that you bought the key from?'

'I think this one came from a bundle I bought from an antique shop in Stonegate. I'm sure I saw it in the window, and I went in, and I got it. I remember because it had the ribbon on it. I can check when I get home?' said Jack.

'I'll go get the food before the lettuce shrivels and we can chat some more, but I think I'll put the letters away for now, they need time to go through, is that ok?' said Alice.

'Yes, that's ok, let me know what you find out, it sounds right up your street' said Jack.

'You know how I like a good old mystery' smiled Alice.

Alice collected the letters up, wrapped them in the velvet cloth and put them back into the box and took them into the dining room, putting the safely away in a kitchen cupboard.

The evening ticked on, Jack and Alice chatted away, eating, drinking, and sharing their summer stories, but Alice's mind was on the box and the story of Charlotte and Hester, especially at the hints in the letter that perhaps they were more than friends.

'Now that's something to look into' thought Alice after Jack had gone. 'Just who were Charlotte and Hester'.

6

A Walk in the Jungle

Alice awoke in a jovial mood, even though it was Monday and her first official day back at work. Sitting on the floor in her living room using the crate as her makeshift desk, she hit the ground running and got through her emails quickly. Most of them were thankyous from colleagues and good wishes for her house move and renovation which put a smile on her face. It would be later in the month before students would be messaging wanting help. She then set about creating the slides for her first lecture of the new term at the beginning of October. Her module on Victorian poverty had been surprisingly oversubscribed. This made her smile as she typed out her notes and set up the software to record her voice so it could be streamed online. Lecturing had changed since Covid, making studying more accessible to everyone, although nothing beat going into the lecture theatre at Kings Manor, one of the most important buildings at one time in York.

Alice's phone rang and was happy to find it was about the furniture delivery, all the pieces of the house jigsaw were fitting together nicely.

'Heck, I better sort out my painting helpers!'

Alice sent out a WhatsApp to her friends on their group chat asking if anyone fancied an afternoon painting in exchange for pizza and wine the following week, and within twenty minutes, she had eight people who'd said yes and two potentials. Alice had bought the paint and paper for the feature walls in the living and dining room, the plaster having dried nicely after the wood burner was installed. Jen and Holly would be there as they were returning from their holiday in Paris the day before.

Alice looked at the time on her phone and decided to do an hours work then she would make dinner. Cooking for one was becoming a chore and ordering a takeaway was very tempting. Online shopping was so good in many ways, but it was sometimes such a temptation to eat unhealthily.

The evening stretched ahead of her with no plans, the house was so quiet, and the nights were beginning to draw in. At the back of her head most of the day were thoughts of Charlotte and Hester. Her enthusiastic brain wanted to read them all immediately, but her work brain told her to be patient. However, she could wait no longer so retrieving the letters from the kitchen cupboard, she set about sorting them into date order. Some had stamped envelopes and others had been hand delivered, perhaps by Anna the housemaid who was mentioned in Charlotte's letter. One envelope contained a letter with a photograph with the name 'Hester Harmson – November 1928 written on the back.

2 Lincoln Place

Belgravia

London

15th November 1928

Dear Charlotte

Is everything alright? I'm concerned that I've not heard from you as you were not at the first hunt of the season. The photographer was there and took this of me, so thought I would send it to you as we said we would swap photographs, I hope you have one for me the next time we meet.

We are staying at my aunts in Belgravia until Christmas, then we are returning to York until Spring. London is quite mad, and the bustle of parties and invitations has been worse than last year. The talk is of finances and the looming crash that my father thinks is on the horizon. He thinks that he is invincible and has moved his businesses and cut back on labourers, and he says that there are signs that this could be really bad too, do you know anything about your fathers' interests? He keeps things so close to his chest about what he does, I hope that all is well there.

Now for some really bad news.

I really do not know how to tell you this, but father wants me to marry his business partners son Peter Haughton. He feels that this would be a good move for me and for the family, but I do not really know him, and he barely speaks when we do meet. He is so old Charlotte, at least twenty years older than me, but because he did something brave in the war, they think he will make a good husband and financially ties things up in a very neat bow for them. But what about me? I have no say at all, and I feel like I'm being dragged along on someone else's journey.

It also means I will have to live in London so far away from you and all my friends, and I just need you close right now. Can you come to Belgravia? Even if only for a few days? If you can come, send a telegram so I know as soon as possible.

I long for the days when it was so simple, and we could go to the park with our chaperone and feel free as birds if only for a few hours.

Sending you much love. Please come.

Hester

Alice stared at the photograph and reread the words. Poor Hester, and poor Charlotte. Alice noted the dates, which were around the time of the financial crisis in 1929, and Charlotte's letter had described the effect that it had on her family. What an awful time to live through. Poor Hester, did she have to marry Peter? Alice spent a few hours combing through the letters and telegrams building up a timeline. By the end Alice knew what her new project was. To find out more about the two women, and she hoped so hard that they had a happy ending. At least that would keep her busy on the evenings.

Alice realised she'd fallen into a rut since the divorce, sitting alone rather than picking up the phone to organise something. Her friends had been such help and support to her, however, knowing what she'd gone through, they didn't invite her to boozy nights out or parties anymore.

The joys of being over 50! thought Alice

She had the weekend to look forward to with her painting pals at least.

The doorbell rang making Alice jump. *And here's me moaning about not seeing anyone!* she giggled to herself as she went to answer the door.

Looking through the spyhole she saw Charlie and another woman stood on the doorstep.

Alice opened the door. 'Hi, is everything ok, was my music too loud?'

'Hey, nah everything's cool, just wondered if you fancied a bit of company?' said Charlie holding out a bottle of wine and big bag of fancy crisps. 'This is my best mate Di'.

Di did a small hand raise in greeting, looking slightly embarrassed.

'Of course, come in, although there isn't really anywhere comfy to sit, my furniture doesn't come until next week,' said Alice.

'Well, if you're up for it, come round to mine then if you like, I can show you my eclectic style' said Charlie laughing.

'Great, let me grab my shoes and will be round in 5' replied Alice.

Alice closed the door. *It's like the universe was listening.*

Alice ran around looking for her shoes and straightening her hair with her fingers. Looking in the bathroom mirror she could see that she looked tired after a day at the laptop. She splashed some water on her face and applied a bit of lipstick, then locking up went next door to Charlie's.

With a hop, skip and a jump Alice arrived at Charlies door which she'd left open. She knocked and heard Charlie shout 'We're in the kitchen'.

Charlie was quite right; she did have an eclectic style indeed. The hallway, a mirror image of her own in size and shape, was like stepping into a jungle, with wallpaper with big palms and leaves and real plants draping from pots mounted on the walls. The original floor tiles sparkled, and if hadn't been for their Victorian patterns Alice thought she could imagine walking into a jungle rather than a house.

'We're in the kitchen, come through,' shouted Charlie.

Alice glimpsed a very smart living room with brown leather wing back chairs and chesterfield sofa as she walked down the hallway into a bright, very modern kitchen with lime green splash backs and shiny white cupboards without handles.

'Wow that is some entrance' remarked Alice 'I was on the lookout for wildlife on my way through, any tigers?'

Charlie and Di laughed.

'Yep, Charlie doesn't do things by halves, ever,' said Di. 'Wait and see what she has done with Valentine's'.

'What have you done with the place Charlie?' asked Alice.

'I'm not going to spoil the surprise, but it's a vast improvement on how it was before. We've got various events planned, there's this one to start with' said Charlie handing Alice a flyer showing an arty photo of a very attractive woman which the leaflet said was called 'Dawn'.

Alice got her phone out and checked her diary, which was daft because it was empty on the evenings, the only things in it were work meetings and her therapy, so adding a social event would be a bonus.

How lovely, maybe the universe was listening thought Alice.

'Come down to Valentine's and I can give you a private tour' said Charlie in a flirty voice.

'Er, ok' said Alice cautiously.

'Only ribbing you! You should see your face, how unflattering for me!' laughed Charlie.

Di by this point was bent double howling with laughter, which at that point Alice realised that they had been drinking for quite a while. 'Charlie isn't used to being rejected'.

'Oh, you jokers' laughed Alice, relieved that she hadn't put her foot in it.

'White or red?' asked Di holding out the bottles.

'White please, just a small glass as I've to be up early for work tomorrow'.

Charlie poured the drinks into glasses on a very fancy tray and Di emptied the bag of crisps into a big bowl and then they both led the way through to the swanky living room. It reminded Alice of a gentleman's club with the hint of museum.

Charlie threw herself onto the settee and Di took the other chair. The alcoves on opposite sides of a retro fireplace were full of books. Alice walked over to have a browse.

'So how have the renovations gone, are you finished now?' asked Charlie.

'Yes, all finished, just some painting to do, but a group of us are going to tackle it on Saturday. Pop in if you're around,' said Alice. 'You've got some real classics here Charlie, I've a bit of a book fetish myself'.

'I like a girl with a fetish' said Charlie seductively 'It's a no from me for the painting. Don't want to get paint on my brogues'.

Alice took a small sip of her wine and then grabbed a handful of crisps to nibble and sat in the other wing back chair which was incredibly comfortable.

'So, what do you do Alice' asked Di 'Besides having a book fetish'.

'Er, I'm a lecturer at York Uni in the archaeology and history departments' replied Alice 'It's my dream job'.

'Cool, so do you dig stuff up?' asked Di.

'Sadly, I haven't been on an excavation for a number of years, I dig around in the archives if that counts?' laughed Alice. She was aware that Charlie was looking at her intently, her head tilted listening, a slight smile on her lips. 'What do you do Di?'.

'A bit of this and that, never found anything I could settle to, I'm helping Charlie out at the minute at her bar' replied Di. 'Keeps the wolves from the door, talking of doors I'm just nipping out for a fag' and she got up and left the room, heading out of the back door.

'So other than working in York, what brings you to the street? Hope you're settling in' said Charlie leaning her head on her arm on the edge of the sofa, her soft hazel eyes looking longingly at Alice.

Shifting uncomfortably on her seat Alice tried to concentrate on the conversation and tried not to meet her eyes.

'I'm recently divorced and needed to find somewhere to live and fancied a project to keep me busy. What about you? Are you from York originally?' asked Alice, aware that she felt like she was sat in the Mastermind chair.

'I'm originally from Leeds but came to York for a quieter life' Charlie said taking a big gulp of wine and then refilling her glass and attempted to top up Alice's.

'No thanks, I've to be focused for tomorrow at work, I get drunk easily these days' said Alice putting her hand over her glass.

'Have you dated since your divorce?' asked Charlie with a smile.

'I'm not sure what I want anymore. I'm not sure I'm ready yet. I just fancy a bit of fun, I guess. It's nice of you to invite me round, makes a nice change' said Alice, taking another small sip of her wine. It was making her feel heady and slightly out of her body.

Di came back in and refilled her glass and sat down with a big puff of air. The air was filled with the smell of cigarette smoke.

'Cheers for that' said Charlie wafting her hand in the air. 'Disgusting habit'.

'How was your date with the girl from the Tod disco?' asked Alice, still not making eye contact.

'Er, didn't last long, wanted commitment, I don't do commitment. Free as a bird I am' said Charlie in a blasé voice. 'Love em and leave em, that's me'.

'You need that tattooing on your forehead Charlie' said Di taking a big gulp of wine.

'Yep, seems so. Can't be doing with clingy women, just makes me want to run a mile. Are you clingy?' asked Charlie, her words beginning to slur.

Di started to laugh loudly. The atmosphere had changed, and the mood had shifted.

Alice began to feel awkward as she wasn't comfortable around drunk people. Charlie and Di had obviously been at the bottle quite a bit that night and Alice didn't like the way the evening was heading.

'Perhaps I should call it a night, thank you for the invitation'

Alice got up, put her glass down on the coffee table and headed for the front door. However, before she could open it, she realised that Charlie was right behind her. She grabbed Alice's waist, span her around and pulled her into a deep, lingering kiss which held such passion that her knees buckled.

Releasing her a little Charlie whispered 'Don't go. Please stay'.

'Let her go Charlie' shouted Di 'You go Alice, I'll deal with Charlie'.

Charlie softened her grip giving Alice the chance to lean back against the wall, her legs feeling very odd, and her heart was racing.

'No, I must go, bye Charlie' Alice opened the door and ran round the wall and to her own house, her hands trembling as she put the key in the door. She stood in the hallway shaking, not through fear, but in the realisation that her body was awake, feelings she hadn't felt for a long time surged through her.

Where the fuck did that come from thought Alice, locking and bolting the front door, turning off switches and checking the back door. She couldn't hear any noise from Charlie's house.

Alice made her way upstairs, heading into her lovely duck egg bedroom, putting on her pj's and climbing under the covers. She laid there wondering what on earth had just happened. On the one hand it was scary, but on the other it was the most thrilling thing that had ever happened to her. She lay there thinking of Charlie on the other side of the wall, butterflies were flapping away in her stomach and parts of her were throbbing, which was a new sensation. She'd never felt like this with Sally. What did it mean?

7

A Day of Delights

The sleep she thought would evade her, enveloped her rapidly, and she slept for longer than she ever did usually, waking to her alarm on her phone.

Alice was usually prepared for the day ahead; she was structured when working and wasn't easily distracted. However, today she found herself staring into her porridge bowl, thinking about the night before, which meant that she was later than normal at her laptop.

She was about to start on her emails when the doorbell rang.

Not thinking to look through the peep hole, Alice swung the door open to find Charlie stood there. She looked very tired and bedraggled, like she'd either slept in her clothes from the previous night or had not been to bed at all. She was stood on the doorstep holding out an enormous arrangement of flowers.

'I'm so sorry Alice; I want to apologise for my behaviour. I could blame the alcohol but that's no excuse. I'm so very sorry.' Said Charlie holding the flowers out to Alice. 'I made a real tit of myself; can you forgive me?'

Alice took the flowers. 'Do you want to come in for a coffee? It looks like you need one'.

'Aren't you working?' asked Charlie.

'Well yes but I think we need to clear the air' said Alice standing aside so Charlie could enter. 'Go through to the kitchen and I'll put these in water, they're beautiful'.

Alice followed Charlie through to the kitchen, putting the flowers on the worktop and looked for her biggest vase, putting the kettle on, and chattering away nervously about the weather, whilst she worked away arranging the flowers. She was unaware until she turned around, that Charlie had sunk to the floor with her head in her hands.

'Oh, hell, what's the matter?' asked Alice kneeling down beside her. 'What's wrong, it can't just be about last night?'

'It's not just last night, I'm at rock bottom with everything. I'm such a loser, I just fuck everything up' cried Charlie who had tears slowly falling down her face.

Alice noticed again how beautiful her eyes were.

'Can I do anything?' asked Alice softly, taking hold of Charlie's hand.

Charlie looked at Alice pulling her hand away. 'Why are you being so nice to me? I was a bitch to you last night' she said crossly.

'Yes, you were' replied Alice 'But I think we need to sort things out.'

'I flipped I guess' said Charlie folding her arms.

'It seems a silly thing to fall out over. If you don't want to commit to someone, then that's your choice'.

'It's not that. I don't like what I do, it makes me angry at myself when it happens. I just get rid of them, before they get rid of me. The lass I was seeing, the one from Tod disco, she called me all the names under the sun, and so she should. I didn't promise her anything, but she presumed that it meant something, you know, having sex, but it didn't. I was just going through the motions. Di's right, I should have TWAT tattooed on my forehead' said Charlie angrily, getting up and headed towards the front door.

Alice followed her quickly. 'Look, we don't really know each other, and I'm not sure what your story is Charlie, but I'm here to listen, stay for the coffee and we can talk'.

'No, I better go, I've been an idiot, and I'm genuinely sorry for last night, I'll leave you to work. I'm sorry.' And with that Charlie left closing the door behind her.

Alice stood in the hallway puzzled at why Charlie was being so evasive. She'd appeared such a confident woman, it felt strange to see the scared woman underneath.

Alice wandered back into the kitchen and saw a folded letter on the floor where Charlie had been sitting which must have fallen from her back pocket. Its heading said 'Alexander Adoption Services' with the previous days date on it. Alice didn't open it further, seeing the heading was enough. She grabbed her keys and went to Charlie's.

Alice knocked on the door, Charlie's car was still parked outside, but there was no reply. Alice knocked again louder. This time she heard shuffling coming from inside.

'Who is it?' said Charlie without answering the door.

'Charlie it's me, open the door, I need to talk to you. You dropped something in my kitchen'.

Charlie opened the door slowly and peered round it. She'd obviously been crying quite hard. Her tear-stained face melted Alice's heart.

'You dropped a letter Charlie, I haven't read it, but I saw the heading. Alice held the letter towards Charlie, which she grabbed and put into her back pocket.

'Can I come in? Please' said Alice in a very quiet, calm voice.

Charlie stood back and opened the door so Alice could enter. Alice entered the jungle and followed Charlie into the living room and they both sat down on the sofa.

She didn't want to presume the reason behind what Charlie had said the previous evening, about not wanting to commit. But Alice had been through similar with Sally who was also adopted, and when they met, she'd said very similar things about commitment. Alice's heart went out to Charlie, and she felt an overwhelming feeling of compassion towards her.

'You saw the heading? Asked Charlie.

'Yes, but I didn't read any further I promise, I just wanted to give it back to you and to make sure that you were alright' replied Alice.

'You may as well know what it's all about, I think I owe you that'. Said Charlie as she took out the letter from her pocket and opened it up. She began to read out loud.

Dear Ms Lowther,

In regard to our correspondence of the 10th of April I'm writing to you to let you know that we've not had any response from your birth mother. It's possible that she has moved from the address

which we held for her through our searches, so we'll continue to explore all avenues where this is concerned.

Yours etc

Charlie folded the letter and put it back into her pocket.

'I've been trying to find my birth mother, but I keep hitting brick walls. She's French and gave me up for adoption when I was six weeks old after she got pregnant to the father of the family that she worked for. My records at the adoption agency said that she went into a mother and baby home until I was born. That's where she left me. I was shunted around children's homes for a bit, then was adopted when I was two'.

'What are your adopted family like?' asked Alice.

'They were nice people, they both died in a car crash when I was 32. They'd been trying to have kids for years, then they got me, and far more than they bargained for. I've always been a bit of a tomboy, climbing trees, playing football and generally being a disappointment to them. Think they wanted a pretty girl, in frilly frocks, but they got me and my jeans' said Charlie staring down at her hands.

Alice reached out and took Charlie's hand into hers.

'I'm so sorry to hear that they died Charlie, that's awful. It's hard losing your parents. You've had so much to deal with. Are you working today?' asked Alice looking straight at Charlie's beautiful eyes.

'No, I'm off for a couple of days, Di is covering for me. Why?' asked Charlie looking straight back at Alice. There was a spark in the air and a moment of total connection between them.

'I wondered if you'd like to go out for dinner tonight' asked Alice, her heart in her throat as she wondered if she'd misread the moment. This was totally out of character for her, and she'd no idea where the confidence was coming from.

'Are you sure? I'm not the best company at the minute. Anywhere in mind?' said Charlie, still holding Alice's hand.

'How about a country pub I know in Gilling? I'll drive,' said Alice. The Fairfax Arms was her favourite place to eat, and the village was divine. It held memories of Sally but also of many fun evenings with Jen and Holly.

'Sounds good to me, but I won't be drinking anytime soon. What time?' said Charlie releasing Alice's hand taking out her phone.

'Shall I pick you up at 6.30 and we can have a nice drive and blow away the cobwebs?' said Alice loading the Fairfax Arms website on her phone and booking a table for 7.30.

'Lovely, do you want my number in case anything crops up?' asked Charlie, getting a business card out of the coffee table drawer.

'Yes, that would be helpful' Alice took the card and punched in the number onto her contacts, sending a text to Charlie so that she'd her number too. Charlie's phone pinged to announce its arrival, she looked at her phone and smiled.

'I have to get to work, but I'm just next door if you need anything' Alice stood up to leave.

Charlie stood up too and this time gently pulled Alice towards her, kissing her in the softest and sweetest way she'd ever been kissed. Either Charlie was very well practiced at this romancing lark, or this was the beginning of something beautiful. Alice didn't want to jinx anything; she was swept away by Charlie and there was something about their interaction that felt like a proper connection.

'Bye Charlie, see you later' said Alice leaving the house.

Somehow Alice managed to make it out of the door and back into her house, her knees were jelly, and she was sure the whole street would have been able to hear her heart beating out of her chest.

'Bloody hell' said Alice under her breath. 'Ok Alice focus. Focus'.

Alice went to her crate and sat down on the floor and loaded her emails. There were lots, and her work phone had a number of messages which she was thankful for to keep her mind occupied.

However, in the afternoon the hours began to drag, so at four o'clock Alice decided to call it a day and got ready for her night out. She wanted to call it a date in her romantic state, but she knew she mustn't jump the gun.

At 6.30 Alice was dressed in her best cream linen dress and jewelled sandals and when she locked the door and turned around, Charlie was already stood outside the gate, opening it for her as she approached.

'You look amazing Alice, wow' said Charlie leaning forward to kiss Alice on the cheek.

'Right back at ya, that suit is stunning, I love the colour' said Alice admiring the midnight blue ensemble Charlie was wearing, with a pale blue shirt and dark tie. Her shoes were as shiny as ever. 'Would you open the drive gates?'

'Of course,' said Charlie, unhooking the gates and opening them wide whilst Alice reversed out.

The drive to Gilling took them up the prettiest of country lanes as they passed through Stillington and Brandsby, with a mixture of pasture and arable land so there was plenty to see as they drove there, and Charlie was like a big kid pointing out sheep, getting overly excited at seeing a horse and rider jumping in a field.

'I didn't see much countryside growing up in Leeds, there are lots of parks, but this is amazing. It's like something you see in a film. What about you Alice, did you get out into the wilds much?'

'I did'. Alice then told Charlie all about Lou and their childhood and horse adventures together, and about her Sunday lunch at her house in Askham Bryan.

'Sounds like a blast. Do you ride well?' asked Charlie with a cheeky smile.

'A bit but it's been a while. Are you being naughty Charlie?' asked Alice giggling.

'Perhaps just a little bit' smiled Charlie.

'Here we are, Gilling is the prettiest village ever' said Alice as she drove down into the village with the stream that ran down the left hand, side and the picture box houses and cottages that lined the pretty street. The Fairfax Arms stood in splendour on the corner of a crossroads, its new orangery looked beautiful in the late summer evening light. Alice parked the car and they both got out and walked over the little bridge.

'We could play Poohsticks,' said Alice.

'We could play what now?' laughed Charlie.

'It's where you race sticks under a bridge, come here I'll show you' said Alice picking up a stick from the side of the road and dropping it into the water and rushed to the other side of the bridge to watch it appear.

'You really are the sweetest woman Alice' said Charlie taking hold of her hand as they walked into the pub.

The manager waved as he saw Alice. 'Hello stranger, table for two, is it? Thought I recognised the name. Come this way. Do you want to go into the orangery or the quiet area?'

'The quiet area please, I think. As lovely as the orangery is, it gets a bit warm for me, is that ok with you Charlie?' asked Alice.

'Of course, us women of a certain age have to be careful of overheating' said Charlie squeezing Alice's hand gently.

They both followed the manager to their table which was near the wood burner, which thankfully wasn't lit, but the tea lights and candles were around the brick fireplace creating a lovely romantic mood. The manager seated them at their table and handed them two menus.

'Can I get you both something to drink or do you want the wine menu? he asked.

'Can I have a still mineral water please with lots of ice,' said Alice.

'Make that a jug if that is ok, I'll have the same' said Charlie sheepishly.

'No problem, I'll get that for you and come back and take your order shortly', and with that he went back to the bar.

'This is a stunning place Alice, did you used to come here a lot, I guess so when the manager knows you! The menu looks good too, wish we had this selection at Valentine's, but the clientele doesn't want posh food, they want burgers and curly fries, but it does give me ideas.' Said Charlie browsing the menu.

A waiter came with a tray with a jug of iced water and two glasses and put it on the table. Charlie, always the hostess poured out their drinks, handing it to Alice with a smile. Raising her glass Charlie said, 'Here's to a lovely evening'.

'Cheers to you too' said Alice clinking her glass on Charlie's.

'What would you recommend' asked Charlie.

'I really like the lasagne they do with the most amazing garlic bread; I'm a carb queen too' said Alice laughing into her menu. 'But the scallops and the steaks are always really nice too'.

'So much choice, think I'll have a steak, thanks Alice, this is really lovely' said Charlie reaching to hold Alice's hand. 'Thank you for this morning, and again I'm sorry about last night'.

'Please stop apologising, it's ok, let's just enjoy the evening' said Alice stroking Charlie's hand with her thumb.

They placed their order, and their food arrived in good time which they both really enjoyed, finished off with a shared cheesecake. The bill arrived and Charlie paid, refusing Alice's offer to pay it or go halves.

'Wow I'm stuffed,' said Charlie. 'That was the best steak I've ever had, thank you for suggesting it. Do you want me to drive back? Share the load?"

'No, I'm ok to drive, I'm wide awake. I haven't felt this alive ever,' said Alice. 'I don't know what this is Charlie, after last night I should be running a mile, but there's something about you, a real spark'.

'I know, I felt it last night when you got cross with me, I know I was very drunk, but I had to kiss you, in that moment I completely sobered up, it was magic,' said Charlie.

'Yes, it was' replied Alice as they walked back to the car.

The journey home was lovely, the two women chatted away and sang along to an 80s CD that Alice had in the car. They were a jolly pair, and the journey was swift as the roads were quiet.

Alice parked her car in the drive, the street was quiet, and it was almost dark. The women got out, Charlie closed the drive gates and Alice locked the car.

'That was a lovely evening Alice thank you' said Charlie taking Alice's hand and walking her to the front door. 'What now? Any chance of a cup of decaf to finish off the night? Can I stay over?'

'I thought you'd never ask' replied Alice.

The two women entered Alice's house and locked the door.

8

The Morning After the Night Before

Alice woke with a start to a storm brewing outside, and a massive crash of thunder. She looked down to see Charlie's arm still holding her, she was relieved to see that she was still there with her and hadn't disappeared in the night. Seeing her naked had been a revelation, an artist tapestry inked all over her body, including the arm sleeves she had already seen. Alice gently turned over in the bed to face Charlie. Her eyes were closed, and she looked so peaceful. Just then there was another crash of thunder and her eyes opened slowly, Alice coming into focus which brought a smile to her lips.

'Good morning lovely, hope I wasn't snoring' said Charlie snuggling closer to Alice, their breasts pushed together which sent a shock wave through the pair in the bed.

'I didn't hear a thing, you looked so peaceful when you were sleeping, I only just woke up myself'. Said Alice. 'Wonder what time it is?' Rolling to reach her phone on the bedside cabinet and waited for her eyes to focus. 'Six o'clock, far too early to think of getting up yet' Alice said snuggling into Charlie's neck.

'I absolutely agree, when there are lots of other lovely things to be doing' said Charlie, slowly touching Alice's hip and moving her hand towards her breast.

Alice let out a small gasp as her body quivered as Charlie's fingers touched her nipple. Her body had never been this responsive before.

Since the onset of the menopause her body had gone to sleep refusing anything to get it going again. It was one of the reasons Sally had gone elsewhere Alice had decided. But with Charlie the chemistry was electric.

Last night when they got home, they went to bed with the intention of kissing only, an agreement made on their way upstairs, instigated by Charlie. However, within minutes that plan had been usurped by incredible desire, and their bodies were responding together. Charlie was an incredible, generous lover, and Alice found herself relaxing to the point where she felt almost out of her body, as Charlie caressed, licked and explored until Alice erupted in a cataclysmic orgasm that resonated around the bedroom. Charlie's body was beautiful with the sweetest pink nipples that Alice had taken great delight teasing the night before. It was an added to surprise to find one of her nipples was pierced which added to the excitement on both sides. This morning Charlie was even more responsive, her body arching as Alice's fingers explored her clit, shuddering in anticipation of the climax ahead. When Charlie came that morning she cried out 'Alice' and she shed tears of joy as they held each other in riding the final waves of ecstasy.

Alice's alarm broke the moment, and she rolled over and switched it off. 'Now that is a lovely way to start a morning', said Alice.

'Other than work what are your plans today Alice', asked Charlie swinging her legs out of bed.

'No plans at all, the only thing on the horizon is the painting party at the weekend, what about you?' replied Alice putting on her robe and socks intending on putting on a pot of coffee before heading into the shower.

'I've some accounts to do at Valentine's and some ordering unless Di has done it already. Do you fancy coming to mine for dinner tonight? About 6?' asked Charlie.

'Dinner would be lovely. Can I bring anything?' asked Alice.

'Just your lovely self' replied Charlie, kissing Alice gently on her neck. 'I'll go now and let you get on with your day or else we'll still be here at dinner time'. Charlie quickly dressed in her trousers and shirt, slipping her shoes on throwing her jacket over her shoulder, giving Alice one last kiss as she headed downstairs.

Alice heard the front door unlock and then open and close. She sat down on the bed in a happy daze smiling. She felt like she was floating on air as she went downstairs intending on making breakfast, but she'd no appetite at all, her stomach was full of butterflies doing loop the loop. Returning upstairs after making a cup of tea Alice picked up here phone and sent a WhatsApp to Jen and Holly.

'Hi guys, I hope you're both having an amazing time in Paris, and you've seen lots of sights and gorgeous romantic walks along the Seine. I've some amazing news you won't believe! Had a date with Charlie my neighbour last night, yes me. I actually went out! Loads to tell you but don't want to interrupt your holiday. Lots of love A x'

Alice pressed send and stood up and headed for the shower, just then her phone rang. It was Holly so she put her phone onto loudspeaker and went into the bathroom.

'Hey! We leave the country for 5 bloody minutes and you've a date! That's amazing, did you have fun?' asked Holly.

'Yes, it's been amazing, not a great start though'. Alice explained what had happened to Holly and after a few seconds she knew she'd been put onto loudspeaker at their end as she heard Jen hooting congratulations. When she told them about the impromptu kiss, she could hear them both gasp.

'Oh my god, that's just nuts, wow, brilliant. I've no words,' said Jen. 'Are you seeing her again? Did she stay the night?' Jen was always to the point and never shirked in asking what everyone else normally didn't.

'Yes, she did but that's all I'll say. Other than it was lovely, and I feel happy for the first time in ages' replied Alice.

'Is this Charlie who owns Valentines? Asked Holly. 'Doesn't she have a reputation? Didn't you say that she was dating someone from the Tod disco? Be careful won't you'.

'Of course, I am, it might just be a fling, or it might be something else, who knows, but I might have fun finding out' replied Alice in a jovial tone. 'All's good I promise'.

'That's lovely, we don't want you to get hurt again,' said Holly. 'We love you; you know that and have your best interest at heart'.

'I know and I love you both too. I can't wait to see you when you're back, you're so lucky to be taking a whole month off together in France,' said Alice.

'I know jammy isn't it. Holly had a shit ton of holidays so why not, only live once don't you,' laughed Jen.

'Very true. I've sorted the decorating party for when you get back, I need Holly's papering skills' said Alice stretching feeling a bit stiff and sore from the previous nights' exploits.

'Will Charlie be joining us? Can't see her as the decorating type' sneered Jen.

'I don't think so, she has the bar and it's a busy night on Saturday's, but I'll ask her again, you should see her house though Jen, the décor is stunning. She's got a great eye' replied Alice, wondering if she should ask her again. Had Charlie been too drunk to remember her asking her before, was she joking about the paint on her brogues?'

'Hope you've chosen some wacky colours. We better go, we're going to Versailles today and need to catch the bus'. Said Jen. 'See you on Saturday' Holly and Jen shouted down the phone.

Alice got into the shower, now beginning to worry. Jen and Holly had vocalised the fears that she'd pushed to the back of her head. Had she made a big mistake sleeping with Charlie? Was she going to get hurt. Would she run away, and it would be really awkward living as her neighbour. Oh god what had she done. Alice's brain continued to catastrophise all through her shower, getting dressed and starting work. By the time she opened her emails the anxiety had risen and was flooding her body with pointless adrenalin. She started her breathing and distraction techniques and even tried to read her emails, but her stomach was churning so hard she had to rush to the loo numerous times to be sick. Once the pains in her stomach had subsided, Alice retreated to bed, curled up under the duvet and fell asleep exhausted.

She was woken by her phone ringing and was shocked to see that it was almost 4 o'clock, she swiped to answer the phone not registering who was calling.

'Hi Alice, how're you doing, how are things with the renovations? Asked Lou

'Hey, yes, all good, just the decorating to finish now, what about you how are you getting on? Did the kitchen fit ok in your studio? Hope you've had a chance to do some painting of the fun kind' responded Alice.

'It looks really sweet in the studio, and I've thrown a bit of paint at a canvas, but it's been so hectic here with plumbers and joiners I haven't really had time to do much. But we've lovely bathrooms now, all modern and with a new Rayburn that means we've actual hot water again. It's the simple things you miss, but we're slowly getting used to the house and its quirks' explained Lou. 'I was ringing for a couple of reasons really. Would you like to come and stay for the weekend and maybe go through the chest, and we are throwing our first dinner party and wondered if you wanted to make it a double visit'.

'That sounds lovely Lou, when were you thinking? I'm busy this weekend having a painting party, you would both be more than welcome to come too, I didn't invite you as thought you would have enough of your own to do' said Alice suddenly feeling guilty for not asking them.

'Don't worry, we're away this weekend in London clearing the last of our things out of the house in Chiswick as it's sold at long last, so it feels like a brand-new start. We were thinking a week on Friday, come over and stay the night and we can go through the chest, then on Saturday night the dinner party. What do you think?' Lou sounded so excited Alice said yes immediately 'And if you wanted to bring anyone that'd be fine too, just let me know a few days before'.

'Thanks Lou, you never know' Alice responded mysteriously.

They signed off and Alice put it into her diary on her phone. She noticed a few texts and one from Charlie sent an hour before. She opened it tentatively.

'Hi lovely, hope you're having a good day. Looking forward to tonight. See you about 6? Cx'.

Alice fired off a quick reply 'Hi Charlie, yes, all good on this side of the wall. See you at 6 x'.

Her stomach flipped again. Two hours to go thought Alice, I better check my emails and then get ready thought Alice. Her phone pinged again.

'Can't wait C x'. Alice tried to picture Charlie on the other side of the wall, sat reading a book in her imagination, when in reality she was probably working still, just like I should have been doing all day, thought Alice guiltily. She grabbed a banana from the kitchen as she realised she hadn't eaten all day, then at long last sat at her laptop and replied to as many emails as she could.

After an hour she'd managed to make a decent impact and had managed to get an appointment at the Borthwick Archives which was attached to the uni library. She smiled as she'd got access to all the records she needed for her research for her module, which would hopefully keep the students interested in the stories of her case studies, noting the date into her diary. There were entries in for the next two weeks which felt good.

She took another shower, leaving her hair to dry naturally, putting on her black jeans, white T shirt and her black converse, and at 6 went around the wall to Charlie's.

Alice knocked at the door and heard Charlie shout 'Come in, it's open'. As Alice walked through the jungle, she could see Charlie stirring something on the cooker top, a tea towel tucked into the back of her black jeans. 'Snap' said Alice posing in the doorway to show their matching outfits.

'Christ that was bloody quick. Normally lesbians merge in a slightly longer time' laughed Charlie beckoning her closer, giving Alice a swift kiss. 'Just at a crucial bit, don't want to burn it. I made the usual dish for a date, a spag bol, hope that's ok?'

'Lovely, but not sure we're wearing the right colour tops, I may end up wearing mine,' laughed Alice. Her fears from earlier simmering down and she began to relax.

'Well, we could always eat naked in the bath, cut out the middle bit' Charlie replied with a very wide smile.

'You're funny. I'm starving I have to admit. Have you had a good day?' asked Alice.

'Not bad, have to admit to having a nap I was jiggered, how was your day?' grinned Charlie. 'Did you keep those students in line?'

'It was fine thanks, no students as yet but won't be long before I'm nursing them along. I had a nap too'. Alice didn't want to admit what she'd been through, she knew it wasn't honest, but she thought that with Charlie being a flight risk it wasn't wise just yet. 'Can I do anything to help?'.

'Could you lay the table in the dining room, and if you'd like some wine open a bottle, I'm not drinking tonight' said Charlie pointing to a rack in the corner. 'I'm just sticking to water. Cutlery's on the side'

'Water's good for me too, got to keep a clear head. I'll lay the table' said Alice picking up the cutlery. 'You haven't shown me your dining room yet, I'm intrigued' Alice said as she walked down the hall and opened the dining room door. What she saw blew her away.

Her eyes beheld a feast of colour and design, a homage to William Morris, with an oak dining table and four cream ladder-back chairs and herringbone wooden floor.

'Wow, this is fantastic Charlie, you've a brilliant eye for design. I love William Morris, is that the Strawberry Thief wallpaper?' asked Alice laying the table which had two candles already lit in the centre, neatly folded linen napkins, a tray with a baguette cut into rounds and a pitcher of water with ice and two tumblers.

'I wondered if you'd know it Alice' shouted Charlie from the kitchen. 'I love Arts and Crafts style'.

'It's stunning, I should have got you round to help me design mine' said Alice going back into the kitchen where Charlie was spooning the Bolognese onto the mound of spaghetti. 'Talking of design, the invite is still there if you want to join us at the painting party on Saturday, no pressure'.

'I could come and help a bit in the morning before I go to the bar, but are you sure you want me to meet your friends?' asked Charlie carrying the bowls through to the dining room. She set them down on the table and switched off the main light leaving the room candle lit.

'No, I'd like you to meet them, whatever happens between us, us lesbians have to stick together! Plus, I need as many hands as possible' said Alice smiling.

'We managed quite nicely with our four hands last night' Charlie said with a twinkle in her eye. 'Are you sure? Who's coming?' Charlie shifted in her seat, looking uncomfortable.

'Are you ok? If it's too much you don't have to come' said Alice using her spoon and fork to load the spaghetti in as careful a way as possible. She could feel the anxiety starting again and wasn't sure if she could even swallow the food which looked delicious.

'Just worried I might have upset one or more of them' said Charlie who was staring at the table.

Alice reached over and took her hand. 'If there's anyone you know we can deal with it together. We all have a past. Anyway, there's Jen and Holly who you've heard of, Andrea and her girlfriend Georgina, Mel and her on and off girlfriend Sukie and Jo and her best friend Nat. Jo and Nat have an odd relationship, one minute Jo fancies Nat, then she changes her mind, then Nat fancies Jo but nothing ever happens. Maybe one day they will get it together, who knows'.

'Sounds like it could be a proper lesbian drama brewing right there,' laughed Charlie. 'Nobody's name springs to mind you'll be pleased to know'.

'Don't worry. Anyway, to change the subject the food looks and smells lovely' said Alice daring to move her fork to her mouth. Within seconds the predicted spillage occurred, and Alice had a large splodge of sauce down her white t-shirt. 'Oh bugger. I should be wearing a bib' said Alice taking the napkin dabbing the sauce but only making it worse.

'Told you that we should be eating this naked' laughed Charlie spooning some sauce and spaghetti, twirling her fork ferociously, then repeating the same spillage onto her t-shirt whilst attempting to get it into her mouth. Alice and Charlie roared with laughter, ending with tears streaming down their faces. Eventually stopping and managing to eat with more spillages, realising that it was too late to save their clothes. After they'd finished Charlie cleared the table then took off her shirt and asked Alice for hers so she could soak them in the laundry.

'Well, this has been fun so far, it didn't take you long to get my top off did it,' laughed Alice. 'Can I help with anything?'

'No, I've got it' said Charlie bringing in two plates with chocolate cheesecake on it. It felt completely safe and comfortable sat chatting and eating with their bras on as though they had been doing that together for years.

'Wow, did you make these too?' said Alice almost drooling at the sight of them.

'No, I cheated and got them from the deli at the end of the street, hope you like them' said Charlie diving into the cake. 'At least I can't make too much of a mess with this',

'Want to bet' said Alice, as part of the crumb went down Alice's bra.

'Need any help with that?' said Charlie with a grin.

'Naughty'. Said Alice retrieving it as carefully as she could. They managed to finish without further incident, then cleared the plates, Alice helping to load the dishwasher.

'Would you like a decaf tea or coffee or are you ok with water?' asked Charlie putting the casserole dish into soak.

'Water's ok with me' said Alice refilling her glass from the jug. 'Do you want some more?'

'Yes please. Shall we go through to the living room and put some music on? Are you warm enough? I can lend you a shirt' asked Charlie.

'Yes please, I'm getting a little chilly'.

Charlie went upstairs and came down wearing a fresh blue shirt and she handed one to Alice. 'It'll be too big for you, but it will cover your modesty and keep temptation out of my eyes. What do you fancy listening to?' asked Charlie going onto Spotify on her phone.

'Anything's good for me, what's your favourite at the minute' said Alice sitting on the sofa. Charlie selected some music, and it came out of hidden speakers in the bookshelves and behind them. The beautiful tones of The Cure 'Just Like Heaven' came on.

'I love The Cure' said Alice snuggling into Charlie who put her arm around her. 'I saw them in Bradford in 1985, one of the best concerts I've ever been too.'

'Really? The Inbetween Days tour? I was there too! What's your favourite song of theirs?' asked Charlie tapping her foot along to the music.

'I'm a sucker for Love Song, it really gets to me,' said Alice. Charlie waited for the song to finish then selected Love Song and started to sing selected lines to her.

Alice sat up and looked at Charlie. 'That was beautiful. You've a gorgeous voice, so much soul'.

'You'll be making me blush' said Charlie who had such a serene look on her face. The bravado that she had when they first met had melted away, and here was the real woman, open and bare, her soul exposed, it seemed like this was the first time that she'd really let herself feel.

'What's your favourite song of theirs?'

'I hardly dare say, I don't want you to judge me,' said Charlie.

'Tell me, it's ok, many of their songs have seen me through hard times' said Alice cuddling onto Charlie's chest.

Charlie got her phone and selected a song. The music and sad lyrics of Sinking came out through the speakers.

They both sat in silence listening to the song. As it finished, they looked at each other, realising that they had both been silently crying. There were no words. Alice knew exactly how Charlie felt, that song could have been written for her adolescence. In the moments of despair before she came out, that had been how she'd felt so often, and since Sally had left her too.

'You've such a beautiful soul Charlie, I hate to think of you feeling so low, it's such a meaningful song, thank you for sharing it with me,' said Alice. 'Can I stay with you tonight? I just want to hold you'.

'That would be so lovely' replied Charlie. And that's exactly what happened. Charlie took Alice up through the jungle into a minimalist bedroom with white walls, white carpet and a large wooden bed with white bedding. They undressed, got into bed and held each other all night long. It was just what they both needed. To feel loved and cherished in the simplest way.

9

A Stitch in Time

Days turned into weeks of whirlwind dates and fun in bed. The joy of exploring each other's bodies and minds was addictive, the need to be together, the need to be enfolded within the walls of both their houses, having sex whenever, and wherever the urge came upon them, which was often, in the blissful first month of their love. The word itself wasn't said but it was felt, to Alice it felt like home.

After another blissful night come dawn nothing was stirring at Charlie's house. Outside, in far off streets, the city was wide awake, and traffic was buzzing around in the rush hour. Alice and Charlie were still curled up together in bed when there was at first a gentle knock at the front door, but as the caller became impatient, the hammering got louder and louder, with intermittent peels from the Ring doorbell. The noise echoed through the jungle and stirred the two occupants in the white bedroom. The knocking continued.

Charlie jumped up, threw on her dressing gown, and ran downstairs to answer the persistent knocking. Alice could hear the door unlock and then a muttering of voices, then she heard raised voices. She sat up in bed getting worried as the person shouting at Charlie really sounded unhappy.

Alice heard the door close and Charlie running upstairs, coming into the bedroom, her face red and angry.

'Who on earth was that? What did they want? Asked Alice throwing on her jeans and one of Charlie's shirts that she liked wearing around the house.

'Di. I missed the fucking delivery this morning. They tried ringing me, but of course my phone's downstairs. She only got to bed a four, so she's mad as hell at being knocked up' said Charlie who looked really flustered and out of sorts. 'Can I get you some coffee or do you have to go?'

'What time is it' asked Alice searching for her phone, realising that the last time she saw it was in the living room.

'9.30. Can't believe we slept in' said Charlie putting on her jeans and shirt.

'Shit, I better get going, think I've a zoom at 10. Sorry I have to run' said Alice giving Charlie a quick kiss, before running down the stairs, grabbing her phone from the coffee table and heading out of the front door. 'Will text you later, bye'.

She'd just enough time to have a quick shower and change of clothes before her Zoom meeting with the head of department and teaching committee. During the meeting Alice was asked to take over as Postgraduate Admissions Tutor the following academic year, which would be a massive boost to her career. After a quick lunch she threw herself into her emails and tasks and before she knew it, it was gone four o'clock. Alice took her phone out of her pocket to find it had died again.

'Damn it' said Alice plugging it in and then began searching the kitchen for something for dinner. On the fridge was the flyer that Di had given her for the folk session at Valentine's which was that evening, and she wondered if she should go and surprise Charlie. It was the first time that they hadn't made future plans before going about their separate days.

Alice checked her phone, there were a few texts from friends confirming that they were coming to the painting party but nothing from Charlie, so she sent a quick WhatsApp to her apologising that her phone had died, and she'd been so busy at work. Changing into a BOHO maxi dress and her DM boots, she straightened her hair, applied some lipstick, grabbed her bag, and headed to Valentine's, noting as she passed that Charlie's house was in darkness.

York was busy even at seven thirty at night, with people heading to the theatre or to the many bars and restaurants. Because it was Wednesday, she wasn't treated to the delights of hen and stag visitors and she enjoyed seeing York in the early evening light, with the Minster lit up and looking magnificent. Alice headed down Davygate and then turned left into Stonegate, one of York's most famous streets.

Valentines was in a medieval building amongst a row of similar designed structures, it's beams looking splendid despite the age. Alice opened the door to see polished wooden floors, art deco tables and chairs, plenty of foliage and a solid wooden bar on the left, and ahead of her she could see a small stage had been set up with a microphone and speakers at the side. The ceiling beams had more leaves and plants draped around them, and she could see the original fireplace had been preserved. There were quite a few tables full of couples and the bar staff were serving amazing cocktails that steamed. Alice couldn't see

Charlie, but spotted Di serving at the far end, so she made her way down through the crowd waiting to be served. Di saw her, but rather than greeting her she frowned.

'Hi, thought I'd come down and hear the folk singer you both talked about, is Charlie around?' asked Alice looking around.

'She's just out sorting something, she'll be back soon I think' replied Di, turning and going through a door marked staff only.

Alice felt the same lurch in her stomach that she'd had the night she saw Sally cheating on her, and despite the warning on the door, she followed Di. Ahead was a corridor with signs for the staff toilets on one door and office written on another. It was from there that she heard heated voices, one of them was Charlie's, the other Di's and another unknown. Alice approached cautiously, looking through the partially open doorway. What she saw sickened her, she felt the vomit rising in her throat. The singer Dawn, who she recognised from the flyer, was naked, protecting her modesty with a hastily retrieved skirt. A visibly drunk Charlie was zipping up her trousers, her shirt unbuttoned, a bra and pants lay on the tiled floor under her feet. The desk had a whisky bottle that was almost empty and two glasses. Charlie looked up and saw Alice, just as she turned and fled back down the corridor, through the crowded bar and out into the street. Her DM boots made a loud clomping noise as she ran as fast as she could, running across Museum Street without looking, and onto St Leonards Place. It was here she had to stop to throw up onto the road, then retreated to lean against the railings, her heart racing and she couldn't catch her breath. She sat on the step that led to number 2 and tried to gather herself to be able to get home, she'd been sick on her dress and she could feel the world closing in on her. She heard someone running from the direction from where she'd come, and looked to see Charlie heading towards her, now fully dressed, a panic spread across her face shouting her name. Alice attempted to stand but found that her legs wouldn't work, she stumbled forward falling face down onto the pavement, hitting her head and passed out.

Alice very slowly became aware of people being around her, an ambulance arriving and being wheeled into a cubicle, all the while dipping in and out of consciousness. She finally came round to find a drip in her arm, a plaster where bloods had been taken, and a doctor asking her if she might be pregnant. They knew her name, but she didn't know how, and she felt so dazed that she answered their questions with a yes and no. No, she hadn't been drinking. No, she hadn't been attacked. Yes, she'd felt faint before.

The doctor explained she was being taken for a CT scan on her head to check for a potential bleed and did she want them to call anyone. Jen and Holly were still away, and she suddenly felt incredibly alone. She'd no one to tell. Charlie had only taken a month to fall back into her old ways and Alice felt an idiot for allowing herself to believe that she would be faithful to her. A porter came and wheeled her to the CT scan and then up to the admissions ward. Because she was so unwell, and the pain in her head was so immense they pulled the curtains around the bed and gave her a mask for her eyes to shield them from the bright ward lights. They took her clothes off and put them into the locker, putting her phone into her hand. Her eyesight was blurred, and she couldn't focus on the screen so when the nurses came to check on her shortly after she asked them to send a message to Jen which they kindly did.

'I'm in hospital as I had a fall in town and I'm in YDH. The doctors want to keep me in for a couple of days and wondered if I could come and stay with you when I come out. Sorry to be a bother but they don't want me to be home alone. I'm turning my phone off as no charger but will check again tomorrow for your reply. Love Ax'. The nurses then turned off the phone and put it into her cabinet. Alice had a cut on her forehead which the doctor had stitched, and there was a large dressing over it and her head hurt very badly and she'd been sick again.

It was a very fitful night with the nurses waking her for checks regularly, so by morning she was exhausted, feeling sick but her eyes weren't as blurred as the day before. She caught sight of herself in the bathroom mirror when the nurses took her to use the loo. The left-hand side of her face was swollen, and bruising was beginning to appear, her chin was grazed and raw and her eye bloodshot. The nurses slowly walked her back from the bathroom which she was glad of as she felt so weak.

Laying on the bed she took out her phone and switched it on. Jen had responded to say they were already on their way home as the weather was foul and that they would come and see her as soon as they got back. Alice felt so relieved, she hated being reliant on people, but last night had really scared her. Her battery was holding steady, so she didn't immediately switch it off. She switched on her mobile data and her emails came through and she quickly fired one off to the Head of Department to tell them of her accident and that she would be in touch soon.

As she was typing her phone pinged and she could see from the banner that Charlie had sent a WhatsApp, then another, then another. It said.

'Come back Alice I can explain'.

'I'm in A&E but can't find you, please message me'.

'The doctors won't tell me anything, I really need to talk to you'

Then one sent that morning 'I hope you're ok, I'm so worried, please call me or send me a message'.

Alice could see that Charlie was online already and she knew that Charlie would see that she'd just read the messages. She paused, wondering whether to reply or not when her phone rang. It was Charlie. Alice quickly answered so as not to disturb other people beyond the curtains.

'What do you want? I don't think we've anything left to say?' said Alice. 'I'm still in hospital. You told me who you were, I should have believed you'.

'I'm so sorry. What have the doctors said, will you tell me that at least? I've no words I can say that will make it better, I could blame the booze, I could blame Dawn, but it was neither of those. I'm a shit and I can't tell you how bad I feel. Can we talk when you're home?' said Charlie, deep emotion in her voice.

Alice was steadfast in her resolve.

'There's no point Charlie. Goodbye'. Alice hung up, curled up in a ball and sobbed.

The doctors had looked at her CT scan and found that there was an intact brain in there, which was a relief, and no fractured skull, however they were concerned about the ECG they'd taken. She was wheeled down to the ultrasound department where a doctor scanned her heart.

It felt very odd to look at the screen at this pumping machine that was so vital to keeping her going. She was surprised to see that it wasn't cracked or broken from the way that she felt right that moment.

The doctor finished and said with some seriousness that there was a problem with her heart, one of her valves wasn't working properly which might explain the dizziness she'd experienced, as well as the fatigue that Alice had explained away as the hard year she'd gone through. Everyone told her that grief was exhausting, so she thought that was the reason for wanting to sleep a lot and needing naps.

'I want to monitor you for a while Alice in clinic twice a year but I'm happy to discharge you today. But if you feel really breathless or faint again, please come straight to A&E, ok? You may have always had a leaking valve, but we need to monitor it. I'll get the nurses to start your discharge papers, have you someone to collect you?' asked the doctor, she was firm but not making Alice too scared at what she might be facing her.

'I've some friends who can pick me up later yes, I'll find out when they will get here and go when they arrive if that is ok, I don't want to hold onto a bed as know you need it,' said Alice.

'Yes, that is true, but for today it is yours as you need it, ok' said the doctor with a smile, and with that she was gone to the next patient.

Alice called Jen and Holly who had just arrived home.

'Mind reader, we were just about to call you. What have you been doing to yourself to end up in hospital, we've been so worried' said Holly through the loudspeaker.

'Can I tell you both later if that's ok. I'm being released today, but you don't need to rush as they said that I can have the bed until you can come and get me, but I'll be so pleased to see you both,' said Alice.' Hope you had a good holiday even though it was cut short'.

'Glad to be home,' said Jen. 'I miss my English grub'.

'Bless you Jen, bacon sandwiches for you then. Sorry guys I just want to lie down and nap, I look forward to seeing you later'.

'Of course, you go rest. We'll be there in a couple of hours. We'll grab some shopping on the way and then we are all set to have our poorly house guest, see you soon, lots of love' answered Jen hanging up.

After a short nap Alice, a nurse brought her discharge papers and they started to get her dressed but realised that what she'd been wearing was badly torn and covered in sick, so Alice told them to throw it out. This meant she was on the bed waiting for Jen and Alice in two hospital gowns to protect her modesty and wearing her DM boots.

'Is that a new fashion statement?' joked Jen lightly, trying to disguise the shock at seeing her friend bruised and battered. She was pushing an empty wheelchair ready to transport her friend safely.

'Yes, do you think it will catch on?'

'Definitely can see it on the catwalks in Milan' said Holly helping Alice to her feet and settling her in the wheelchair.

Alice thanked the nurses on the ward as she was wheeled out, then held her breath whilst in the lift as they always scared her. Soon she was wheeled out into the fresh air and Holly put the brake on whilst Jen went to get the car. It felt so nice to be out of the ward and to feel the sun on her skin. She noticed the reactions of people seeing her face before entering the hospital and those gathering around in huddles to smoke.

She was reminded of one of her favourite songs by the Editors 'Smokers outside the hospital doors'. Some were wired to drips sat in wheelchairs but were still puffing away unhappily. The sight made Alice think of her lovely dad in his final days. If he hadn't smoked, if he had given up sooner, maybe he would still be here, she just wanted her dad right then to give her a big hug and make her feel better. She felt overwhelmed by sadness of his loss, despite it being nearly twenty years ago. *Grief sneaks up on you when you think you've it under control* thought Alice.

Holly was stood behind Alice chattering away about their holiday so didn't see as the tears poured down her face, stinging her scrapes on her face. She managed to wipe the tears away and contain herself as Jen pulled up outside the hospital entrance. Holly helped her into the back seat making sure the gown didn't fly up and flash everyone and then returned the wheelchair to the reception.

'We thought we could collect some of your things from your house on the way, have you got your keys? Asked Holly.

'Yes, they're here in my bag' said Alice, she suddenly felt scared to go home, what if Charlie was there and tried to talk to her. She looked at the time and saw it was almost four o'clock, maybe Charlie wouldn't be there.

The street was busy as they drove down it with people returning from work. Her car was in the driveway so Jen parked as close as she could to the front of her house. Charlie's bedroom window was open, and her car was outside. Holly helped Alice out of the car and unlocked the front door for her and into the garden chair in the living room.

'Right tell us what you need, and we'll get it for you,' said Jen.

'My clothes are still in the suitcase upstairs in my room, and can you bring the box we found from the fireplace, my laptop and my phone charger are all I need really, oh and the usual bathroom stuff. Thank you, you're both so kind, I don't deserve you, I just need to get out of here' said Alice as who broke down. She'd wanted to hold it together until she got to their house, but she just couldn't hold it in any longer.

'Jen, can you get Alice's stuff, and we'll get her home quickly. It's ok, we've got you' said Holly kneeling next to her and holding her close. 'You've been in the wars. We wanted to get you back before we asked anything, we know something big has happened'.

Jen set about her tasks bringing the wash basket down too and all of Alice's things and went to load the car. Holly helped Alice walk to the car and they set off to what she felt was sanctuary.

10

Sanctuary

It's certainly true that friends know the inner workings of your heart. Alice only needed to tell Jen and Holly the bare essentials of what happened with Charlie for them to be able to help their friend, not only heal from the short-lived affair, but to recover from the trauma of her fall and discovering her bad heart. Jen had said that it seemed surreal that someone with such a kind heart could have one that was defective.

Work had been understanding about her couple of missed days, but thanks to the TLC from her friends she'd managed to work from the sofa and her bed, whilst they fussed around her like two mother hens.

There had been no further contact with Charlie, and she'd cancelled the decorating party as she wanted to be fit and well to join in, not just sit there and give instructions. The decorating could wait until she was well again. Being able to work at her friend's house gave Alice the space to catch up on her module planning and emails, so she would be ready for her potential promotion. That was an important thing to aim for thought Alice, something positive to focus on. Jen and Holly went out for the day on Sunday and were dropping into Alice's house to collect the post on their way back, which gave her a free day to do some research on Charlotte and Hester's story. She had the letters and the beautiful photograph of Hester. The fact that she'd collapsed outside Hester's house wasn't lost on Alice. The women she had begun to fall in love with had walked in her footsteps and she in theirs.

She slowly began to plot out their story.

Timeline of Charlotte and Hester

Charlotte was born in 1910 at Newington Villa on Tadcaster Road, York to Charles and Amelia Hope. They were an affluent family, and she was home schooled with a governess. She met Hester Harmson at one of her mother's charity fetes at St Stephen's Orphanage which was further up Tadcaster Road. The girls were both 14 when they met and formed an instant bond.

Charles Hope lived on private means with money inherited from his father who was a banker, however he lost a great deal of it in the stock market crash in 1929 meaning that the family had to move into the house that Alice would later buy. Charles died in 1931. From the letters Charlotte was told it was an accident but newspaper articles it was clear that he had jumped in front of a train. Charlotte continued to live with her widowed mother until she died in 1933, the death certificate stated that her cause of death was emaciation, and Alice wondered if she'd given up on life due to grief. The house was left to Charlotte who lived there for the rest of her life. There was no one to pressure her to marry, so she could be single unlike poor Hester. The 1939 Register stated that she was in Bootham Asylum.

Hester Harmson was also born in 1910 to George and Esther Harmson and lived a very affluent life and they had the best of everything. George's family-owned mills and breweries in Yorkshire and money was no object for anything. Their main home was in Kensington, but the children were brought up at 2 St Leonards Place, York and spent their summers either in London or Bath. The family were only mildly affected by the crash, her father adapting the business and diversifying. Once Hester reached the age of 19 her family started to pressurise her into marrying, a number of suitors were thrown in her path, each one she rejected.

Charlotte and Hester realised their love for each other at this point and with Charlotte losing her place in society after the death of her father, and then her mother, it was hard for them to be together so they wrote letters and visited when they could.

The separation was painful for them both, and Hester was distraught that her father was making her marry his business partners son Peter Haughton who was 20 years older than her. He was a strict forceful man who having gained the rank of Captain in WW1 treated his staff, friends and family cruelly, but his drive and social position were attractive to Charlotte's parents, and her inheritance when her parents died would mean he would be even richer. The marriage went ahead in the summer of 1937 and Peter would travel the UK and Europe looking to expand the business and to make more money.

The couple lived in Kensington but whilst he was away working, Hester took every opportunity to be in York with Charlotte, snatching what time they could together.

Charlotte's parents were both killed in a motor accident shortly after her marriage, and the will left her a substantial amount of money which would have given her financial freedom, but just as she was thinking of leaving Peter, she found that she was pregnant.

Charlotte was devastated as it was the realisation that Hester was having sex with her husband, and also that she was completely trapped in the marriage. This sent Charlotte into a tailspin which led to her having a breakdown and she was admitted to Bootham hospital for mental health treatment. After she was released a month later, she returned to her home in St Stephen's Road and waited for Hester.

However, being in touch with Charlotte was too painful for Hester so she stopped writing to her and concentrated on raising her daughter Eliza and trying to be a good wife, but Peter became more distant, drinking excessively and was aggressive when he felt she wasn't being the wife he wanted. It was almost a relief when in 1939 Peter was called up to serve in the army. Forever secretive, Peter didn't tell Hester where he was going, and would send very few letters to her. She stayed in Kensington until it was felt it was too dangerous for her to be in London, so she moved back to York and leased a house in the village of Nether Poppleton. She tried desperately to stay away from Charlotte, but one day she could take the separation and loneliness no longer and she went to her house on St Stephen's Road.

Charlotte, who at that point hadn't been long out of Bootham was in a very sorry state, not eating and not taking care of herself. She collapsed at the door when she saw Hester. So Charlotte took her to her house as there was food and she knew she would be able to take better care of her there. She slowly nursed Charlotte back to health, spending hours reading to her, talking and saying how sorry she was for abandoning her. It was at this point that she knew that she could not live without her.

She knew that she could not send a letter to Peter telling him she was leaving as he was away fighting, so she decided that the next time he returned on leave she would tell him then.

He sent a telegraph in the winter of 1942 to say he was at their home in Kensington and that he would be travelling to York the following day and said he would be staying at the Station Hotel and asked her to meet him there. Charlotte was anxious as to why he wouldn't just come to the house in Poppleton, and her fears were realised when Hester didn't return after meeting with him. She thought that she'd decided to stay with him, but the following day a telegram arrived from the County Hospital from Hester to say that she'd been admitted there after being attacked by Peter.

Charlotte rushed to the hospital to find a very badly beaten Hester, who had been admitted with internal bleeding and broken ribs which the doctors had operated as she had a punctured lung. Her face had been badly bruised, and she was unrecognisable. However, her prognosis was good, and she was allowed home after a week.

Peter was arrested and taken to Wakefield Prison awaiting trial. He had exploded when Hester had told him that she was leaving and had attacked her in the lounge of the hotel in front of the staff. He had also been charged with assaulting two police officers who arrested him at the scene.

Hester returned home and was cared for by a private nurse and Charlotte whilst awaiting the trial date, however Peter was found dead in his cell the week before they were due in court. This left Hester with enormous guilt and shame for what she felt she'd caused, but this was eased when his army records showed that he had been acting in this aggressive manner for some time and had been AWOL when he arrived in York. The post-mortem showed that he had been suffering from a brain tumour which had caused the change in his behaviour and that if he hadn't killed himself, he would have died through his illness.

Charlotte and Hester moved into St Stephen's Road along with Eliza, who loved her aunt and didn't question why the two adults slept in the same bedroom. They had a cleaner who came in every day, and *despite the fact that the Hester could have afforded to buy any large mansion or estate that she wanted, she chose to make her life with Charlotte in the end terraced house in York, with the woman that she loved. In 1965 Hester fell ill and died in the arms of the woman who had made her life complete, Eliza was away with her London relatives when she died and became an extraordinarily rich woman in her own right.*

The final note in the box was written by Charlotte in 1965 which read: -

Hester my darling, my life, my love. I love you more than all the stars above in the night sky and will love you always and forever.

Charlotte died in 1966 from a heart attack and she left the house to Eliza. It appeared from what the deeds and Charlie had said that she lived there at the end of her life.

Eliza had married in 1972 to a Lance Hazelwood and they had a child born in 1973 called Katherine but that is where the story ended. Lance had died in the 1980's in YDH leaving Eliza a widow but there was no record that Alice could find for Katherine.

Alice knew that she must try and locate Katherine as she should have her grandmothers' letters, but then again it might come as too much of a shock about having a lesbian grandmother. The women's story was fascinating and really deserved to be written up properly and shared, the history of lesbian women was very thin on the ground, and it really needed sharing Alice felt. But first she had to try and find Katherine. She really needed to get back home to look at the deeds again.

She began to feel very tired so snuggled down on the sofa and was asleep when Jen and Holly arrived back home with fish and chips. The lovely aroma roused her from her slumber, and she sat up and slowly made her way into the kitchen, following her nose.

'Hey, that smells divine, have you had a good day?' Asked Alice, getting knives and forks out of the drawer and putting them onto the dining table. Holly was putting out the salt, vinegar and tomato ketchup whilst Jen distributed the food, stealing the odd chip when no one was looking, or so she thought.

Holly and Alice were giggling watching Jen think she wasn't being seen. 'Having fun over there Jen?' said Holly laughing.

'I'm starving! It's a long time since lunchtime, a girl has to keep her strength up' said Jen bringing two plates of food over to the table, and then going back for the third.

The three women sat and ate, the couple sharing their day in Harrogate, going to the spa and then to Betty's for lunch, followed by a walk in Knaresborough on the way back. Alice was now ready to share the news about the box and the story that she'd uncovered, both from the letters and her research. The pair sat listening intently, Holly looked emotional when she heard the pain that Charlotte had gone through as well as the abuse that Hester had suffered. They both agreed that Alice needed to keep going, write it up fully and then find Katherine if she could. Maybe with her inheritance she could have moved abroad, because with money, the world was open to her.

'You've got to find her; Charlotte and Hester were a brave and amazing couple. It makes me feel so emotional thinking how much they fought to be together, it's a proper lesbian love story' said Holly, reaching for Jen's hand who she could see had a wobbly bottom lip and was staring at the wall so as not to cry.

'I'll do my best, I promise, maybe I should find the antique shop in Stonegate to see if they have a record of where that key came from. I really believe it's the original to the box. Bit of a long shot though. I'll send Jack an email tomorrow. Would you like to read some of the letters? I've been through them all now, such beautiful penmanship and words, I wish someone would write letters like that to me,' said Alice.

'Talking of letters, let me get your post' said Holly and she reached down and took them from her bag on the floor and passed them over to Alice.

Most of them were bills, a postcard from her aunty from her holiday in Spain and then a hand delivered letter which Alice opened with a frown as she didn't recognise the handwriting.

It said: -

Dear Alice

I'm writing this to you as I don't want to bother you again on the phone when you're unwell. I saw you come back today to get your things and I wanted to come out and see you, but I didn't think I would be very welcome. I'm so sorry that you were so badly injured, and you've hurt your beautiful face, I don't know what happened to make you fall so hard, but I couldn't run fast enough to catch you. I called the ambulance and stayed with you until they had you safely inside it and gave them all your details. They wouldn't let me ride with you so I ran to the hospital and waited in A&E but because I wasn't a relative, they wouldn't let me know anything other than you'd been admitted, and I was so worried.

I can't express to you how guilty I feel about what you walked in on, there are no excuses that I can make. You've seen how messed up I am, and it was wrong to start anything with you whilst I'm in such a bad way.

That awful bloody day I started drinking as soon as I got into work, I hadn't heard from you, and I thought you'd changed your mind about me as you ran out without making further plans and I panicked. The right thing to do would have been to knock on your door but I couldn't face you rejecting me. I hit the whiskey as soon as I arrived at work, Dawn arrived shortly after, and one thing led to another. I'd convinced myself you didn't care. I got your text about your phone dying when I was running after you. I'm so very sorry. I can't ask for forgiveness as I don't deserve it. You're honest and beautiful, and you need to be with someone who loves you deeply for the woman you are. I wanted so badly to be that person. You made me feel like a normal person, that I could talk to you about anything and that I have known you forever, but I threw it all away.

I'm putting this letter through your door as I'm going into a rehab facility in Windermere, Di has a friend who went there, and I was lucky to get a cancellation. I need to get my head and health sorted for myself. I don't know how long I'll be away; it could be a couple of months or longer, so when you come home you don't need to worry about seeing me. Di is checking on the house every few days, so don't be surprised if you see her, and she has taken on the role of Manager at Valentine's until I come back and decide what I should do with it. She's been a good friend to me. I don't know why. I honestly don't deserve anyone being kind to me.

I hope that one day you'll forgive me.

All love

Charlie x

Alice passed the letter to Jen and Holly waiting to see what their reaction would be. Holly looked sad, but Jen looked mad as hell.

'What the fuck makes her think that she can write a letter like that and be forgiven?' said Jen.

'I don't think that she wants to be forgiven, or at least she doesn't expect to be. I don't know her story Alice, and I don't want you to tell me, but she sounds in pain, and I'm pleased that she is owning her behaviour and going into rehab. I think I know which one she means as I've referred patients there before. If she sticks to the programme, it will really help her start a new life. But she'll need to be there for three months at least. Don't beat yourself up for trying Alice, you're so kind-hearted you want to believe the best in everyone' said Holly giving her a hug.

'Are you ready to talk about what the doctor said at the hospital, can you remember which doctor you saw?'

'It was a female consultant in the cardiac department, does that help? She was tall with short brown hair and had red framed glasses which I thought was funny as she looked like Timmy Mallet in them' smiled Alice. 'All I know is it's called tricuspid regurgitation, but I'm sure you'll know all about it'.

'Have they put you on medication?' Asked Holly.

'No not yet, they want to monitor me for a while but said that if I get breathless to go to A&E straight away which really scared me. I literally feel like I've a ticking time bomb inside me waiting to explode' replied Alice, who looked at Holly hoping for answers.

'Ok let's not worry too much, if you aren't on medication that is quite low risk, and I know you would say if you felt unwell again. I know it isn't news anyone wants to get, but it isn't too much to worry about right now. You're here and safe, and we'll look after you. Stay as little or as much as you want until you feel ok about going back home. Now come here and give me and Jen a big hug, you're in safe hands' said Holly as the three of them stood and hugged in the kitchen.

'And don't you be thinking or worrying about that Charlie,' said Jen. 'You deserve so much better. Now, do you mind if I've the last of your chips Alice'.

The three women burst out laughing at Jen with her hollow legs, who was guaranteed to lighten any given situation and Alice felt thankful for her lovely caring friends as they all cleared the pots and washed up together. Alice thought that it was the simple things in life that meant the most.

Going up to her room Alice got out her journal and wrote what fell out of her head onto the paper.

As the autumn leaves fall

They scatter on the floor like my dreams I had of you.

The dream of life eternal, love and care

Drifted dreams that blew around my heart so fleetingly

The life I'd imagined doesn't compute anymore.

You've built up your wall, and although I see glimpses of you within

You won't reveal your heart enough to allow it to beat to the rhythm of mine

It feels so cruel, years of hurt that I can't help heal.

So I will kick around the leaves around my heart and pray for peace for us both

As we part and move away on different paths.

As she settled into bed that night, she reread Charlie's letter. She felt sorry for her and wished her well out into the universe. 'Goodnight Charlie' she whispered into the darkness.

11

Charlie's Journey

Charlie sat in the queue of traffic on the A59 outside Harrogate. She felt like she was fleeing a dragon that was intent on swallowing her whole, heading towards a mountain that she wasn't sure that she could scale. She felt sick with fear and had already sweated through her t-shirt. She hadn't touched a drop of alcohol in the week since seeing Alice fall, and she felt such remorse and anger at herself that she'd barely slept.

Di had really lost her shit with her, and it was needed, she deserved to be publicly flogged for what she'd done. So, after a lot of coffee and talking with Di she'd contacted a rehab clinic in Windermere and signed up. She'd decided to drive herself there with just a small bag of clothes, her phone charger and her sketching things. She'd visibly lost weight in just that one week of not drinking or eating much, and had left behind her lovely house, her suits and polished shoes. What faced her she knew would be gruelling and ugly, facing into the demons that she'd shoved in a box for so long.

The traffic subsided and Charlie manoeuvred her car around the outskirts of Harrogate out onto the road passed Blubberhouses, and up to what felt like the top of the world. Open fields and stone walls with miles and miles of white sheep littering the hills, driving down a road that at times felt like a rollercoaster ride of its own making. When she'd driven with Alice to the pub and seen such amazing countryside it had excited her, but this time it made her sad and she wanted to blinker herself away from the beauty. She drove to Skipton and parked and stopped for a coffee and bought a sandwich in case she felt hungry later, spotting postcards with horses on that she'd the sudden urge to buy and send to Alice. She felt a pang in her stomach every time she thought of her which was a totally new experience.

Time was ticking on, so she headed back to her car and set out on the road which led towards Settle, then Kendal and then down to Windermere. The Briar Rehab Centre was a large white house on the top of the hill looking down over Lake Windermere. The view was incredible, seeing the lake, woods beyond and the boats bobbing along taking tourists on excursions. But Charlie wasn't here to sightsee, she was here to sort herself out and make sense of her life.

She went through the entrance and a middle-aged man greeted her, booked her in and took her to her room on the first floor which overlooked a beautiful well stocked garden. The greeter was talking away to her but she couldn't take anything in, it was all a blur and garbled in her head. Once in the room she could see a group of men and women sat on the grass in a circle meditating which made the scenery look even more peaceful.

'If there's anything you need you can use the room phone and dial 1 for reception 24 hours a day and there is an itinerary of your week on the desk. Just take your time to settle in your room and we will see you downstairs later' he said. His lanyard said Toby.

Charlie nodded and Toby left.

Her room was big, with an old fireplace, large bed, en suite and a desk and chair, dressing table and large wardrobe. Unpacking took Charlie a minute as she'd brought so little with her. On the bed was a t-shirt, sweatshirt and some jogging trousers in navy blue, which the details said everyone wore whether they were staff or patient whilst on site. The brochure said it was to remove the pressure of what to wear so you could just focus on the self.

The itinerary for the week began with a group gathering in the conference room at 6pm, which gave Charlie a couple of hours to settle in and eat her sandwich. The schedule started at 7am and finished at 10pm each night and was a mix of therapies, group work, individual counselling and exercise to replenish both the body and mind. Charlie wondered if she'd the energy for it, as lately she'd been so tired each afternoon, she often had a nap. Maybe it was being in your 50's, the menopause or the amount of sex she and Alice had. She set an alarm on her phone and laid on her bed for a while feeling drained after the two-and-a-half-hour drive. Within what felt like seconds her phone alarm was peeling out, she quickly turned it off, freshened up in the bathroom and put on the t-shirt and joggers that had been left out for her, and headed down to the conference room.

There were already a few people in the room and Charlie took a seat on one of the chairs which were placed in a circle in the middle of the room, there was soft classical music playing and those already seated were looking everywhere but at each other.

As 6pm approached more people joined until there were 16 people seated with one chair spare which was filled by a young woman with a clip board and name tag that said Dr Hanson.

'Good evening all, I'm Dr Hanson and I'll be one of your therapists during your stay. Some of you'll be here for some time, but others will leave before that. Everyone is on a different journey so there is no judgment if you're here for longer'. She then set about handing out stickers and a pen to write down their name which was then stuck to their t shirt, first names only. She then talked about the process and daily tasks which were aimed at keeping the mind busy, whilst giving the body a chance to rest and learn new coping techniques. However, she stressed that the most important part of the journey was to talk. 'The more you put into the sessions, the more you would get out' she enforced.

Charlie's first official session was at 9am the following day for an assessment with the doctor to decide on whether medications would be needed. This had never crossed Charlie's mind. She'd never been keen on drugs, which was hilarious thinking of what poisons she'd put into her body through alcohol over the years. She knew there were drugs you could take that made you very ill if you had any alcohol, but she'd never considered them, but at this point she was willing to do anything that the doctors said.

After the introduction they were all shown around the large house with an assortment of therapy rooms, spa treatments, art room (which grabbed Charlie's attention) and then went into the dining room for a 'light supper' which consisted of a variety of salads and fruits. Charlie was glad that she'd eaten her sandwich earlier. She felt too weary to talk to anyone, and it seemed that everyone else felt the same. Just being here felt exhausting, and she was desperate to get back to her room.

As they headed out, they were all given a journal which they were encouraged to write in each day. Charlie couldn't face it that evening, so she headed up to her room, put on shorts and t shirt and went to bed. She lay there listening to the noises of the house. The creaking of floorboards above as someone was pacing, up and down, in the next room she thought she heard someone crying, and she heard fire doors opening and closing regularly. She was just dropping off when there was a loud door banging, then a car door and then the noise of a car speeding off. Charlie wondered if someone had left, or maybe a member of staff was speeding off home for the night, but she didn't have the energy or inclination to find out.

After a fitful night she was woken at 6.30 by the morning call on the room phone. She had to be down for breakfast at 7am which was just enough time to shower and dress for the day in the blue outfit. The dining room was silent but for the scrapping of a spoon on a bowl, or knife on toast, all eyes were cast down as though eating breakfast was the most important thing happening.

Charlie took a bowl and poured cornflakes and milk, took a spoon and went to an empty table. There was a pot of tea on the table and cups, so she poured herself some, her hand slightly shaking making the lid rattle. She was aware as she ate that more people had entered the room and repeated the same process, and a couple joined her at her table. They too kept their eyes down as though in a silent prayer.

A woman of similar age to Charlie joined her table, sitting down in an aggressive pose leaning far back, lifting the front legs off, her hands stuffed deep in her pockets. She didn't have a label on her sweatshirt, and her facial expression was one of defiance as she glared around the room. She began to shuffle about, running her hands through her short, black spiked hair in an agitated manner, and Charlie could see out of the corner of her eye the other people at her table looking uncomfortable.

It was a relief when some people who looked like they worked there came in and stood at the front of the room. Dr Hanson cleared her throat.

'Good morning, everyone, I'm Dr Hanson. A couple of you weren't here for the introduction last night so I will have a brief word with you after breakfast. As you'll have seen, we have a meditation class every day straight after breakfast at 8 which, gives you a chance to ground yourselves for the day. I know not everyone will have tried this before, but as with everything we do here, please give it a go and allow yourself to feel as we guide you through it. I also want to introduce you to the team today who will be showing you around whilst you acclimatise yourself to the building, the routines and we can work out with each one of you a specific plan to help you achieve the most out of your stay here' said Dr Hanson, who then asked each member of staff to introduce themselves.

Each of the staff took it in turns to introduce themselves, there was a dietician, an art therapist, yoga teacher and finally a psychologist who said that she would be running the daily therapy sessions.

Dr Hanson stepped forward again.

'If you can all follow me to the meditation room, we will start the morning off with a group session, then as you all know we will be having individual sessions with each of you, have you all got your times?'

There was a general murmuring of agreement from the group as they stood and followed Dr Hanson.

Charlie had just walked out of the dining room when she heard loud banging behind her, and when she turned she saw the angry woman from her table very agitated raising her chair above her head and threw it across the room.

She screamed 'I'm not here for this shit, you can't fucking make me stay. Don't fucking touch me' as Dr Hanson and another large built man approached her.

The remainder of the group were ushered from the room and down to the meditation room and closed the door leaving the angry woman behind. Charlie had seen many angry drunk women in her years working in bars, and she'd been one herself on many occasions, but it felt strange to see it in this quiet house when last orders hadn't just been called.

The meditation room had many bean bags, floor mats and large cushions scattered around a highly polished wooden floor. Large windows gave views over Lake Windermere and there was light classical music coming from the speakers. Dr Charlton the psychologist muted the stereo as they all took a seat around the room. Charlie opted for a large cushion as she was unsure if she would ever be able to extricate herself from a bean bag with 52-year-old hips and knees.

Dr Charlton then talked the group through a body scan meditation where you closed your eyes and allowed yourself to feel each individual part of your body, tensing and releasing it as you moved from bottom to top, her voice was soft and soothing, but Charlie felt very tense despite this. She tried very hard to feel her muscles relax beneath her, but instead she could feel her jaw tensing, the vein on her temple throbbing. She had a quake on her right hand that had been more pronounced since her arrival and Charlie put it down to nerves, but in reality, she knew she was in withdrawal. After the session came to an end the door opened and Dr Hanson came in and asked Charlie to come with her to her treatment room.

Charlie followed, her heart in her mouth dreading what was to follow.

Dr Hanson's office had a large resplendent oak desk and wooden swivel chair which she took a seat in and beckoned Charlie to take the chair opposite.

'Good morning, Charlie, nice to meet you one to one. Have you settled in, ok?' Dr Hanson asked.

'So so' replied Charlie. 'I've never done this before'.

'It's a positive first step. Today I want to talk about what brought you here, what medications you're on and what your expectations are'.

'Not sure where to start to be honest other than I'm here to stop drinking and stop my behaviour around it. I've made too many mistakes because of it, or because of who I am. I make too many bad choices and I want to make good ones. Did you say medications next?' asked Charlie.

Dr Hanson nodded.

'Other than HRT I don't take anything else. I haven't done any illegal drugs in a long time' answered Charlie. 'I just want to stop drinking and be normal'.

'And what do you see as normal?' asked Dr Hanson

'To live without the need to drink whenever anything goes wrong, when I feel rejected. Not to feel anxious at what the future holds for me, I've messed up so badly' said Charlie putting her head in her hands, to cover the tears forming in her eyes, discreetly wiping them away.

'Do you want to tell me about that now Charlie?'

Charlie shook her head. She felt too embarrassed at crying in front of the doctor at her first session.

'That's fine Charlie we can talk about that at another session, it's early days. I've noticed you've a slight shake to her hands. I've the results of the bloods you had done before you came here, and I'm pleased to say that your liver function was ok which is a positive sign. When did you last have a drink and how much do you drink in a week?' asked Dr Charlton making notes.

'I haven't had a drink in over a week, I don't drink every day, but I do when I have any kind of emotional upset, once I start, I can't stop. I've hurt too many people with my behaviour' explained Charlie.

'And have you thought about how you're hurting yourself too Charlie?' asked Dr Hanson.

'Not really no' answered Charlie.

'Well, this is something that we can work on whilst you're here. I'd like to start you on 10mg of Diazepam. This helps both with alcohol withdrawal and also with anxiety. You won't be on it for long, but it will help you in the short term alongside the other therapies we have here. Was there anything in particular you wanted to be involved in or were looking forward to?' said Dr Hanson.

'I'd be interested in the art therapy. I like that sort of thing. I'm not keen on taking drugs,' said Charlie. 'But I will try anything to not feel like this anymore'.

'Good, I'm glad to hear that. Art can be very therapeutic, and you'll have the freedom to explore a range of techniques. We also have sessions where your family can come into the centre for joint therapy and to visit you. These can be very helpful for when you leave, so that they can be part of your journey too. Is that something that you would be interested in?' asked Dr Hanson.

'I don't have any family. And I'm not sure if my friend Di would want to. There is only one person I want to see but I've hurt her really badly and I don't think she'd come' said Charlie sadly.

'We can work on that together in our sessions. So, I will start your meds tonight when you've had dinner which will help you relax and sleep. I would also recommend that you maybe don't contact your friends for the first few weeks until you settle in, and we can talk through how you want to progress with things. We'll meet every few days and you can always journal what you want to talk about. We're here 24 hours a day if you need anything, or someone to talk things through with. Is there anything you'd like to ask?' asked Dr Hanson.

'How long do you think I'll be here?' enquired Charlie.

'As you're here voluntarily you can leave anytime unless we feel you're a danger to yourself or others, but I'd allow for 90 days to give yourself as good a chance of recovery as possible, I know it feels like a long time, but it's the beginning step of the rest of your life'. Dr Hanson looked at her watch. 'If you make your way down to the dining room everyone will be there for coffee shortly and then we will do an introduction session with everyone, this sometimes happens naturally and sometimes it doesn't'.

Charlie said goodbye to Dr Hanson and headed down to the dining room, the table and chairs were all lined up in a row now, with coffee cups on a separate table. Toby arrived pushing a large trolley with a tea and coffee urn with assorted jugs.

Charlie took a cup and poured herself some coffee and took it to the French doors, opening them up and stepping out onto the terrace. Inhaling the fresh cool Windermere air, she closed her eyes and wished the 90 days away.

12

For the Love of Horses

The weekend had been such a tonic Alice didn't want to leave Jen and Holly's, so after a group discussion it was decided that she would stay there until she went to Lou's on Friday.

The furniture from Lavender Interiors was delayed a fortnight, they weren't happy about it, but Jen was quite forceful over the phone and the painting party was rearranged to the Saturday before. Her friends returned to work after their break and caring duties on the Monday morning, Alice was installed in Holly's office which had a serene air and she worked away happily there all week, slowly building her strength as her bruising went down after turning a multitude of colours. On an evening she cooked for her friends, and they talked over food and hot chocolates, discussing Holly's hectic work schedule and Jen's electrical adventures rewiring old houses that week. She'd apparently become obsessed with looking under floorboards in the hope of finding another mystery box.

Jack had replied to Alice's email and told her he'd bought the key from Ellekers on Stonegate, and in turn she'd called the shop about it. They had the details of the seller, and so Alice gave them her email address and phone number to pass onto them, with the intriguing message that she'd found something in the house that belonged to them. She really hoped that it would lead her to Katherine and not be a dead end.

Alice had tried to call off her weekend away with Lou as her face was still a mess and her dressing was still on her head. The stitches were dissolvable, but she didn't like looking at the cut on her head, it made her remember Charlie and she didn't want that. She didn't want to think about that until she was stronger and had come to terms with what was going on for her. However, Lou wouldn't hear about it and said she'd a lovely surprise for her.

So, on Friday morning she was just packing her things when Jen came into her bedroom with a pile of freshly laundered clothes. She was a dab hand with an iron, it was like the clothes lay down and submitted to her.

'These are yours love; shall I just leave on the bed?' asked Jen. Alice nodded as she was concentrating on folding neatly which wasn't her forte.

'What's the weather like this weekend, do you know?' asked Alice. Jen started to laugh at her.

'You really need to get to know your phone Alice, it can tell you a multitude of things, you can be such a luddite,' laughed Jen.

'I forgot, what am I like! I'll be ready soon if you're still ok to drop me off at my house' asked Alice putting the clothes Jen had brought up into her suitcase, however whilst trying to get them to fit she realised one of the items was Charlie's shirt which she'd loaned her after the meal. She remembered that she'd thrown it into her wash basket which the girls had kindly washed for her. And there she was holding it in her hands staring at it. 'This is Charlie's, I should get it back to her somehow'.

'Nah chuck it, best place for it,' said Jen.

'Jen! No, I'll try and catch Di one day when I'm back home. Ok I'm ready to go.' Alice had opted to be casual and wear her black jeans and a sweatshirt and her ankle boots, she didn't have any country clothes, but she was sure it wouldn't matter.

Jen drove her home so she could collect her car and drive to Lou's. After Jen had gone, she went inside to check her post and make sure the house was ok. There were some things in the fridge that were practically walking on their own which needed throwing out, so she sorted that and then left the house. She glanced at Charlie's house all the windows were closed and the shutters were half shut. Her stomach lurched and she felt sick again, with a mix of wanting Charlie and the repulsion at what she'd done.

The ring road was heaving so Alice diverted and took a nostalgic trip down her childhood streets, past the farm where she kept her pony Misty, and up onto the country lane cutting out the traffic jam. Askham Bryan was as lovely as ever, and she quickly parked her car next to a Range Rover and an Audi convertible and went round the back of the house to the kitchen door. She knocked and Henry answered.

'Welcome Alice, come on in. Crikey you've been in the wars, Lou is just upstairs, let me go shout her' and with that he walked down the hall and bellowed up to announce her arrival which reverberated around the house.

'Coming' replied Lou and there was the sound of a door closing and Lou walking down the stairs. She appeared in the kitchen dressed in jodhpurs, boots and was carrying a riding crop. 'Just like old times, eh?' She walked over to Alice, gave her a hug. 'Your poor face'.

'It's much better than it was. What a get up! Have you got yourself another horse?' asked Alice, clapping her hands.

'Yes, as a celebration of selling the house in London I bought myself a horse, do you want to come and meet him? Said Lou.

'Oh my god yes, a hug with a horse is just what I need' said Alice feeling very giddy. Horses had been such a huge part of her childhood and she missed the thrill of riding and all the wonderful smells that having a horse entailed, even the mucking out.

'Follow me, this is the big surprise, not just the horse' said Lou leading the way, grabbing a scarf from the coat stand as they left the house.

As they approached the entrance to their garden Lou turned and said she was putting on the blindfold so Alice couldn't see, as long as it wouldn't hurt her. Alice agreed, she hadn't quite expected this, but she trusted Lou.

She led Alice through the gate, across the small lane and she could hear her opening the gate to the old stable yard. She led her to what felt like the middle of the complex and then she was told to remove the scarf. Alice couldn't believe her eyes. All of the stables had been totally refurbished, doors had been painted, windows repaired, and it gleamed like new. There were bales of straw and shavings in the small barn and every stable had a new horses name on it.

'Have you opened up the yard again or gone mad and bought a lot of horses?' laughed Alice.

'No, it's quite something, as you know we were wondering what to do with it and had pretty much decided to leave it until next year, then a woman in the village came round and asked to rent the whole thing, I negotiated with her a bit and in the end, I have my studio and one stable, and she is renting the rest. Come and meet Harvey, he's such a gentle giant' said Lou who was beaming from ear to ear and looked like a teenager again.

She made a clicking noise and heard clomping of metal horseshoes on the concrete in the stable. A large piebald horse's head and neck appeared over the door giving a small whicker.

'Oh, my goodness Lou, he's beautiful. Such a kind eye and gentleness about him. I'm smitten' said Alice stroking his muzzle and head and leaning in to put her face against his to inhale the wonderful horse aroma. He stood there totally still letting Alice get her horse fix. It had been a very long time. 'I'd forgotten how amazing it is to be around horses. You're so lucky getting to relive your childhood again'.

'I know, but you're welcome anytime you need a horse fix. Do you feel up to a little ride, can you get a hat on with your dressing?' asked Lou.

'I'm not sure but willing to give it a go,' said Alice.

'Look at us being so safety conscious, all those years of riding without hats bombing around everywhere. We were fearless.' said Lou going into the tack room and bringing out a very sparkly new hat. 'This is mine and it might fit you' she said passing it to Alice who slowly put it on her head, the peak sat just above her dressing, she did up the strap and it fitted like a glove.

Lou went back into the tack room and brought out a rather lovely black saddle and pelham bridle with two reins. She quickly tacked up Harvey who stood like a total gentleman whilst she adjusted the throatlash, nose band and fastened the chain under his chin loosely.

She then expertly put on his saddle, attached the martingale and did up his girth.

'You never forget how to do the important stuff,' said Lou. 'It just feels totally natural'.

She led Harvey over to a very large mounting block, pulled down the stirrups and Alice climbed the steps and put her foot into the stirrup, mounting him quickly and gently. 'Gosh he's a bit bigger than our ponies isn't he, feel like I need altitude pills,' said Alice. 'Shall I just ride on the top rein, or does he need both?'

'Yes, that's fine, he probably doesn't need the full pelham, but he looks so elegant in it. I'll downgrade to a snaffle I think, see how he goes in that. Do you want me to lead you for a bit?' asked Lou, their horse chatter and language just naturally came back, and it really felt like old times.

'Yes, just for a bit, I'm out of practice. Is he just for pleasure or are you aiming to compete?' asked Alice feeling totally at ease on Harvey who was very chilled and laid back. It wasn't long before Lou let go and Alice was riding him on the buckle.

'I'm not sure, I quite fancy learning some dressage, but for now I'm happy just plodding down the lanes. It's nice sharing the yard as I always have someone to hack out with if I want. Henry tried riding too, but it isn't for him, so I think he's taking up golf. We are fitting into the village nicely and it's lovely to have a community. Tomorrow night I've invited a few of our new friends and neighbours for dinner as long as you're sure it won't be too much for you?' asked Lou.

As they walked together down the lane up to where the fields went on for miles Alice could see Lou's fields with various horses in them, it was so nice to see them being used again. Harvey picked up pace a little as he approached the gateway and let out a whinny to his friends, who lifted their heads but decided the grass was much more fun and ignored him. Poor Harvey.

'No, it's fine, I might have to have a nap in the afternoon, but I'm just looking forward to hanging out with you all. I wasn't sure what clothes to bring so I brought too many,' laughed Alice. 'Do you want to swap and get on?'

'No, it's ok, I rode this morning, let's head back and we can turn him out then go and have some dinner, is that ok or do you need a rest beforehand?' asked Lou as they walked back to the yard, Harvey felt more sluggish walking away from his friends.

'No, I'm ok so far, thank you for letting me ride Harvey, it's made my day'. Alice untacked Harvey in the stable and put on his very posh leather headcollar and led him down to his field. Once released he galloped off to join his friends bucking and farting as he went. 'Aren't horse amazing'.

'They really are. We had so much fun didn't we back in the day' said Lou with a hint of nostalgia. 'Horses know just how to make you feel better, they're very good therapy'.

'Is everything ok Lou? Are things working out being here with Henry?' asked Alice. Lou looked so sad suddenly after appearing so happy.

'It's been difficult; therapy is hard, and it's a culture shock moving here after the buzz of London. Henry's bored and wants to go back to work, but I think it would be a big mistake, lots more talking is needed, I think. But anyway, we aren't here to worry about that today, we're here to have a nice weekend and we can worry about all that another day. Now, for supper I've thought we could have a stir fry, how does that sound then watch a film with a bowl of popcorn?' said Lou changing the subject.

'Sounds lovely, let me help with the cooking and you can tell me all about the village gossip and if you want, we could have a look at the chest?' Alice then told Lou about her box of letters and the lesbian love story that had come out of it. 'Have you had a chance to look through yours?'

'A lot of it was old bills and invoices and photographs of Aunt Agnes when she was young and some when she was at school. There were some letters, but we struggled with the handwriting, so we saved them for you as know you probably have a better eye than us.' Said Lou as they walked into the kitchen pulling off her boots and washing her hands.

'I'll just grab my suitcase, and then can I freshen up? I smell of horse, which is lovely, but I fancy changing into something cosy,' said Alice.

'Great, I'll show you to your room and you can see the new bathrooms' said Lou with pride in her voice.

Alice quickly collected her suitcase and headed back into the house. Henry was waiting to carry the case upstairs and into a pretty double bedroom which faced the back garden and beyond. The room was wall to wall Laura Ashley with a sun burst mirror over the fireplace. The Divan bed and matching plush headboard looked so appealing and Alice felt that she could happily climb under the comforter and fall asleep right at that moment.

'What a beautiful room, I feel very spoilt'. Said Alice unzipping her case and starting to look for something to change into.

'There is a new ensuite through this door with a shower in it, but if you wanted a bath there is one next door? Come and have a look,' said Lou.

The new bathroom was amazing, a large walk-in shower, a claw foot bath, basin and loo. It was very modern but didn't look out of place with the wooden panelling that had been installed around the room and painted a sage green.

'It's so lovely Lou, but I think I'll just have a shower and be down with you soon if that's ok' Alice said walking back into her room.

'Of course, just take your time, I'll be in the kitchen if you need me' said Lou closing the door.

Alice had a lovely shower and changed her dressing as it got wet when she washed her hair. She put on some cream linen trousers and a t-shirt and headed back downstairs into the kitchen. Lou was chopping peppers and already had a pile of mushrooms and onion, the wok poised ready to perform on the Aga. 'Anything I can do to help?'

'No, it's ok, just take a pew and tell me all about your house and what's going on with work' said Lou chopping quickly and expertly without chopping her finger off.

Henry uncorked some red wine and poured two glasses, Alice had declined as she was still taking tablets for her headaches and was sticking to water. The three of them chatted as Lou tossed the vegetables and retrieved the rice from the microwave. 'I know it's cheating but I can't seem to cook rice without burning it, this saves time and pan washing'. Alice smiled; it was good to see that Lou was still the same in some ways as she was years ago. The number of pans she went through in cookery classes at school, as everything seemed to burn as they were too busy chatting, which they often were. The trio ate, laughed and shared funny work stories until it became apparent that Alice was over tired, and she was sent to bed with a hot chocolate and told to have a lie in.

She was asleep as soon as her head hit the pillow and her body did as it was told, and she slept in until after 9. Lou and Henry had gone out, leaving a note to help herself to breakfast and that they would be back at 12. After making some toast Alice sat and read the Guardian in the living room which was unchanged since her last visit which was a relief. The old gymkhana photos made her smile once again. It had been so lovely to ride Harvey and Alice decided to go and see him in his field. She pulled on her boots, grabbed a carrot from the veg rack, borrowed Lou's jacket and headed down to the field. She shouted him but he was having none of it, the grass was far more tempting than a stranger calling him. So, Alice went into the field to give him the carrot instead. He lifted his head briefly to eat the offering but then wandered off casually.

She went back into the house and carried on reading the Guardian until Lou and Henry returned, she'd felt uncomfortable being in the house alone as though she was intruding, but that feeling passed once they were back, arms full of bags of groceries for the dinner party.

Alice was banned from helping, other than to pod some peas and choose the music whilst Lou and Henry cooked. They worked well together, unconsciously knowing what the next stage was, who was doing what, it was like watching a well-timed play. It was ambitious thought Alice for them to make a beef wellington, but the prepared roast would not have looked out of place in a Michelin Star restaurant. Alice gave them a round of applause she was so impressed. Eventually they relented and let Alice put on the tablecloth in the dining room which had been replastered and painted in a muted baby blue with the long mahogany table and chairs as the magnificent centre piece. There were eight place settings which kept Alice out of the kitchen and busy placing glasses, cutlery and placemats with a centre piece silver candelabra that was on the sideboard.

Henry came through with the red wine to let it breathe and said they were going up to change as everyone would be there at 6.30 so Alice went up to her room and put on the same linen dress she'd worn for her date with Charlie, fixed her hair and put on a small amount of makeup. She felt great, except for the dressing on her head which took away from the full effect of her outfit.

She heard voices in the kitchen as she descended the stairs and saw a small gathering of people near the door, three men in suits and ties and one woman in a red dress, stood with her back to Alice, who had her black hair tied back in a fancy bun.

'Hey everyone, this is my friend Alice, I told you all about. Alice this is Robert and his partner Tony, our neighbour Clive, and do you remember our old riding pal Harriet?'

13

When It Feels Like A Dream

Alice felt floored. Her childhood crush was stood right there in front of her, and she was completely speechless, she just stood there with her mouth open looking bonkers.

'Wow Alice, you haven't changed a bit' said Harriet walking towards Alice who still was gawping.

'Er hi Harriet, what are…… erm' stuttered Alice.

'Are you ok Alice, do you need to sit down, have you overdone it today?' asked Lou clucking around her anxiously, worried that her friend was ill in her charge.

'Is it hot in here?' asked Alice suddenly feeling flushed and her legs were wobbling again.

Lou put her arm around her and walked her onto the patio and sat her on a chair, Henry appeared with a glass of water at her side. Alice felt foolish and blindsided. She took a few gulps of water and her temperature returned to normal after a few minutes.

Alice realised she'd made a bit of fool of herself, maybe she could blame the bump on her head. 'Sorry about that, maybe I've overdone it a bit,' said Alice.

'Let's all go through to the dining room; do you want to sit it out Alice and just go to bed?' asked Lou.

'No, it's ok sorry Lou. Can you just help me through though, my legs feel a bit wobbly'.

They walked through to the dining room just as there was a knock on the door. Henry went to open it and she heard a woman's voice and then the door closing. Lou settled Alice in a chair between Clive and Tony, and then she took the seat at the head of the table. Robert started to pour the wine and the chat was light as Harriet sat opposite her shortly followed by Henry and the new arrival who sat next to Harriet. She was tall with short dark hair and she looked familiar to Alice, but she couldn't place her. She realised that she must have been frowning and staring at her whilst thinking about it, as then Lou said: -

'Alice this is Grace, she lives at the house at the top of the lane, Alice is my old school friend I told you about'.

'Hello again Alice, how's your head doing now, healing nicely? she asked.

Alice realised with a start that Grace was the doctor who had told her about her heart problem. She looked different in her trouser suit and without her red glasses. Plus, Alice thought, I was concussed so I've a good excuse for not recognising her.

'Yes healing nicely thank you, apologies, I didn't recognise you without the white coat. I was a bit dazed when I saw you last,' laughed Alice. 'And Harriet I'm sorry I flaked out on you earlier, I've a good excuse' Alice smiled, pointing to her head, worried she was coming across like an idiot.

'Don't worry, Lou's told us what happened, looks like a nasty bump on your head. Did Lou tell you I'm renting the yard?' asked Harriet.

'No, she didn't, what a lovely surprise, so those are your horses with Harvey?' asked Alice deciding to keep to safe topics. Bizarrely for all the years since the crush she'd wondered how she would feel seeing Harriet again, and she honestly felt nothing at all once she started talking to her. She'd felt shocked to see her, but there were no stirrings. Alice laughed to herself, how the brain works and plays tricks on you. She realised that Harriet was speaking whilst she'd been off in Lala land.

'Yes, I've dressage horses which some are home bred. When Clive and I lived near Lancaster we had our own yard, but we've had to move back up here to be near our parents who have health issues. We haven't been able to find anywhere near here with land as yet, so we're renting a barn conversion and are on the lookout. The first thing I did when I knew we were coming back was come and talk to Lou. I was so sad to hear about Agnes. She was such a lovely lady'.

'Yes, she was, such a shame I didn't get to see her before she died. Our lives have taken us all in different directions. Lou let me ride Harvey yesterday which was the first time in decades. I ache in places I forgot I had,' laughed Alice.

'Well, if you fancy it, Grace and Lou are going out for a hack with me tomorrow if you wanted to come along, I can always lend you one of my old guys. Would be like old times' asked Harriet.

'Absolutely if that's ok with you all' Grace nodded as did Lou who was handing round the starters of smoked mackerel pate on melba toast.

The starters were quickly consumed and then the men cleared the table, leaving the women to talk life, horses and village gossip. Alice sat back and listened as they chatted away, it was certainly a lovely village but also had lots of intrigue, such as who had taken the flowers from around the font in the church, the couple who were getting married last weekend, but the bride jilted him at the altar, and the village pond having plastic ducks in it, and who'd put them there. It was so nice to listen to funny, normal conversations.

Henry, Robert, and Clive came in carrying plates of food for everyone, then went back for tureens of vegetables. The beef wellington looked amazing and there was a lull in the conversation while everyone helped themselves to food.

'Have you lived here long Grace?' asked Alice.

'I was born here but went away to boarding school, then off to medical school. I came back when I got a job at YDH a few years ago. My parents still live in the house, and I've the annexe at the back. It works well and handy for work. What about you Alice? You said that you knew Lou from school?' replied Grace.

'Yes, we were at school together and had ponies, I had mine in Woodthorpe down the road, and we used to ride out together and do mad gymkhana things. It was so much fun back then, we didn't have a curfew really and our parents would send us off with a pack up and not see us again for hours, and there were no mobile phones if anything happened. We had so much more freedom than kids today' said Alice wistfully.

'Do you have children Alice?' Grace asked helping herself to some broccoli and carrots.

'No, I don't. My wife and I didn't want children, what about you?' asked Alice.

'No, the opportunity never arose, my partners weren't into it, and I was so busy with my career it passed me by, but that's ok. I'm in a good place now, kids would have been nice though, but hey ho, it is what it is' replied Grace.

Alice wondered if she was batting for the same team as her, her gaydar had been pretty faulty in the past.

'Do you go out into York much' said Alice fishing as subtly as she dared.

'Not really, there aren't many places to go other than Valentines' grinned Grace who knew exactly what Alice was fishing for.

Alice grinned back. Their little secret. Her stomach lurched when she heard the bars name again, but she brushed it away. The others around the table were eating and chatting so hadn't realised their conversation. It was always nice to meet a fellow lesbian out in the wild, we need to stick together laughed Alice internally.

The conversation flowed and she and Lou reminisced about school uniform disasters as they tried to adapt them, hair colours that had gone wrong and the school disco with smuggled in vodka and orange. Clive and Harriet told tales about their trips abroad and Tony and Robert, who were the quietest of the group, spoke about their garden designs, many of which had been created around the area.

The women cleared the main course away and Lou served out Eton Mess into delicate bowls. 'It was a raspberry pavlova, but I tripped over, and it went crashing onto the island' laughed Lou putting the bowls onto a tray with a jug of cream and carried it through to the dining room.

Henry was just popping open a bottle of champagne as they entered the room and poured it into eight glasses and passed them around. Alice had been on water all evening but took a glass. As soon as the bowls had been distributed and everyone seated Henry stood and raised his glass.

'Thank you all for coming, it's been such a lovely evening and it's been nice to get to know you all more. I just wanted to make a toast as the meal draws to a close, to thank my lovely wife Lou for being so supportive since we moved up North, and to you all for accepting me as a southerner into your lives. So, here's a toast to Lou, the love of my life, and my whole world. To Lou' Henry said raising his glass. Everyone followed suite and raised their glasses too.

'To Lou' they all said in unison. Alice took a small sip of champagne and looked down the table to see tears in Lou's eyes, she looked so happy in that moment, she really hoped that they could sort out their differences and make a good life here in North Yorkshire.

After dinner they all went and sat in the garden as the evening was still warm and the clear sky showed them an array of beautiful stars. Candles in lanterns lit the table and around the patio, it was so pretty, and it felt so nice to be out of York, breathing fresh air and be surrounded by kind people.

Grace came and sat down beside her and looked upwards too.

'I'll never tire of seeing a night sky, it's amazing isn't it. Makes you feel so small knowing how big the universe is,' said Grace.

'It really does, so relaxing to sit here in the quiet'. Alice replied continuing to look at the night sky. She was unconsciously thinking about Charlie, she hoped she was ok and not struggling with rehab. Sometimes when you look up at the night sky and wonder if the person you love are looking upwards too. It somehow made them feel closer. Alice wondered if she should try and write to her, but maybe that would make it worse. She just didn't feel like their chapter was closed.

'A penny for your thoughts' said Grace 'you were miles away there, Lou asked if you wanted anything to drink?'

'Sorry, I was drifting off then, yes another glass of water would be lovely thanks, it has been such a lovely evening, thank you both for inviting me' said Alice beginning to yawn.

'I prescribe bed for you Alice, get a good night's sleep so you're fresh for the ride tomorrow' said Grace putting on her best bedside manner.

'Yes doctor,' laughed Alice. 'What time are we setting off in the morning?'

'9.30 if that ok, we'll take it steady, our days of bombing around the country are pretty much over' said Lou passing Alice a glass of water.

Alice stood up and said goodnight to everyone and made her way up to bed. It was 10.30 and she was so tired, she quickly undressed and climbed under the comforter. She could hear laughter from the patio below and she smiled as she drifted off.

She was woken by Lou at 8.30 with a breakfast tray with cornflakes, toast and coffee. Over her arm she'd a pair of cream jodhpurs.

'Morning sleepy head, you looked so peaceful I didn't like to wake you. Thought you might like breakfast in bed. Harriet dropped these in for you as you're about the same size, and I have spare boots. We were the same size feet I remembered! I loved borrowing your DM boots, but you never wanted my stilettos. The clues were there,' laughed Lou.

Alice took the tray and ate the toast and half the cornflakes, the coffee really sparked her awake, it was like rocket fuel. 'Wow!' said Alice.

'It's a special blend from a place we went to in London, always got Henry out on a morning. I'll leave you to get ready. Harriet and Grace are tacking up, so we don't need to rush'.

'Thank you, Lou, you've been so kind, I feel totally spoilt' said Alice finishing off the coffee.

Lou took the tray down and Alice had a quick shower and then dried off quickly. Putting on jodhpurs was an art that she'd got out of, and it took a couple of good heaves to get them pulled up. They showed every lump and bump. Alice put on her baggy sweatshirt which covered a multitude of sins, including the Eton Mess from last night.

Lou was ready when she went down and gave her the option of long or short boots. Alice opted for the long ones, which were leather, very new and looked so expensive. She caught sight of herself in the mirror on the way out and she looked the part. Lou shouted her back and she took a picture of them both. 'We can compare it to the old ones we've, got,' said Lou.

They went over to the yard, and the four horses were tacked up and ready. Harriet and Grace shouted morning across the yard whilst finishing off various buckles.

'This is Max Alice; he's so laid back he's asleep' said Harriet beckoning her over and passed her a riding hat that looked like the one Lou had loaned her the other day.

Max was a dark bay chunky old chap, with a black mane and tail and he looked at Alice as she approached. 'Don't worry Max, I won't ask much of you, be gentle with me'.

One by one they used the mounting block. Harriet's horse Monty was very impressive, he held himself so well, his neck arched and chomped on the bit in a knowing manner. Grace, who was also borrowing one of Harriet's, was already astride a black thoroughbred who looked very sleek and polished. Harvey being a typical piebald had a grass stain on his bum where he'd made the conscious effort to make himself look untidy. Alice smiled at Lou in the knowing way horse people do.

They set off down the lane and crossed over down a busier road that led to the A64 but turned off before they reached it and followed a winding road to Askham Richard. They rode two abreast on the small track that led towards fields that Harriet had permission to ride on the set aside, Alice felt safe on Max, who was really taking care of her. As they reached the set aside, Harriet asked if everyone fancied a moving it up a gear off road, which Alice, although a bit nervous agreed to. So, they set off at a steady canter across the field, all the horses very happy to stretch their legs. Grace, Lou and Harriet were excellent horsewomen, Alice felt more like a sack of old potatoes, but she kept up with them and didn't fall off so that was a bonus. They looped round the front of the prison in Askham Richard on their way back, past the old stable building, which was now converted into very spectacular houses, then down a short lane back home. The horses knew where they were, and their strides picked up as they neared the yard and the thoughts of feed.

They all dismounted in the yard and untacked together, laughing and joking about who was going to be the stiffest in the morning, then led the horses back to their field. They were too hungry for grass to run around but took it in turns to roll. Harvey achieving even more grass stains.

'I told you to buy a bay,' laughed Harriet. 'Saves a ton of elbow grease, but he's a darling, I'll admit that'.

The four women had coffee on the patio before Harriet had to leave to go to her parents for lunch, so Lou cleared the table. Grace stood up to leave and turned to Alice and asked if she could have her number if she ever wanted to go out for a drink or something, so they swapped numbers. It was totally platonic on Alice's side, and she was sure on Grace's too.

As the party broke up, Alice helped Lou empty the dishwasher and put things away, and then went and packed her case, giving the jodhpurs to Lou on the way into the kitchen. Henry was at the church cutting the grass again as there was no service that day, so she didn't get to say goodbye, but thanked Lou for her many kindnesses and set off back home. She'd had such a lovely weekend but was ready for some time alone.

Her house was bathed in sunshine as she arrived back, almost as if to say it was pleased that she was home. Alice went in with her case, loaded clothes into the washing machine and put Charlie's shirt on her bed, after deciding to return it she was unsure if she could.

She sent a text message to Jen and Holly to tell them she was safe at home and had such a lovely time, then taking her laptop to bed she put on Charlie's shirt and watched Pride and Prejudice which was her favourite thing to watch when she was unwell. The bed no longer smelt of Charlie, but she couldn't face changing the bedding just yet. She just wanted to feel her close. She knew she should have been angry, but she just didn't feel that at all, Jen was feeling all that on her behalf.

There was no food in the house, so Deliveroo was her best friend, and she ordered some Tofu Phad King and lovely jasmine rice which she ate in bed. After a short chat with Jen on the phone she switched the light out and putting Charlie's letter under her pillow fell asleep thinking of galloping horses and dark starry skies.

14

All Work and Some Play

In the blink of an eye, it was the start of term and induction days and a whirl of welcome parties. It'd been so nice to see her colleagues in person rather than over zoom, and to sit down and plan the term ahead. Another joy was meeting her master's students, who were a mix of young and old, men and women, who were all very keen for reading lists and assessment questions way before the first lecture.

It was also lovely to be able to walk into work every day, the early autumnal weather was mild, with bright sunshine in the early mornings. The leaves were starting to turn as she walked past Bootham Park, and children from the private schools looked pristine in their new uniforms. Today she was taking her students on a walking tour of York, to look at the buildings they would be studying in one of their modules, finishing off with a visit to the York Minster Undercroft.

One of her favourite places was Herbert House, with its misshapen beams and its scary lean onto the street. Alice hoped that the students would like it too, some of course did, but others only wanted to go inside to buy Gin. She attempted to keep their attention by a walk up the Shambles, but the younger students only wanted to look in the Harry Potter themed shops, rather see or hear about the lovely architecture and its history. Alice began to feel frustrated; this was the first seminar for them on her module, and some of them were just not engaging. By the time they'd walked down Petergate and stood outside the Minster, Alice decided that she needed to do something.

She told the twenty students to split up into two groups, deliberately mixing the age groups, then sent them into the Minster to explore and told them to meet her at the entrance to the Undercroft in an hour. She felt tired, she hadn't walked that far in a while and her whole body ached. She took a seat on one of the large stones outside the Minster, which had been placed there for security, and was just checking her phone when she heard someone say her name.

She looked up and saw Di.

'Hi, sorry I didn't see you there,' said Alice.

'Nah worries, you were busy with ya students. You ok?' asked Di who took the opportunity of stopping to roll a fag.

'Ok thanks. Bit busy with new term starting. How are you?' asked Alice, but that wasn't the question she wanted to ask.

'I'm a busy bee. We're starting quiz nights next week and thinking of doing karaoke, not sure if it'd bring anyone in' said Di, lighting her roll up and taking a big drag.

'Karaoke isn't my thing, but the quiz sounds fun. Let me know details and I'll pass around' said Alice although she wasn't sure if she ever wanted to step back into Valentine's ever again after her last visit.

'Shall do, I'm slumming it next door to you now as I got kicked out of my flat. They're turning it into an Airbnb the bastards. Just got it how I liked it too.' laughed Di.

'Bloody hell that's shit,' said Alice. 'Glad that you've got somewhere to stay. If you need a cup of sugar, just ask' smiled Alice, she really wanted to ask the question, but she felt tongue tied and anxious.

There was an elephant in the room, except they were stood in the middle of York, the person and event that neither of them could mention. Charlie.

She bit the bullet.

'How's Charlie? Have you heard from her?' asked Alice cautiously.

'She rang me yesterday. She's struggling, they don't let her have a minute's peace, and isn't allowed her phone. She sounded a bit drugged up'. Said Di. 'She's sorry what she done to you. She proper liked you'.

'Hope she can sort herself out' said Alice 'Will she be there long?'

'Not sure. She's free to go whenever she likes but she wants to do the full lot' replied Di stubbing out her fag on the floor and putting the stub in her back pocket. 'But who knows with Charlie, only time will tell'.

'I guess so. Better go and see where my students are. Who knows what trouble they'll have got into' laughed Alice nervously. 'Take care'.

Alice walked away, not waiting for Di to say goodbye, she'd wanted to say give Charlie my love, it was on the tip of her tongue, but she couldn't. She went into the Minster, paying her entrance fee and went in search of her students.

She looked at her watch as she entered and realised that she'd twenty minutes before she'd to meet up with them and so she went straight to her favourite part of the Minster, the Chapter House with its beautiful, vaulted ceiling.

Alice took a seat in one of the stalls and enjoyed the silence around her, the echoes of voices from the main building floating in as she looked skyward. There was such beauty in the world thought Alice, but sadness enveloped her heart and she felt heavy and weak. She was struck by the fear about her future, if she'd one at all. Would her body give out on her before she could find her happiness. Before she could see Charlie again. The thought of jumping in her car and going to Cumbria struck her very strongly, but she didn't think that would be helpful for Charlie, nor herself. Why did life have to be so complicated?

After a relatively peaceful time in the Chapter House, Alice walked to the entrance to the Undercroft where most of the students were waiting. It was an amazing place to visit for archaeologist, theologist and historians alike. With its layers of history dating back to the Roman occupation of England up to the present-day Alice thought that it would have enough there to keep her students talking and interested. After the visit they all went their separate ways with instructions to research and write about the history of the Minster into their journal. They were then told that this would count towards their assessment, which the younger students were not happy about that as they hadn't really been paying attention. Alice was too tired to really care and decided to leave them to it and headed back to her office. Her colleague asked if she fancied heading out for tea in a restaurant, but Alice was too tired and asked for a rain check. After a cup of tea and a final check of her emails she started the short walk home.

In the final weeks before the start of term her friends had come and taken care of the decorating, Holly was an expert at wallpapering and she'd made the rooms look amazing, all subtle blues, creams and greens with a feature wall to make it extra special. The furniture had been delivered from Lavender Interiors which looked very homely in her front room, and the dining room was all ready for having people round for dinner. If only I had the energy thought Alice.

As well as being super decorators, her friends, under the instruction of Jen, each brought Tupperware containers with meals for the freezer so that she could settle in and relax after work which made Alice feel so humbled. She really had found out who her friends were over the past few months, so she decided to plan a dinner party for them all as soon as she felt up to it. It wouldn't quite be up to the standards of the ones Sally, and she used to hold, but Alice didn't care about all that anymore.

Tonight, was potluck from the freezer as the label had come off, but it looked and smelt delicious whirring around in the microwave and Alice made a pot of tea and ate in the dining room, watching the light fade as the sun went down. She hadn't had time to read her personal emails for a few days, so she opened them up on her phone and after deleting a number of offers to marry foreign princes she found an email from the antiques shop where Jack had bought the key. It read:

Dear Alice

We've been in touch with the original owner of the key. She is currently out of the country at present and will be in touch with you in due course. I hope that she can answer some of your questions.

Kind regards

Ellekers.

Now that was exciting news thought Alice. 'She' would be in touch. Alice really hoped that it was at least someone connected to Charlotte and Hester. In the meantime, she'd managed to find out a little more about Hester, and found a few photographs of her in society newspapers, although there were no photos of Charlotte. The houses where they had both lived still existed, including No 2 St Leonards Place where she'd collapsed a month ago. She'd written to the owners of both houses to see if there was still a family connection, but they would've changed hands many times since the 1920s, but they kindly invited her to have a look round. That was where she was due tomorrow after work, following a day at the Borthwick Archives. Throwing herself into work was the only thing she could think to do while she tried hard not to think about Charlie.

It had been two months without Charlie. Her brain screamed that she never had Charlie. It was a fling, it was nothing, Alice meant nothing to Charlie. She was the first person she thought about each morning, and the last when she went to bed. She'd read the ink off the paper from the letter Charlie had written her, it was still under her pillow and although she'd changed the sheets, she hadn't changed the pillowcase she'd slept on. Alice knew that she needed some kind of closure, but she knew that writing to her was not an option. She didn't want to upset her by sending a heavy letter and potentially set her back in her recovery. Alice knew she had to be patient and see what happened when she came home, and her therapist had agreed that she needed to have a conversation with Charlie whenever that might be.

Until that day came she'd lots to keep her busy. She was officially the next Masters Admission Tutor and was being included in more committees and decisions on departmental policies. So as always in life when your private life is crap, something else improves.

The following day it was pouring with rain. York always looked so beautiful, even when everything and everyone was drenched. It also meant that everyone who used their bikes took their cars instead, so the roads were worse than ever. Alice sat in the traffic as it crawled towards the main campus, hoping that she would find a parking space when she got there. She was lucky and found a space near Health Sciences and walked the short distance through the library into the researcher's heaven of the Borthwick. The records were all set out for her, and she'd a gorgeous couple of hours scouring the archives for the information to build her module content, making notes and taking photographs so she could work through it all later. The time flew and when she headed back to her car, it was still raining, and she felt like a drowned rat by the time she got in. She repeated the slow crawl back to Kings Manor and had just enough time to dry her hair under a hand dryer in the toilets before she was due at St Leonards Place.

A very short walk later, with a borrowed umbrella and department camera, she stood outside No 2 St Leonards Place, looking down at the pavement where she'd collapsed, Alice took a deep breath and knocked on the shiny black door using the brass knocker.

The door was opened by an elderly gentleman.

'Good afternoon, I'm Alice, I have an appointment to see Ms Lunby at 5 o'clock,' said Alice.

'Ah come in, she's just on the phone' he opened the door wide and indicated for Alice to go in. 'I'm her dad James, Molly won't be long. Come through to the drawing room'.

Alice was pleased to see that the rooms had been restored beautifully, the high ceilings with lovely coving and a centre rose, the original fireplace looking resplendent taking centre stage. The room had been elegantly furnished with white walls giving a mix of old and modern. It made Alice smile. She heard footsteps on the hall tiles.

'Hi Alice, sorry I had an urgent work call. Take a seat and tell me more about your project.' said Molly. She was tall and elegant with very short spiked grey hair which she ran her long fingers through as sat down.

Alice took a seat on a large leather sofa.

'Can I get either of you something to drink?' asked James.

'No, I'm fine thanks' replied Alice and Molly concurred. James took a seat in a high back chair near the fire.

Alice told Molly how she'd come across the letters and the story that had evolved from them, the place that this house had played in the drama, and a little about the family.

'I'm hoping to turn it into a book because I'm very interested in hidden lesbian stories. I won't use your full address, but it would be really helpful to have some photos of the original features if that would be ok? Have you lived here long?'

'Yes of course, what a fascinating project. I look forward to reading it' said Molly 'I bought the house about three years ago, but I'm not here very much because of work. You look familiar Alice, where have I seen you before? Do you work at Kings Manor?'

'Yes I do' replied Alice.

'Are you the lass who took a tumble outside a few months ago?' asked James.

Alice had been dreading this, how embarrassing.

'Yes it was. So sorry if I disturbed you' answered Alice blushing and feeling like it had been a mistake to come here.

'Don't be daft lass, we heard a commotion outside so went out to look. Are you ok now? That's all that matters,' said James. 'Are you sure I can't get you a glass of water or cup of tea'. He looked like he thought that Alice might make a repeat performance.

'No I'm fine, I'd had a bit of a shock and passed out, all's good now' said Alice trying to change the subject.

'That woman was really upset wasn't she Molly, she wouldn't leave your side for a minute, she said she was a friend of yours. Did she catch up with you at the hospital as they wouldn't let her in the ambulance, kicked up quite a fuss and ran after it when it left' said James, gesticulating with his hands and getting quite excited.

'She gave all your details to the ambulance crew and was really distressed. We offered to take her to the hospital, but she shot off,' said Molly. 'Did she find you at the hospital? We were worried about you both and did ring, but they wouldn't tell us anything'.

'That's very kind of you, yes she found me' said Alice really desperate to change the subject.

'Sorry we've embarrassed you, as long you're ok now. Shall I show you around now or are you desperate to get away?' asked Molly.

'Yes please do show me around, that would be lovely thanks' said Alice prepping the camera, remembering the real focus of why she was here. To retrace the footsteps of Charlotte and Hester.

Molly and Alice then spent a pleasant half an hour walking around the house taking photographs. It felt lovely to be in the house where

Hester and Charlotte had fallen in love, maybe in the very drawing room that she'd just been sat. Many of the original features had been kept, and it was easy to picture the house from the late Victorian and Edwardian era. The main area that had been changed was the kitchen, so Alice only took a photo of the old bell box which was still in place, after the butler's pantry, scullery and old kitchen had been extended and updated.

'Thank you so much Molly that has been so helpful. Once I know where the project is heading, I'll email you. Lovely to meet you both' said Alice heading for the front door down the hallway Hester and Charlotte would have walked, down the step into the street. Alice could picture Hester's photograph all dressed up for her days hunting and the budding romance that had started there.

Alice walked back to Kings Manor, it was now rush hour and she could hardly hear herself think, she collected her car and took the short drive home following the slow plod of cars down Bootham.

As she cooked dinner she called Jen to fill her in on what had happened with Molly and James and how Charlie had acted after her accident.

'She's a wrong un, I know you Alice, you forgive too easily, don't want you getting hurt again,' said Jen.

'I know, it was just a bit of a shock to hear about it all again. Anyway, what's happening with you both?' said Alice trying to change the subject which was becoming a theme today she thought.

'Work is as busy as ever for me, Holly has some news though, let me shout her' said Jen, and she heard her walking away and shouting, followed by footsteps coming downstairs and muttered voices.

'Hi Alice hope you're ok,' said Holly. 'I've been asked to become a partner at the practice; can you believe it'.

'I absolutely can, it's so well-deserved Holly, congratulations! Now that calls for a celebration, unless you've something planned together?' asked Alice.

'No, we were thinking the same, let's organise a meal out or something really soon, will text you later,' said Holly.

'Great, look forward to it. Plus, I want to have a housewarming too so lots to look forward to' said Alice, feeling joyful and thankful to have such lovely friends and things to plan.

All work and no play makes Alice a dull girl.

15

The Needle and the Damage Done

Rehab was a bastard Charlie decided. She didn't miss drinking at all, it felt good to wake up unmuddled and without a hangover. However, the constant evaluation of her mental health and the restrictions were really beginning to get to her. She'd been here two months, and a few times she'd wanted to walk, something that many of those that started with her had done already. Some of whom had left already. Most went quietly in the night, but with others there was shouting and the slamming of doors as they left the building.

The girl who had kicked off on the first day was still here, some days quiet, other days screaming at the world for the anger that she held deep inside her. Group therapy had been rocky, Charlie found it hard to open up at all. Dr Hanson reiterated often that the sooner she opened up, the quicker she would be ready to leave.

The only highlight to her day was the frenetic journalling she did every night and the art classes which she had asked for more of. In both she worked hard, filling two journals already and she'd almost finished a painting of the lake view from the garden. She hadn't bonded with any of the other patients, everyone was on their own journey, their problems wrapped around them like old mouldy clothes. They all wanted to shed them, but in a way, they had been their comfort for so long they were hard to discard.

At the end of another gruelling session with Dr Hanson, she was asked how her journalling was going. It was then that Charlie told her that she'd filled almost two of them. Dr Hanson suggested that she write a piece to read out at their next session. Charlie wasn't sure if she could do that and put up some resistance.

'Ok Charlie, I understand your reservations at sharing. Let me be open and frank with you. You're a businesswoman like me. I started the centre to help people, for there to be somewhere for those in need to come to and recover. But it isn't a charity, it has to pay its way and have clients come, work hard, recover and build a foundation for when they go home. You started here so well, intending on working hard to return home, but we haven't touched on anything deep, everything has been peripheral. You're spending a lot of money to be here Charlie and I think that the time has come to either dig deep and really work on your issues or for you to leave. I don't say this lightly, you've coped really well with not drinking, but if you continue to keep everything bottled up, one day you know that you'll pop and be back to where you were.' she said, her voice no longer calm and soothing, today she was firm and forceful. 'Do you want that, Charlie? Is this just something that you want for the rest of your life?'

Her words felt like a slap to the face. Charlie sat up straight.

'You're right. I've been coasting. It's eating me up. I can't get the words out'. Her voice wobbly with emotion. 'I just want it all to stop'.

Charlie doubled over rocking, hugging herself sobbing. The dam had broken.

'It's ok Charlie, let it out'. Dr Hanson paused, and the room fell quiet except for the sobs and the creaking of her chair. After a minute or so Charlie sat up and wiped her eyes, taking a tissue from the box on the table.

'Take some deep breaths. I know that it hurts but it really is better out than in. The next time we meet I want you to have written a piece to read out either to me or to the group. Write it as a story if that helps. It's a big scary step I know, but you can do this' enforced Dr Hanson. Here's another journal if you need it'.

Charlie nodded and took the book and left. She went to her room and changed into her outdoor clothes, there was a walking trip around Bowness with Toby, and she wanted to get out and stretch her legs before her next art session. It was a small group that wandered down Kendal Road into the village, past pubs and shops and down to the lake where tourist boats were moored. They followed the road left and onto Glebe Road and they were all bought an ice cream.

Charlie broke away from the group, walking across the grass and took a seat on a bench on the green. The black wood had been graffitied, most had become illegible through time. She looked closely and faintly she could see JW loves CL indented into the wood that had been painted many times since it was carved there. Charlie wondered if JW still loved CL. She somehow doubted it.

Charlie could clearly remember Johanna carving their initials into that bench thirty years ago after a heavy night out in the club that overlooked the lake. Afterwards they'd sat on the bench, drinking wine straight from the bottle. Johanna had used her Swiss army knife to carve their initials into the wood, drunk with love after being brought here by Charlie for a romantic weekend.

It hadn't lasted of course. Johanna had left her for Charlie's best friend, which had been a new hideously painful experience. One that hurt deeply, to lose her best mate and her supposed soul mate in one go. That rejection by the two people who were supposed to love her the most had been a catalyst. A catalyst of years of loving and leaving to avoid being hurt. So by coming back to Bowness to where it had all started she had hoped that she could process what was going on inside and face into it all.

Toby broke away from the client group. He'd seen Charlie sitting alone on the bench, holding the squashed cone in her hand, the ice cream melting down her hand. She was staring off into the distance, over the still water but he could see from the anguished look on her face that inside there were raging rapids pulling her under.

'Charlie' Toby said gently. 'Are you ok? We're just heading to feed the swans, do you want to come with us, or do you want to go back to the centre?'

'Can I just sit here for a bit on my own. I just need some head space, is that ok?' asked Charlie worried he would insist on staying with her.

'Ok, we'll be half an hour or so but will come back and get you. Do you need anything?' asked Toby pulling out some baby wipes from his rucksack and handed them to her.

'Yes, have you got any paper and a pen with you or a spare journal? I just want to write something down' asked Charlie hopefully.

'Hang on' said Toby, reaching into his rucksack. 'I've a notepad you can use, and you can borrow my pen' Toby ripped some used pages out of the front and handed Charlie the now empty pad.

'Thank you' said Charlie as Toby went back to the group and headed off towards the boats.

Charlie sat back with the pad and began writing.

I'm starting this journey at the end. The final thing that has brought me here.

It started off as such a beautiful day, broken by my best friend Di hammering on my front door, angry and disgusted, thinking that I had been up to my old tricks. But that was the thing, I really wasn't. Being around Alice felt different to any of the other woman I have ever been with, and there had been a lot of women.

Before I met Alice, it was always the thrill of the chase. To kiss the most beautiful woman in the club, party or pub, to be seen leaving with her, then to have sex with them but never letting them touch me physically or emotionally. This was followed by the morning after the night before, feeling grubby and disgusted at my behaviour, and just wanting them to leave. The words of anger often ensued from some, but not all. Some were like me, just wanting to be seen leaving with the attractive butch lesbian, like I was some kind of trophy.

All this of course went hand in hand with booze. Binge drinking more and more regularly whenever I found that I just couldn't cope with the feelings inside. Some days the thoughts in my head were overwhelming, and I couldn't deal with what my brain kept throwing at me.

I was drinking more with the tension of trying to find my birth mother, to get answers to the many questions I have been fretting about all my life. When I found out I was adopted it became a universal mystery of who I was, and why she rejected me. Did she think the baby in front of her was a disappointment, and that I would continue to disappoint all my life?

My adoptive parents certainly were. They'd wanted a girlie girl to fuss over and pamper but all I had wanted to do was climb trees and play football with the boys. I'd done well at school, especially at art, but that wasn't a profession my parents were happy with, so instead I took some hospitality courses at college and then travelled the world running bars and restaurants. This led to many encounters with women, my appearance at first was unusual and I was someone who fascinated women and men alike. There were good encounters and bad ones, women were both intrigued by the woman in the suit, men sometimes saw me as a threat. There were a couple of times where I got into near dangerous scrapes, only extricating myself by using charm and wit. These encounters and experiences have made me form a thick skin, and I never let anyone near my heart.

The one relationship I had that lasted a few years was with Johanna, a woman I met in Spain, and although we had a fractious relationship, I thought that she was my person. We came here once to Bowness and stayed next door to the centre, she was my world. I was so happy with her. She was the first woman that I said I love you and I absolutely meant it. I thought that we would be happy, and we had so many dreams and plans. But then unexpectedly she left me for my best friend Sue, which was hilarious as Johanna had always said she hated her. In fact, it was the opposite.

We'd bought a bar and flat in Benidorm which was really successful and fun, and I thought life was all good, but it really wasn't.

When she broke up with me, we sold the flat and bar and I moved back to England. I went home to my adopted parents for a few months but then they were killed in a car crash, so I was all alone. They left the house to me in Chapel Allerton and for a while I stayed there, slowly going through their papers. That's when I found out more about my adoptive mother. It didn't help knowing how young she was, not then. As I've got older, I've rethought it, but back then I just felt such rejection. I couldn't see the positives.

So, for years I travelled the world, buying and selling houses and bars, buying wrecks and turning them into successful businesses and pretty houses. Leaving a trail of unhappy women in my wake. Then I discovered York and it's calming beauty, a lovely home and a few bars and restaurants to have fun with.

Taking on Valentines in hindsight, had not been the best of ideas. Di, my best friend had been really against me buying it, but I was pig headed and bought it anyway. I had the best of intentions, bringing an LGBT friendly bar to York, and at first it had been great fun. However, the temptations of the availability of booze, and women hanging on my every word led me to make a lot of wrong choices. It was a relief to close it for the refurb and I could just focus on the parts that I enjoyed the most, designing the dream space.

Then in June I was doing my neighbourly duty and went round to say hello to the new owner. I'd seen two women go in, and had recognised Jen, although not by name at that time. And then I met Alice, and although it was a brief conversation, I was aware of what a lovely person she was, and every time I saw her something inside me shifted but I didn't know what it was then. She was intriguing and her kindness shone out of her, I wanted to know more about her but of course I did the opposite.

I stupidly had the most excruciating time with a girl from the Todmorden disco. I didn't know why I had agreed to a second date with her. Guilt of her coming over from Hebden Bridge to see me, and maybe a chance to put right what I'd done wrong for all these years, but it hadn't worked out like that. The woman had said some horrible things, how I'd used her, promised her things and made me feel disgusted at myself. I couldn't remember what I'd even said as I was too hammered, and certainly couldn't remember promising any form of long-term commitment.

I was just getting sorted after that episode, reopening the bar and dealing with the marketing of new events when the letter arrived from the adoption agency to say that they'd no success in finding my birth mother. I hit the bottle with Di and then had the urge to go and see Alice next door. It started off ok and we were all having a lovely time. I realised then how much I liked her, in fact I couldn't stop looking at her. I just wanted Di to go and leave me alone with her, so when she went out for a fag, I flirted really hard with her, but I don't think she noticed which amused me. Di came back and I carried on drinking, I knew I should stop but suddenly felt I needed Dutch courage to ask Alice out. Then I upset her, I can't remember what was said but she got up to leave and I wanted to stop her. I followed her to the door, took hold of her and kissed her. It was in that moment I knew I was falling in love with her.

I barely slept but hadn't been drinking since Alice left. I paced the floor, threw up, wrote a million notes to her. I just didn't know what to do with myself. After Di left, I went to the florist and got the biggest bunch of flowers and went round to her house as soon as I thought she would be up and working. She was gracious and kind, she showed me such love, love I didn't feel I deserved, she didn't make me feel bad or blame me in any way. She is a breath of fresh air in a world that is full of uncaring people. She was so lovely to me, and I threw it all away. After a few weeks of gorgeous dates it all went so wrong.

One morning I missed a delivery at work, I was so engrossed in Alice that I forgot, and Di was angry with me, Alice left my house and said she would message me later. As the hours ticked by and I heard nothing from her I just thought that she didn't want me anymore. I had to go into work as there was a gig that night and when I hadn't heard by 5, I just started drinking. Then the singer, Dawn arrived, and we started drinking together. I'd met her before, and we'd had a bit of a dalliance, so when she made a pass at me again, I thought fuck it and just went along with it. I just didn't care.

Then Alice turned up out of the blue, she walked in on us. Di had tried to warn me, but it was too late. I ran after her once I'd got dressed but she'd a head start on me. I saw her ahead; she'd been sat on a step, and I saw that when she tried to stand up, she just collapsed on the floor and hit her head. I rang the ambulance and stayed with her until they came, then ran to the hospital but they wouldn't let me in. After that I had a very brief call with her, but she obviously so angry with me. Since then, I've been in turmoil because all I want is Alice. If I never had another drink again, I wouldn't care. I feel so guilty for what I've done.

I spoke to Di who told me about your clinic so I came as soon as I could. That is why I am here.

Charlie looked up and saw Toby and the group approaching her. She closed the notebook and walked up to meet them. They made the short walk back to the centre, Charlie trailing behind, mentally drained at what she'd just relived. She went back up to her room as she'd an hour before dinner, not that she was hungry. She went over to the desk and sat and wrote a letter to Alice. The one that had been in her heart since arriving in Bowness.

16

If Not Now, When?

The term was whizzing by, and they were already halfway through it. The younger students had started to get to grips with the step up required for studying a Masters, both in commitment and in intellect. From their contribution in seminars, it was clear that they'd really buckled down and stopped the late-night clubbing, which had been evident at the start of term. With the mature students, years of experience had taught them how to cope with a steep learning curve and the demands of academia.

As the nights drew in, Alice found that she'd become a bit of a hermit, coming home from work, eating, planning and sleeping. She occasionally went out for meals with Jen and Holly which were always great fun, and she was still planning her housewarming at the end of term, but the evenings were generally long and depressing. She'd seen Di in passing heading to and from work, but other than that there had been no more news of Charlie. She'd sat writing a letter to her many times but had thrown them into the wood burner rather than send them.

Yet another dull night in front of the television loomed ahead with a bowl of crisps and a hot chocolate, Alice jumped when suddenly her phone rang. The number wasn't one she recognised, and she answered cautiously.

'Hello, can I speak to Alice please' said the caller in a soft, gentle voice, the accent unrecognisable.

'Speaking' said Alice puzzled.

'I'm Kate Hazelwood, Ellekers have been in touch with me in regard to something you have that belongs to me?' she said quizzically.

'Oh, my goodness, hello Kate. I recently bought a house on St Stephen's Road which I believe once belonged to your grandmother? I've been updating the house and found a box that I believe belonged to her. I was wondering if we could possibly meet up so I can tell you about it?' said Alice hopefully.

'Wow that's amazing, really? I would love to hear more about it, I'm back in the UK now and plan to be in York next month, how about the 12th of November,' asked Kate.

'Yes, that's fine with me. Why don't you come to the house, unless that would be too painful?' said Alice cautiously.

'No that would be lovely. I'm staying at The Grand, so it isn't far to walk' asked Kate.

'Perfect with me, how about 2pm?' suggested Alice.

'Wonderful, see you then, I look forward to it' said Kate hanging up.

Alice wrote the date in her online diary and brought out the box from where she was storing it in the dining room. The red ribbon on the key, and the matching ribbon that Alice had retied around the letters held so much turmoil, love and honesty she was so keen to share with Kate, but also worried at what her reaction could be.

'No going back now' thought Alice, putting the letters back in the box, locking it and putting it onto the coffee table.

'Alexa play 80s hits' ordered Alice. The first track played quietly 'Alexa volume 5'. Louder music came out of the speaker, playing Cyndi Lauper 'I drove all night', Alice sat back and thought of the lyrics. How often had she had these thoughts going round in her head recently, she'd plotted the journey to Charlie so many times on her phone she knew the route so clearly. She could be there in just over a couple of hours, the temptation was great to just jump in the car and go.

She'd talked this over with Joyce and she'd suggested that it might be a good thing to go, but maybe wait until Charlie indicated she wanted to see her, and as Di had said she wasn't having visitors nor had her phone. No, it wouldn't be right decided Alice.

The pang in her stomach of longing had often kept her awake at night, combined with the worry and concern of how she was doing. She just needed to know what the hell had happened. Why did she do it?

Joyce had voiced her concern that she'd transferred her loss of Sally and her previous life straight onto someone who was as confused as she had been when they first met. This jolted Alice awake thinking that she was going down the same path again, but the feelings she had for Charlie were far more than she ever remembered having for Sally.

Jen had suggested that she just needed someone to love and perhaps she ought to get a cat. 'Not bloody helpful Jen' Holly had declared, and Alice had agreed.

She knew that what she needed was closure.

Her doorbell rang and Alice looked at her Ring app and saw Di stood there. Alice answered the door.

'Hey, thought you were home, heard the music' said Di who was leaning against the wall.

'Sorry is it too loud? Do you want to come in?' apologised Alice.

'Nah not too loud, just don't be playing any Bananarama or I'll have to complain then,' said Di laughing.

'I'll bear that in mind,' laughed Alice.

'Just wanted to drop this in, Charlie sent me a letter and included one for you too, guess she is saving on stamps, tight cow' smiled Di.

'Er ok, thanks. I wasn't expecting to hear from her' said Alice taking the envelope from Di like she was handling a grenade.

'Catch you later, got a night off and heading to town with me mates' and with that Di was gone into the night.

Alice locked the door and headed back to the sofa, staring at her name on the letter. Charlie had beautiful penmanship. Slowly and carefully, she tore open the envelope and took out two sheets of paper.

Dear Alice

I'm sorry if getting this letter is unwanted or a shock to receive. Di told me she saw you a few weeks ago and you'd asked how I was, so I thought I would put pen to paper. It's taken me a number of weeks and efforts to get what I want to say straight in my head and feel it's only fair that I'm honest with you.

Coming here has been difficult, more than I expected it to be. It isn't necessarily not drinking or being away from home, it is having to face into the issues that are deep rooted, and which have blighted my life for so long. I didn't tell anyone why I chose to come here to Bowness, because I haven't shared much of my past with anyone, but I wanted you to know because you deserve me to be truthful.

Thirty odd years ago I came here with my first love Johanna, we met when we were young, you know when you think everything was forever. The weekend here was absolutely blissful, and I honestly thought that this was the person I was meant to be with. Anyway, we were together years, travelled, bought and sold houses and bars and were on the up. Then I found out she cheated with my best mate. I was floored. It meant the end of not just my relationship, but also the end of the business and my best friend all in one go. The months sorting everything out, the anger and animosity were crippling. I just wanted to run away but I couldn't, I had to stay in Spain and sort everything out whilst she flaunted her romance under my nose. It was cruel and I found myself drinking more and more as a way of coping, but also to just forget on a night when I couldn't sleep. Once everything was sold and split, I headed back to Leeds to stay with my parents. They were disappointed in me, they'd loved Johanna, the first girlfriend that they'd actually liked, but blamed me for the split despite my explanations. Like I told you before I was always a disappointment.

I'd only been back with them three months when they were killed in a car crash heading for a holiday here in Windermere. I'd paid for it for them, knowing that they'd love the beauty of the hills and lakes, but then they died coming here. On a holiday I'd paid for. So, it was my fault, or at least I thought it was for so many years, until I came back here and talked about it for the first time.

That's why I had to come back here, to where things began, and things ended. I felt it was the only place I could really bottom out, and I have. It's been painful and I've really worked my arse off, and the doc has said I can leave whenever I want, but I am going to stay until the 12th of November. There are still a few things I need to get straight and one of them is with you.

Would you consider coming to see me here? I know that's such a lot to ask, but I really want to clear the air with you before I come home. There are so many lovely places to stay here, and I could give you the details if you wanted them. I have my phone back now which I switch on after dinner about 8 if you wanted to ring or text me.

I understand that this is a big thing to suggest but I needed to ask.

Hope to hear from you.

Charlie x

Alice read it again, taking it all in. Looking at her phone she saw it was almost 8 o'clock. Should she ring? Should she not? Should she hide her head in the sand?

Alice paced the floor reading the letter again, there were no emotions for her within the letter, maybe it really had been all in her head, and she knew that she had to find out what Charlie wanted to say. She dialled Charlie's number. It rang four times then she heard Charlie's voice.

'Hi Alice,' said Charlie. Alice's stomach flipped hearing her voice.

'Hi thanks for the letter and for being so honest about things, it can't have been easy to relive it,' said Alice her voice quaking, her body was suddenly very cold and shaky.

'Are you ok? I know it's a lot to ask you to come here but I think it'd help us both before I come back. I totally understand if you won't' said Charlie, her voice soft took Alice back to their night on the sofa listening to The Cure.

'Yes, I'm ok, busy with work. When you say help us, what do you mean?' asked Alice her hands were shaking holding the phone, so she put it on loudspeaker and set it down on the coffee table.

'What I did to you was awful Alice, but what we had felt so special. I know it's fucked up, I know I fucked up, but I really want to talk to you face to face, to know if what I'm feeling is real. I know that sounds bollocks, I'm not explaining myself well, sorry' said Charlie her voice tapering off.

'I think I know what you mean. We need to clear the air if nothing else. When do you want me to come?' asked Alice not giving away how much she'd thought of driving there to see her over the past few months.

'Whenever you like, the therapists are happy with me to do this now, I feel more together now than I have in years. I'm happy to pay for your stay if you wanted to get a room somewhere' offered Charlie.

'No, you don't need to do that, I could come on Friday? I don't have any meetings so could set off in the morning and be with you for lunch? Are you allowed out? Sorry, that sounds such a rude question' asked Alice embarrassed.

'I'm not in prison Alice,' laughed Charlie. 'We could go out for lunch if you like and take it from there? There's a lovely Italian, I could book us a table for 1?'

'That sounds good' said Alice relieved at the suggestion. 'I'll look at booking a room. Can you text me your address or do you want to meet in Bowness?'

'Let's meet in Bowness. I'll text you directions'. said Charlie.

'Great thanks' replied Alice.

'It's so lovely here despite the work. So peaceful' Charlie took a deep breath 'I'm looking forward to seeing you'.

'Er, me too. Do you want me to bring anything? I could ask Di if there is' asked Alice.

'No ta, all's good'

Alice's head was swamped with all she wanted to say right then and there, but knew she had to wait. It wasn't the time to do it, and it wouldn't resolve anything for them.

'Ok, I'll see you on Friday' Alice said firmly. 'Take care'.

'Bye Alice, you take care too' replied Charlie and she hung up.

Alice sat back and looked at her hands which were still shaking. She wanted to tell Jen and Holly but knew they'd probably talk her out of it. She knew she needed to get her head straight before she spoke to them.

Probably best to sleep on it she thought.

But of course, that night there was little in the way of sleep for Alice. She tossed and turned, her head over catastrophising every scenario she could think of.

The following morning she bit the bullet and called Jen, but Holly answered.

'Morning, Jen's ill honey. How're you doing?' said Holly sounding breathless.

'God, is she ok, what's up? Asked Alice. 'You ok? You sound awful'.

'We've both had covid and feel grim' said Holly coughing.

'Why didn't you tell me? I could have brought you things,' said Alice.

'It's ok, we've survived on takeaways, and knew you'd want to come and play Florence Nightingale' laughed Holly until she started coughing again. 'We're both negative now thankfully. Let me take the phone up to Jen, she'd never forgive me if I didn't let her tell you how she's more poorly than anyone else!' said Holly.

The sound of her slowly climbing the stairs was in stark contrast to how she normally bounded up them. She then heard Jen coughing and the sound of a creaking bed.

'Hey Alice, has Holly told you I've been proper poorly? I was rough as owt' said Jen with a croaky voice.

'Yes, she said you were both ill, sorry to hear that. Are you feeling any better now?' asked Alice.

'Yeah, just about. I got up for a bit today, buggered me up well and proper' wheezed Jen. 'How's you?'

'I'm ok, work's full on but I'm loving it. Is Holly there? Could do with some advice if you're both up to it?' asked Alice. 'If you're both not well enough it can wait'.

'Nah, it's ok, think we could both do with something to think about other than covid' responded Jen. 'Hit us with it'.

Alice took a deep breath and told them about Charlie's letter and phone call. There was silence at the end of the phone, then she told them about going to see her on Friday in the lakes. Again, there was silence.

'Are you both still there?' asked Alice.

'We thought something like this would happen. What does your gut tell you?' enquired Holly, although she could hear Jen chuntering in the background.

'I want to go; I know she hurt me, but there's unfinished business. I miss her. She's the first person I think about when I wake, and the last before I go to sleep. I need to see her' said Alice breaking down. 'Sorry. You're probably disappointed in me'.

'We're just worried about you. When are you going?' asked Holly,

Alice composed herself.

'Friday morning, it's years since I've been to Windermere. I'm staying for Friday and Saturday night. So if things go pear shaped with Charlie, I can have a break,' said Alice.

There were muttered voices as Jen and Holly discussed something.

'Oh god are you really mad at me?' said Alice concerned.

'No, we thought something like this would happen. How about if we came too? I don't mean to meet Charlie, but to be there if you need us. We could do with a break from York too, what do you think' asked Holly.

'Er, are you sure you're both well enough? Alice took a moment to think about it. 'Ok why not. Sounds like a lovely plan'.

'Will you drive the two invalids? Not sure we're up to driving that far. Jen is googling hotels, there's a nice spa there which I think would be just the tonic we need. We won't get in your way I promise, just be there for back up should you need it' said Holly reassuringly.

'Of course. I'm staying at the West Lodge; That has a spa. Is that the one?' asked Alice.

'Yes. A lovely road trip and weekend away, looks bliss. Just what the doctor ordered' joked Holly.

'Brilliant. I'll pick you up around 9.30 on Friday morning then. If it all goes wrong, we can have a girlie weekend instead,' said Alice. Who felt relieved she was going with friends to support her.

After finishing her call, she sent a WhatsApp to Charlie to let her know what was happening on Friday and where they were staying, as she didn't want to just arrive mob handed. Charlie replied with that was a brilliant idea and she was looking forward to maybe meeting them properly at the weekend. Alice heaved a sigh of relief. Please let everything be ok she wished.

17

Romance or Tragedy?

Charlie paced the floor of her room, her bed strewn with clothes with labels still attached that she'd bought in Windermere over the past week. She was regretting not bringing something smart to wear, but she'd found a couple of outfits that would suit a variety of occasions.

Her call with Alice had gone better than she'd expected, but she felt sick to her stomach at actually facing her in person. She'd booked a table at Villa Roma for 1 o'clock and had been up since 6 trying to mentally prepare for what could happen. Dr Hanson had arranged for her to attend a meditation class and a session with her before she was due to leave for lunch to calm her. But in reality, taking a handful of Diazepam wouldn't have touched the butterflies in her belly, nor the thoughts whirling around her head.

She looked at the clothes wondering whether to go smart or casual, her hair desperately needed a cut. She'd a floppy fringe, and it was all well over her ears. She'd had the same barber for years and didn't dare go elsewhere just in case they made a hash of it. She put some hair putty in and attempted to make it lie down but it seemed to have a mind of its own.

Opting in the end for black shirt and trousers, she took a final look in the mirror and headed out to meet Alice just before 1. She knew she was checking in early to her hotel so Jen and Holly could chill out and had given her directions to the lakeside where she wanted to meet her. The weather was remarkably mild for November, the trees were now bare, but the views across the lake were stunning. She was early and she took a seat on the lakeside watching the swans and ducks cavorting around, the soft lapping of the lake was very soothing and Charlie, although on high alert closed her eyes to focus on the soft sound of the water and to still the noise in her head.

'Hi Charlie, are you having a nap?' asked Alice suddenly.

Charlie jumped. 'God, you made me jump' she laughed. 'Hello Alice'. Her heart was beating out of her chest. Alice looked stunning, wearing a pair of black linen trousers and red shirt she looked so beautiful. 'You look amazing Alice'.

'Thanks. It's so beautiful. Have you been out on a cruise?' asked Alice looking out over the water trying to think of something to say as suddenly she had no words.

'No, I haven't but I thought we could maybe go on one this afternoon if you like?' replied Charlie, her mouth so dry she struggled to get the words out.

'Let's see how lunch goes first' replied Alice, her face was colder than Charlie remembered it, her soft, gentle blue eyes were now grey.

'Of course, shall we have a little tour of Bowness before lunch. How as the drive here? How's your hotel? Charlie rambled.

'Yes. It's all good,' said Alice.

The noise around them, the lake lapping loudly, the cars passing and the horn from a boat filled the air around them.

Charlie wished she knew what Alice was thinking, her stomach was in knots, and she was restraining herself from taking her into her arms and holding her.

'Let's go this way,' said Charlie heading towards Villa Roma where they found the restaurant only partially occupied, and they were seated in a corner at the back. It had been a recommendation from Toby that made her make a booking there, however the place looked shabby and rough around the edges. Charlie hoped she hadn't made a mistake booking there. The waiter brought them two menus and took their instructions for water, a hot chocolate and a latte. The menu had lots of choices and there was a pause in the conversation whilst they decided what to order.

'Have you eaten here before?' asked Alice, who was focused on the menu which was shaking slightly as her hands trembled.

'No, I haven't, someone at the centre recommended it. Are you ok Alice, you're shaking?' said Charlie, reaching over to touch Alice's hand. Alice flinched, pulling her hand away.

'Don't Charlie. Let's order and we can talk ok?' said Alice. She'd stopped making eye contact and when not looking at the menu she was looking out of the window to the lake beyond.

'I'm sorry Alice, I just ……' Charlie tailed off, she'd no words as she was so taken aback by her reaction.

The waiter appeared with their drinks and took their food order. Alice opted for the Ravioli Genovese and Charlie although feeling queasy chose Risotto Tosca knowing damn well she wouldn't be able to eat it. Not until Alice said something.

Alice was wringing her hands on her lap and biting her lip and Charlie could see that she'd tears in her eyes.

'It's ok Alice, take your time. There's no rush' said Charlie calmly hoping to put Alice at ease, but the silence continued.

The waiter appeared with two bowls of food which smelt and looked delicious. Alice picked up her fork and started moving her food around, and Charlie, at a loss at what to do, did the same.

Suddenly Alice dropped her fork, stood up and rushed in the direction of a corridor where the toilets were signposted. Charlie sat there frozen; she didn't know what to do. The waiter approached and Charlie got up and followed Alice into the toilet. One of the cubicle doors was closed and she could hear retching coming from inside.

'I'm sorry, let me take you back to your hotel,' Charlie said totally distressed at how upset Alice was.

Alice flushed the toilet and came out of the cubicle. She was ashen and shaking and walking forward to the sink she looked very unsteady on her feet. Charlie instinctively leapt forward and took hold of Alice, fearful that she was going to faint. She helped Alice rinse her face and then helped her back to the table in the restaurant as the nearest place to sit her down.

The waiter came over and asked if all was ok and he suggested ringing for an ambulance but Alice, who had regained some colour indicated that she didn't want that.

'I'm so embarrassed, I've been worrying about coming so much this week I think I've worn myself out' Alice took a sip of her water, shaking a little less.

'Do you want me to get you a taxi to your hotel or shall I walk you?' asked Charlie.

'I'm ok now, let me just gather my thoughts and we can talk if that's alright?' said Alice, dabbing her eyes with her napkin.

'Take your time, there's no rush at all. Shall I ask for our food to be warmed up?' requested Charlie.

'No it's ok, I don't think I can eat it, but do you think they have any bread I could have just to settle my stomach?' asked Alice.

Charlie stood up and walked to the reception desk where the waiter was sat, she could see that the booking list was pretty empty for the day. She asked him for some bread, and he went into the kitchen returning a short time later with a baguette cut into chunks and some butter in a dish. He took the bowls away uneaten, and Charlie assured him there was nothing wrong with it, but the bread would be fine. It seemed such a waste of good food but neither of them could eat.

They sat there eating the bread and commenting on how sad it was that the restaurant was empty when Alice suggested that they both go back to her hotel so they could talk privately. Charlie paid the bill, and they walked back slowly up the hill to the West Lodge.

They both walked into the beautiful white building through to the reception where Alice collected her key, and they went up in the lift to the second floor. The room was luxurious, with a large bed, desk and sofa with a wall mounted tv. Charlie took a seat on the sofa and Alice sat on the bed. Alice's colour had fully returned to normal, and she looked so pretty sat on the bed, her legs dangling down over the edge.

'After thinking about this for months I don't know where to start. You broke my heart. I know it was just the beginning, but I was swept away. I thought you felt the same. I fall hard for people, I always have, and that's my problem not yours, but what happened with THAT woman hurt. More than Sally, or maybe on top of Sally I don't know. Is this what everyone does, is there something about me that makes people cheat? I don't know what you want from me,' Alice shouted, her voice clear, loud and full of passion. She got off the bed and was pacing up and down. Standing in front of Charlie she screamed 'WHAT DO YOU WANT FROM ME?'

Charlie wanted to hold her, but after her previous reaction she backed away.

'Let me explain. I tried to in my letter.' Charlie took a deep breathe. 'I told you before that I leave women before they can leave me, but it's a self-fulfilling prophecy isn't it.'

Charlie walked over to Alice who was leaning against the patio door shaking. She could see that she was shocked at the outpouring that had come from her mouth. Taking her hand, this time Alice didn't pull away as Charlie put her arms around her and pulled her in close. She could feel her heart pounding out of her chest, Alice's heart was doing a similar dance to hers which she felt through her hands on her back. They stood, wrapped in each other for some time, not speaking, just breathing in tandem, both taken aback by the anger that, although expected, had been a surprise to them both by its force.

'I just want to make you happy Alice. Nothing can take back what I did, but I want to spend the rest of my life showing you how much I love you' said Charlie with such feeling in her voice she became chocked up.

Alice pulled back slightly and looked into Charlie's eyes.

'You love me?' questioned Alice, her voice raised. 'You don't even know me. How can you love me. After what you did, how can you say you love me?'

'Because I do know you. I started falling for you the moment I first met you. I have no doubt that we are meant to be together. I will apologise EVERY, single, minute, of EVERY single day until you believe me. I love you Alice'. Charlie sat down on the sofa and put her head in her hands. 'Do you want me to go?'

Alice frowned and turned to look out of the window. 'No. I came to sort things out with you.'

'Ask me anything Alice, I'm an open book. I've nothing to hide from you,' said Charlie taking a seat at the desk, swivelling the chair around to face Alice.

'Ok, have you seen Dawn or anyone else since that night?' asked Alice.

'No one. You can ask Di; she knows what a mess I was after it all happened. I don't want anyone else, all I've thought about is you. If I could turn the clock back, I honestly would' replied Charlie. 'I've worked hard since I got here and have come to this conclusion Alice. I love you and I want to spend the rest of my life with you. It's as simple as that. You're my ONE'.

'You make it sounds so easy Charlie,' said Alice. 'It isn't that easy'.

'I know it isn't' said Charlie beginning to feel defeated. 'Please tell me how I can make this right. Will you at least let me try'.

'I don't know Charlie' replied Alice, her voice quiet and sad.

'Will you at least tell me if you've any feelings left for me' requested Charlie.

'I wouldn't be here if I didn't still have feelings for would I? It isn't as straightforward as what I feel Charlie,' said Alice.

'I know that, but do you still have feelings for me?' insisted Charlie.

'YES! I LOVE YOU' shouted Alice, who sat down hard on the bed and burst into tears, rolling on her side and curled up into the foetal position.

Charlie knelt in front of her, took hold of her hand and brushed the hair out of Alice's face.

'That's a good start then isn't it. We can work through this; I know we can,' said Charlie softly.

Alice sat up and pulled Charlie towards her, running her hands gently over Charlie's face, over her forehead, cheeks, touching her lips, then slowly leant towards her and kissed her. Within seconds they were kissing passionately, Charlie felt such relief, she let herself go completely as Alice undid her shirt and she undid hers. They were both breathing heavily, the intensity of their passion for each other exploded, and they felt a mutual frantic need to be as close as they could, as fast as they could. Within a minute they were both naked on the bed, still kissing, hands holding each other, desperate to wander, but restrained for now. Just to be close to Alice is all Charlie wanted right then.

'I love you Charlie' said Alice 'I have for such a long time. I love you'.

'I love you too, god I love you' said Charlie as Alice moved lower to kiss her breast. 'No Alice, it's ok, let's take our time. I want you so badly, but I want you to be totally sure'.

'I AM' said Alice gently pushing Charlie back down onto the bed. 'I want to show you just how much I love you'. Her tongue gently flicking Charlie's nipple. Charlie lost the battle there; her body was trembling as Alice's fingers slid deep inside her.

'Fuck me Alice' she begged.

'Oh, I will my love' replied Alice 'I absolutely fucking will'.

18
Friction and Fireworks

It was still dark outside, and Charlie and Alice were still wrapped up in each other, when there was a knock at the door.

'Alice, are you there? It's Holly,' came the voice from behind the door.

'Hang on,' shouted Alice.

Alice jumped up, grabbed her complementary bathrobe, and opened the door slightly, poking her head around it. Charlie took the opportunity to grab her clothes and went into the bathroom to get hastily dressed.

'Is everything ok?' asked Holly quietly.

Alice looked back and saw that Charlie had gone into the en suite.

'Er yes, just here with Charlie, are you both ok?' replied Alice guiltily.

'I rang and I couldn't get through, is your phone off or is it the reception? asked Holly.

'Do you want to come in, sorry I'm being rude' said Alice opening the door fully. 'Charlie's just in the bathroom.'

Holly stepped through the doorway. 'I just wanted to make sure you were ok. Jen and I were wondering if you'd both like to go out for dinner. We've booked a table at Villa Roma for 6.45 as the receptionist recommended it, no pressure if you've got plans together' suggested Holly.

'Hang on, let me ask Charlie' Alice knocked on the bathroom door 'Charlie, do you fancy going out for dinner with Jen and Holly?'

The door opened and a redressed Charlie emerged.

'Nice to meet you' said Charlie smiling knowing Holly would be able to see the recently vacated bed and Alice's clothes on the floor. 'What do you think Alice?'

'Ok sounds a plan, shall we walk down or shall I take us in the car?' asked Alice.

'Think a walk and fresh air would do us both good, Jen is feeling better after a nap, honestly covid has really floored her' said Holly. 'Will knock for you about 6.30 if that's ok?'

'Great, I don't even know what time it is?' said Alice looking around the room for her phone, finding it in her discarded trousers on the floor, it was 5.55.

'Lovely, look forward to it' said Holly making a swift exit.

'Well, that was funny, god what will she think' asked Alice.

'I'm sure she was just happy to see you smiling, I know I am' said Charlie taking hold of Alice's hands. 'Fancy a shower together, that looks like a super duper one in there' grinned Charlie.

'Lead the way' said Alice smiling as Charlie led them both into the bathroom.

True to her word Holly knocked on Alice's door at 6.30, and the threesome went down to the reception to meet Jen who looked washed out sat on a sofa.

'Hi Jen, this is Charlie, Charlie, meet Jen' smiled Alice.

Charlie raised her hand in greeting.

'How are you feeling? Are you sure you don't want me to drive us all down? You look really tired Jen'.

'Charlie' she said giving a cursory nod. 'Ok you twisted my arm. Feel like I smoke 200 fags a day, sodding Covid' said Jen standing up gingerly.

Holly hooked arms with her, and they all headed to the car park. Jen positioned herself at the front passenger door, almost like she was marking her territory, so Holly and Charlie got in the back.

When they arrived at Villa Roma it was practically empty. The waiter from earlier in the day was there, as was an older man in a suit at the desk.

'Hi, I booked a table for four at 6.45 for Holly' she stated.

'Lovely, this way please' said the waiter looking at Alice. 'Are you ok now Miss after earlier?'

'Much better thank you' replied Alice feeling embarrassed.

'Why what happened?' snapped Jen glaring at Charlie.

'Nothing, I just had a funny turn, it's ok Jen' said Alice calmly.

'Well as long as that's all it was' said Jen sitting down next to Holly, directly opposite Charlie.

'I know what I've done was very wrong, and I'm sorry for hurting her. I've told her everything, I just want to be given a second chance' said Charlie passionately. She took hold of Alice's clenched hand on her lap. 'I love her, I honestly do'.

'Well time will tell won't it' snarled Jen.

Holly put her hand on Jen's, it was a table of clenched fists and jaws. The waiter approached to take their drink orders. No one wanted alcohol, which with the high tension was probably a good idea. Instead, the waiter brought a large jug of water with ice and then approached for their food order. Alice and Charlie ordered the same food as at lunchtime, and Jen and Holly ordered two different pizzas to share.

'What's your room like?' asked Alice trying to break the silence.

'It's gorgeous, does yours have a hot tub? Asked Alice.

'Absolutely! We're going to fire it up and try it out, have you got one too?' asked Holly.

'Yes, although I think it might be a bit cold, will see though'. said Alice sipping her water and buttering a piece of baguette, she was ravenous having not eaten properly all day.

'So are you staying with Alice then Charlie or do you have to go back to the rehab thing' said Jen in a loud voice, looking like she hoped to upset Charlie.

'No, I'll go back to the centre tonight, not because I 'have' to,' replied Charlie calmly. 'I'm free to come and go as I please Jen'.

'Has it helped Charlie?' asked Holly trying to defuse the situation. 'I've heard good things about it'.

'Yeah, it's been hard work, but I feel so much better than I was. It's why I asked Alice to come here. Thank you both coming to support her' replied Charlie, who Alice could see had really started to relax despite Jen firing daggers at her from across the table.

'I'm glad to hear it's helped,' said Holly. 'I know it won't have been easy'.

The waiter arrived with their food and then there was silence for a while as they all ate, with lots of positive noises. Jen and Holly shared theirs and Alice and Charlie did the same. The food was delicious and soon the waiter was clearing clean plates. They all opted for tiramisu for dessert.

'Oh, my goodness, this is divine, I don't think I have ever had a nicer meal' said Holly and the others agreed.

'I don't understand why it's so empty,' said Alice.

'I think it just needs a revamp and good marketing' said Charlie. 'It wouldn't cost that much'.

'Maybe you should have a word with the manager Charlie' suggested Alice.

'Maybe, but not today. Tonight, is about getting to know you both and seeing Alice, that's all that's important right now' said Charlie holding Alice's hand and looking adoringly into her eyes. Alice returned the gaze and smiled.

'Do you only renovate bars and restaurants' asked Holly.

'And houses, but I could do it for other businesses too I think, it's something I've been working on whilst I've been here. I wanted to tell Alice this in private, but I've decided to put a permanent manager in

Valentine's and focus more on design work. I enjoy it more, and until I came here, I didn't realise how much I enjoy being creative' explained Charlie.

'Wow that's a big decision, very brave, but I think you'd be amazing at designing other places without the hassle of running them,' said Alice relieved to hear that she wasn't going to be working there anymore.

'Is that so you're not tempted by women and drinking then Charlie' interrupted Jen. 'Can't be easy with all them women throwing themselves at you'.

'Look I know why I was doing what I did, and drinking was part of that, but that is the past, and this is my future' said Charlie reassuringly.

'Time will tell with that won't it' snipped Jen, glaring at Charlie across the table.

'I know,' replied Charlie. 'It's been a long journey, and I know it's not over'.

'Well....' Said Jen who was cut off by Holly.

'Anyway, the meal was lovely, and it's been fun, but I think we need to head back to the hotel?' asked Holly stroking Jen's arm.

'Of course, let's head back, you both look really tired,' said Alice.

Charlie raised her hand to attract the manager who came over and brought the bill. They split it four ways although Charlie offered to pay it.

Alice drove them all back to the West Lodge in silence, and Jen and Holly said goodnight and went to their room.

'That wasn't as bad as I was expecting' smiled said Charlie. 'What would you like to do now Alice? Shall we go sit somewhere?'

'Let's go sit somewhere for a while, although I have to admit I'm rather tired. Do you want to meet up again tomorrow or are you busy?' asked Alice.

'I'm free whenever you want, we could go on a boat ride or whatever you'd like to do,' said Charlie.

'How about coming to my room at 9.30 and we can go from there?' asked Alice yawning, the day catching up with her.

'Sounds good to me. I'm going to let you go to bed now, you're tired and we've all day tomorrow to plan what we do next' said Charlie holding Alice's hand, and under a clear night sky, where every star was shining brightly, she kissed Alice goodnight and looking skyward after, as Charlie walked away, Alice saw a shooting star and made a wish to the universe.

'Night Charlie' said Alice waving into the darkness.

The following morning Alice, Jen and Holly breakfasted together in the dining room, there was so much choice, but Jen who really wasn't well, hardly ate anything. Holly prescribed a day of rest for them both and told Alice to have a lovely day with Charlie.

Alice returned to her room for a quick shower, and just as she put on her robe Charlie messaged her good morning, which she replied to excitedly, adding that she was free now if she wanted to come over to which Charlie replied, 'On my way'.

Within 10 minutes Charlie was knocking at her hotel door and Alice threw herself into her arms, kissing her with such force that took her by surprise.

'Good morning Alice' said Charlie coming up for air. 'Did you sleep ok?'

Alice took Charlie's hand and walked them both to the bed and they sat down.

'I did, I think it must be the gorgeous fresh air here, just eaten half my bodyweight in croissants for breakfast. Did you eat too?' asked Alice.

'Yeah, it's all healthy fare at the centre, I do miss a full English though! How's Jen and Holly today?' asked Charlie with trepidation.

'Jen still isn't right, she couldn't eat much so Holly has ordered her to bed, I wish you'd order me to bed too' smiled Alice coyly.

'Your wish is my command' said Charlie forcefully. 'Tell me what you want me to do to you'.

Alice visibly quaked. 'I'm all yours' she said, standing to take off her robe. She stood naked in front of Charlie, their eyes locked in the deepest of lustful gazes. 'I want you to make me come hard'.

'Slow or quick?' said Charlie kissing Alice's breasts, avoiding her nipples.

'Quick' pleaded Alice.

'Not a chance' said Charlie kissing her neck, her fingers tracking slowly up and down her spine. 'I'm going to make you beg me to come. Get on the bed on all fours'.

Alice did as she was told, her full round arse facing towards Charlie, who climbed on the bed behind her, continuing to trace her fingers from the top of her spine, down her back, between her cheeks and then slid the tip of her finger into her, moving it in slow circles. Alice let out a gentle moan, leaning back attempting to push the finger deeper, Charlie pulled out, repeating her finger movement from the top of her spine, down and then slightly into her. Alice attempted to sit deeper onto the very tempting finger, only for it to be removed, she groaned again.

Leaning forward Charlie cupped Alice's breast, tweaking her nipple hard making her let out a small yelp. 'Harder' she begged. Charlie obliged. Alice groaned louder. Continuing to caress and tweak in alternate movements, Charlie slid her other hand down onto Alice's full bush, her fingers playing with her pubic hair just above her clit, Alice leant down onto the fingers which slid onto it, letting out a shudder as she did so.

'Naughty' said Charlie moving her hand away, leaning back and repeating the fingers up and down her spine.

'You bad, bad woman' giggled Alice, 'Please touch me!'

'Where?' smiled Charlie.

'You know where' she said shyly.

'No, tell me,' Ordered Charlie.

'Deep inside me, please' pleaded Alice.

'Deep inside where Alice, tell me' Demanded Charlie.

Charlie pulled back, repeating her fingers up and down her spine, sliding her smallest finger only part way again, Alice was so wet by this point she was finding it hard to restrain herself. The noises were divine music to her ears.

Pulling her small finger out totally she slid three fingers as deep as she could, Alice's muscles tensing onto them letting out a loud gasp. Slowly she slid her fingers in and out, Alice was so tightly gripped onto them that Charlie couldn't have pulled out if she had wanted to, she could feel her pulsating inside as the climax built up. Pulling out gently Charlie rolled onto her back next to Alice, kissing her and pulling her up towards her.

'Sit on me, I want to taste you, hold onto the headboard' Charlie demanded, as Alice straddled Charlie's face, sinking her wetness onto her awaiting tongue. Charlie knew she wouldn't be able to last much longer, the intensity would be too much for Alice, so she flicked her tongue, sucked very gently, then just as she knew she was on the edge, slid one finger inside, holding it steady against the fleshy bulb of the enigma that is the G spot. Alice's body erupted, her muscles tensing throughout her body, she let out the deepest of groans repeatedly, dipping on and off Charlie's tongue until she sank down onto her arms on the headboard, releasing Charlie.

'Oh my god, what was that? I've never felt anything like that before' said Alice shakily.

'Come lie down next to me' said Charlie.

'I don't think I can move' laughed Alice 'They're frozen' she said moving her legs slowly and gingerly.

Charlie knelt up next to her and putting her arm around her waist, pulled her gently down onto the bed. 'Are you ok? Was it ok?' she asked.

'Was it ok? My god Charlie, my body is utterly gone. That was the most intense thing I've ever experienced. God you're hot' said Alice.

'You're hot too, you look so sexy from all angles' said Charlie with a smile.

'I'm blushing! Now what can I do for you?' said Alice beginning to unbutton Charlie's sodden shirt. 'Oh god is that me?'

'Yes darling it's all you, you were so wet. I may have to go back and get changed!' said Charlie.

'I have one of your shirts with me that you leant me ages ago, I wanted you to have it back, so I packed it' laughed Alice.

'Well that is just perfect, thanks. Now where were we?' said Charlie moving closer to Alice. 'I need you to show me how much you just enjoyed yourself'.

Alice happily obliged.

After a beautiful morning in bed Alice and Charlie dressed after showering and headed into Bowness to find a tearoom for lunch. They ordered plates of savouries and cakes and laughed all the way through eating it. It was a busy tearoom, but they were so enthralled by each other's company that they didn't notice anyone else. After lunch they walked to the lakeside and took a boat tour around the lake and marvelled at the boats in the marina and the fantastic views. As they arrived back into Bowness Alice's phone rang. It was Holly.

'Hi, is everything ok?' asked Alice

'No, not really, I'm not happy about the way Jen is today, I think she's got a chest infection and her temperature is up, so we are going to get a taxi to the hospital in Kendal, I'm so worried about her,' said Holly.

'No let me take you, I can be at the hotel in ten minutes,' said Alice. She explained to Charlie what was happening, and they both rushed back to the West Lodge.

When they got there Jen looked really pale, and Holly and Charlie helped her into the car despite her protests. They drove to Kendal as quickly as they could and went into the A&E department. Holly spoke to the receptionist, who then called a doctor who took them both through to where the cubicles were. Alice and Charlie took seats in the waiting room. It was relatively quiet compared to how A&E had been at York.

'Can I get you something from the vending machine Alice? Water? Coffee?' asked Charlie.

'No I'm ok thanks, I really don't like hospitals' said Alice thinking about the last time she was in one. A flash of sadness appeared in her eyes and Charlie noticed it straight away.

'Shall we go and sit in the car, would that help?' asked Charlie.

'Yes I think it would, I'll just text Holly and tell her,' said Alice.

Once in the car Alice decided to tell Charlie what had happened when she was in hospital, explaining how they had discovered the heart problem and how she felt like she was living on borrowed time.

Charlie sat with a stunned look on her face. 'What have the doctors said? Did I do this to you?'

Alice took hold of Charlie's hands which were tense, with a pained look on her face.

'No, of course not. I could have had it since birth, it could have developed over time, they don't know. At the minute there isn't any treatment needed, just if I start to feel dizzy or breathless, they will want to see me again, it just knocked me off my feet finding out'.

'Don't you dare get ill, I couldn't bear it, I'm sorry that I put you through what I did' said Charlie with such emotion in her voice they both burst into tears hugging.

Just then Holly knocked on the car door window making them both jump.

'Sorry guys, I was right, she has a chest infection, so we're just waiting for some antibiotics and then we can go back. Are you both ok?' asked Holly concerned that they were both tearful.

'Yes all fine, I just told Charlie about my heart thing' explained Alice 'but we can talk about that another time, getting Jen back to bed is more important'.

'Don't worry Charlie, we've got Alice for a long time to come' said Holly heading, back into the hospital.

Jen and Holly came back to the car shortly after, so Alice drove them back to the hotel. It was already dark when they got there and after parking Jen and Holly went inside, deciding to order room service and that an early night was in order.

Getting out of the car and stretching her legs Charlie suggested that they walk down into Bowness and look at the lake. As they walked down, they stopped and bought fish and chips to eat at the lakeside. As they sat looking out across the lake fireworks started on the other side, to their left, right and behind. The sky was full of spectacular colours, shapes and squeals as they exploded around them. They both sat there looking skyward as the display expanded above them, both smiling and pointing out the various shapes of love hearts and stars.

'I'd forgotten that it was bonfire night,' said Alice. 'I feel I've got romance on top of romance' she laughed. 'Is this why you wanted to come down here Charlie?'

'I could lie and say yes but I hadn't a clue either, isn't it lovely though' said Charlie putting their chip wrappers into the bin and then returning to the bench and pulled Alice closer. Although they were wrapped up warm, they were still really cold.

'Shall we go back to my room and see the fireworks from the balcony, we could brave the hot tub?' suggested Alice with a smile.

'That sounds a great idea, once we're in the water, I'm sure it'll be fine' replied Alice.

They both walked briskly back to the hotel and once in the room Charlie quickly read the instructions for the hot tub and switched it on. Neither of them had a swimsuit with them, so switching the light off in the bedroom they both snuck into the hot tub naked, hopefully unseen. The bubbles and warmth were lovely, and Alice and Charlie laid side by side watching the fireworks across the night sky.

'This is absolute heaven Charlie; I really don't want to go back tomorrow,' said Alice. 'When are you coming home?'

'I'll be leaving here next week; I want to see if I can gain any interest in my design work so want to crack on with that when I get back, but mostly I want us to be together. I don't mean move in with each other as it is too early for that, do you agree?' asked Charlie floating so she was in front of Alice, her legs astride her. 'What do you think?'

'Now how am I supposed to concentrate with your gorgeous body enticing me like that' said Alice pulling Charlie in closer.

'I know how can you resist? But seriously, how do you feel about it?' asked Charlie slightly pulling back.

'Yes I agree, it is far too early for the whole moving in with each other, but are we even proper lesbians if we don't,' laughed Alice.

'Very funny! How would you feel about going back to dating each other? What do you think?' said Charlie.

'It's going to take time for me to trust you, you do understand that don't you?' said Alice looking concerned.

'Of course, but if we keep talking, and if something comes up that's worrying you, please just talk to me, I promise I'll do the same,' said Charlie. 'It's a long road for us both, but I think we're so good together, that's got to be a good place to start doesn't it'.

'I can think of another lovely place to start with too Charlie' said Alice pulling her closer by the waist, her other hand finding its way between her thighs. 'What do you think?'

'Absolutely. It's a very lovely place to start' said Charlie putting her hand between Alice's legs, her other arm pulled her forward gently, so she was directly over one of the jets which completely intensified the sensations rushing through her body. Alice gasped. The jets and Charlie's hand blew her mind, the fireworks going off overhead as she reached an immense climax masked the loud groan that escaped her mouth as she came. Charlie kissed Alice softly as they held each other.

'God Charlie, you've truly finished me off, I'm floating, one of us needs to get a hot tub for the garden!' She said smiling.

Charlie laughed 'Now that is a lovely thought. Is it ok if we get out? I'm becoming a prune'.

'Hope there's no one down in the garden' giggled Alice scrambling out putting on her bathrobe and passing the other to Charlie.

'Would you mind if I stay over tonight, I just want to hold you and go to sleep with you' asked Charlie.

'That'd be lovely' said Alice feeling so happy. She'd wanted to ask Charlie but hadn't wanted to push it.

'Perfect, I'll just call the centre and let them know so Toby isn't waiting up for me' said Charlie getting out her phone making a quick call.

The sky was still erupting with distant pops and bangs from fireworks as they both snuggled under the duvet and drifted off on a sea of happiness.

19

Where There's Love, There's Hope

All was quiet in the hotel, it was so peaceful laid there snuggled up to Charlie who looked so serene, that Alice really didn't want to move. She slowly, and quietly leaned over to get her phone to look at the time. She knew she had to check out at 10, but she really didn't want to. Her phone showed it was 8.10am so time really to get up for breakfast, she wished she'd thought to order it in bed for them. Charlie began to stir, rubbing her eyes and sitting up on her elbows.

'Morning, think I feel I've been asleep for a month, these beds are so comfortable,' said Charlie. 'I sleep so well with you beside me, mmm come here and let me hold you before we have to start the day, is it late?'

'It's just after 8 so I need to get up I'm afraid' said Alice laying with her head on Charlie's chest. 'I better message Holly and see how Jen is.'

'Ok love, sorry I don't want to hold you up' said Charlie kissing Alice on the top of her head and then went into the bathroom.

Alice raised her voice 'They're having breakfast in bed, they just ordered it, do you fancy it too? I need to tell them I had an extra guest anyway'.

'You twisted my arm, could I have a full English? I've really missed having one, is that bad of me?' laughed Charlie.

'Not at all, think I'll have the same, can't think why I'm so hungry' said Alice with a cheeky smile.

Alice dialled reception, requesting two breakfasts and explaining that she had a guest who needed adding to her bill.

'Let me know how much I owe you' offered Charlie.

'It's ok Charlie they aren't charging me, I've already paid the single supplement anyway, and I'm happy to stand you a breakfast just this once' giggled Alice.

'Cheeky' said Charlie jumping onto the bed and proceeding to tickle Alice making her laugh very loudly.

Alice's phone then pinged so Charlie released her, sitting back on her elbows smiling.

'It's Holly, Jen isn't much better so she is thinking they should stay on for another couple of days and getting the train back. Let me have a look at my diary on my laptop' said Alice going to her suitcase and retrieving it. She sat on the bed, opened it, waiting for it to boot up, Charlie leant forward and kissed her naked shoulders making her quiver. 'Naughty'

'Well, what's a girl to do!' said Charlie innocently.

Alice leant in as her calendar loaded.

'Do you want me to pass your glasses Miss?' said Charlie. Alice turned and looked at her and she was wearing them on the end of her nose like an old school mistress. Alice started laughing and took them off her, giving her a kiss.

'You're so funny'. Alice put on her glasses and studied the screen. She knew she'd things on Monday but nothing in person. There were two supervisions by Zoom and a seminar, so Alice knew that there was no rush to get back, and by the look of her diary she could stay and work until Thursday morning when she'd a lecture at Kings Manor.

'Would you mind if I stayed until Wednesday? Everything I have until Thursday is online so I can work from here' asked Alice 'I don't want you to feel pressured by me staying longer'.

'That would be fantastic, not pressured at all, what a lovely surprise. I'll need to go back to the centre after breakfast to change and I have some final sessions to do this week, but we could get together on an evening? What do you think? I'd really like to stay over if that wasn't too much for you?' Said Charlie.

'Perfect' said Alice. 'Let me ring reception again and see if I can keep the room a while longer, they'll be sick of me ringing'.

Just then there was a knock at the door, and after a frantic search to put on bath robes, Charlie opened the door. A waiter brought in a trolley with two trays with tea, coffee and plates of food and toast.

'Thank you' said Charlie offering him a tip that she'd retrieved from her trousers.

'That's all set, we can stay here until Wednesday morning. Ooo, the food looks amazing' said Alice as Charlie took the metal cover off one of the plates. 'Not sure how I'm going to eat this without making a mess, maybe we need to eat it in the bath, like we should have your spag bol'.

Charlie laughed, then manoeuvred the trolley in front of Alice and then took her tray and sat at the desk. 'Ta da' she said.

'Ingenious' smiled Alice.

'OMG I've missed bacon' exclaimed Charlie.

'It does feel naughty but rather nice, like someone I'm looking at right now' smiled Charlie. 'I'll head back to the centre in a bit and get some clothes for later if you want to go out for dinner tonight?' asked Charlie.

'Perfect, shall I ask Jen and Holly too do you think, or just us?' enquired Alice 'I know you haven't hit it off with Jen'.

'No, invite them along, I'm not shying away from it Alice, I can take whatever Jen throws at me. How about if I come back about 1 if you wanted to go out somewhere this afternoon? I could do with taking my car out for a run, it's been stood for weeks' asked Charlie.

'Ok I'll ask them,' said Alice. 'A drive out would be lovely; I'll have a look at the tourist board in reception for ideas'.

'Wonderful love, right I'm going to get ready and get off. Have a lovely morning' Charlie got dressed, kissed Alice tenderly goodbye and headed back to the rehab centre.

Alice got ready then went to see Jen and Holly in their room on the floor below. Jen was sat on the sofa, with a little more colour than she'd the day before, but definitely not her normal self.

'I've booked to stay until Wednesday so there's no rush to get back' said Alice. 'How's the patient?'

'Jen's temperatures up and down, and I know it's only a couple of hours drive back, but it seems such a shame to go back when we haven't really left the hotel.' Said Holly. 'Are you sure you don't mind staying?'

'I've got my laptop so can work from here, thankfully everything's online, so all's good.' answered Alice.

'So, where's Charlie this morning?' asked Jen in an unfriendly tone.

'She's just gone back to the centre to change and sort things out. She's going home soon. It's been magic Jen' said Alice smiling kindly at her friend. 'She loves me, I genuinely believe that'.

'Yeah, but you're in a love bubble right now, everything's rosy, what happens when she's tempted again? Will she cheat or start drinking again?' said Jen.

'I have to trust what she's saying' responded Alice.

'Do you? Once a cheater, always a cheater' said Jen loudly.

They were both visibly shaken at the venom in Jen's voice.

Holly sat down next to Jen. 'That's a bit harsh Jen, doesn't everyone deserve the benefit of the doubt. Look at the effort that she's making being here, she looks like someone trying to make amends. Neither of us want you to get hurt again Alice, but I think she's really trying to sort things out. It must be costing her a lot of money to do this'.

Holly retrieved her medical kit and got the electronic thermometer out and stuck it in Jen's ear.

'38.5, back to bed for you Jen I'm afraid'. Holly guided Jen to the bed and settled her. 'Here's two paracetamols, take these and snuggle down and sleep lovely. I'm just going to go out for some fresh air whilst you rest, is that ok'.

Jen nodded, swallowed the tablets and laid down on her side, her face like a petulant toddler. Holly indicated to Alice to follow her out of the room and they both walked silently down the stairs and into the bar area where they ordered two coffees.

'Sorry about that, she really isn't herself. I'm sure she doesn't mean what she's saying. We're both worried about you, but you're a grown woman and if you're willing to give Charlie another chance, so am I. Jen will come round in time. Did she ever tell you about her parents?' asked Holly with a serious tone to her voice. 'Not that I have ever met them, as you know she only sees her mum rarely, and I've never wanted to rock the boat for her'.

'I know her father was abusive to her, it's why we all bonded wasn't it, because our parents were so anti-gay we became our own support group' smiled Alice.

'Her father had multiple affairs and it's really affected her, she had to leave for her own sanity. I know she misses her mum a lot. I've tried to encourage her to get in touch now her dad's dead, but I think she's too scared to. That's why she's being so hard on Charlie because of the cheating. She loves you, we both do, but she doesn't trust her yet. Once she's better I'm sure she'll try harder' said Holly hugging Alice. 'It's lovely to see you smiling again'.

'It feels so lovely to be smiling again! Do you both fancy going out for a meal tonight. If Jen isn't well though I totally understand if you can't,' said Alice.

'That'd be lovely, let's see how she is later, I think she should just be sleeping, but you know Jen, strong willed as ever, even when ill,' laughed Holly.

'Yes, she's definitely that,' said Alice.

The waiter came over bringing them two cups of coffee, cream and sugar and the two of them relished in the rush of caffeine. Alice could see the strain on Holly's face.

'Is everything ok between you two?' asked Alice.

'Yes and no. Jen's hard to live with when she's ill. I'm patient. But oh my god, she'd test the patience of a saint!' said Holly excitedly.

'Bless you. Why don't I sit with her for a while after my coffee so you can go out and stretch your legs? You look like you could do with some fresh air' suggested Alice.

'I'd really appreciate that. Here's our door card, I've my phone if you need me, but I'll only be a couple of hours, just need to clear my head for a bit'.

'No worries. I'm not meeting Charlie until 1 so that gives you loads of time. I'll just grab my laptop first. Go on, off you go. Enjoy' said Alice standing to hug her, then she turned and went out into the cool November air.

Jen was still asleep when she went into the room. All was quiet in the hotel and Alice sat with the laptop on her knee facing the window so she could see the lake and beyond. It was so tranquil here; it seemed a shame to have to go home and leave it all behind. Alice sorted out the details for the following day and answered some work emails and then checked her personal ones but there was nothing very exciting in them.

Her phone buzzed; it was a text from Charlie. 'All good here and cleared for staying over with you until Wednesday and I check out of here on Saturday morning. How's your morning?'

Alice felt flips of joy in her stomach as she sat smiling at her phone, sending a quick reply that all was well, and she was in Jen's room whilst Holly had some time out.

'What's that' said Jen from the bed, she sounded very short of breath.

'You made me jump, sorry I had it on vibrate so I didn't disturb you' said Alice apologetically.

'Well that worked well didn't it' replied Jen crossly who was sat on the side of the bed leant forward wheezing badly.

'Sorry Jen, Holly's just gone out for some fresh air, and I said I'd sit with you' said Alice shocked at her friend's tone and her breathing. 'You don't look right Jen; I'm going to call Holly'.

'Just fuck off and leave me alone' she gasped.

Ignoring her protests she called Holly's number, quickly explaining what had happened.

Jen stood up and tried to wrench the phone out of Alice's hand. 'Bloody leave me alone, fuck off.'

Alice managed to get Jen to sit down who was incredibly hot to the touch and sweating profusely and her breathing sounded short and raspy. She spoke slowly and gently to her, trying to calm her down. After a few minutes Holly arrived, but it felt like an eternity. She immediately got the oximeter and put it onto Jen's finger. It measured 92 and was flashing.

Without talking to Alice, Holly stood up and took out her phone and dialled 999. 'Ambulance please' she said hastily.

Alice sat on the bed next to Jen trying to placate her, but nothing was working when Charlie knocked on the door and came in.

'What's up?' she asked.

'It's going to be a few hours before they can get an ambulance here, can you take us Alice?' Holly begged.

'Of course,' replied Alice. 'Does the hotel have a wheelchair?'. She dialled reception and nodded at Charlie, who left the room to go and collect it.

Returning shortly after, Charlie pushed the wheelchair into the room. Looking around the room she saw a pair of slippers and put them on Jen's feet despite her lashing out her legs at her. Then between them all they managed to get her into the wheelchair.

Arriving in the car park Charlie took charge.

'Let me drive, you two sit in the back of my car, it's bigger than Alice's'.

Nodding they guided Jen into the back of Charlie's Jeep and once she was safely strapped in they set off. The road was busier than last time and the atmosphere in the car was very stressful. Alice was trying along with Holly to calm Jen, but she could see how distressed she was, panicking that she couldn't breathe properly.

As soon as they arrived at the hospital Charlie went and found another wheelchair.

'Look, we could be here quite a while I think, so please go back to the hotel. I'll ring when there's news' said Holly as they all walked into the A&E department.

'We'll stay to see what happens and then go from there. Just message when you know more,' said Alice.

A nurse arrived and after Holly explained everything, she was wheeled straight into the cubicle area. The department was very busy, with some obvious, and other nonobvious ailments, and the fact that Jen was wheeled straight through highlighted the seriousness of the situation.

Alice and Charlie went and sat on a bench outside the hospital waiting to hear from Holly.

'It was just awful Charlie, she was so aggressive, not like my lovely Jen at all. I'm so scared' said Alice bursting into tears.

Charlie put her arm around her and pulled her in close.

They sat there for some time, ambulances coming and going. Some with lights and lots of rushing, others slow and without sirens. Charlie went and got them both warm drinks, and they took a walk around the outside of the hospital, finally admitting defeat of the cold and went and sat in Charlie's Jeep. About an hour later Holly texted to ask where they were and came out and met them at the car alone.

'They've put her on oxygen and IV antibiotics, and they've fans going like crazy trying to get her temperature down. They'll be keeping her in for a few days, I'm really worried about her breathing' Explained Holly. 'Can you take me back to the hotel to get some things for her and me and bring me back. So sorry that we're spoiling your day'.

'Don't apologise, tell us what you need, and we'll go and get them from your room and bring it back, you stay with Jen,' said Alice.

Holly texted a list to Alice's phone, gave them both a big hug and the room card. Within an hour they returned with a bag of things for Holly and Jen, and sandwiches and drinks. They also brought Alice's car, so Holly could drive back that evening as there was nowhere for her to stay.

Returning afterwards to the hotel, both wrung out with tiredness and stress. It felt as though they hadn't breathed properly for the past few hours. They laid fully clothed on the bed holding hands in silence, watching the tv with no volume waiting for news.

Alice sat up suddenly, 'Shit Charlie I haven't asked how you got on today at the centre, so sorry my head's a shed' apologised Alice.

'It's ok, you don't need to say sorry. It was ok, I set out with Dr Hanson a few things to do this week, but mainly I want to spend time with you and Holly if I can help you both' said Charlie reassuringly.

'Let's see what Holly says when she comes back. I don't want you to miss out on anything important' said Alice, rolling onto her side and resting her head on Charlie's chest.

'I love you' said Charlie tenderly.

'I love you too' replied Alice feeling safe and secure in Charlie's arms. She closed her eyes and listening to Charlie's steady beating heart she drifted off.

Around 9.30 Holly knocked on the door looking exhausted.

'How's Jen?' asked Alice going to sit next to her friend and Charlie put the kettle on.

'She's improved a little now she has oxygen, and the IV antibiotics should speed things up a bit, they think she has bronchitis. God I'm so tired, I had to leave as visiting was over and Jen was sleeping. They think that she'll be in for a couple of days. Thank you for driving me around today, I really appreciate it and for lending me your car.'

'Hey, it's ok that's what friends are for. Do you want me to order you some food?' asked Alice.

'No, it's ok, I just want to go to bed I think. I was so scared I was going to lose her. I don't know what I'd do without her' said Holly sadly. Alice gave her a big hug as the tears fell, rubbing her back and letting her friend release all of what she'd been holding in all day. Alice caught Charlie's eye who was making tea and smiled at her.

Charlie brought over a cup of tea and handed it to Holly.

'Thanks Charlie' Holly took a sip and nearly spat it across the room. 'Oh my god, how many sugars?'

'A few, thought you needed something sweet for shock?' replied Charlie smiling.

'I feel so bad for leaving her, I don't think we've had a night apart since we first met. I'm sorry for what she said to you Charlie, she isn't well' said Holly taking another smaller sip of her tea.

'It's fine, she just needs to get better, and she'll be back home with you in no time. Are you sure you don't want anything to eat?' asked Charlie forever the polite host.

Holly shook her head and put the teacup down on the table. 'I think I'll just head off to bed now. Am I ok to use your car again tomorrow Alice?'

'Yes of course, I'm working all day and don't need it. Hope that you can get some sleep tonight, if you need us just knock, ok?' said Alice hugging her friend again. 'Love you'.

'Thanks, love you too, night, night Charlie' said Holly leaving for her own room.

'God what a day' said Alice beginning to get undressed 'Would you mind if I go to bed now, I'm shattered.

'I was about to say the same, don't worry love. Shall I order us breakfast to the room again? It'll be less of a rush for you tomorrow'. Asked Charlie.

'Yes please, but just fruit and yoghurt for me, don't think I could face another full English, 7.30 ok for you?' said Alice who felt exhausted and a little sick.

'No problem' replied Charlie, picking up the phone and dialling reception putting in their request.

Alice was already in bed when Charlie got off the phone, so she undressed and joined her, turning off the lights by a switch at the side of the bed and they curled up together awaiting sleep and to rid themselves of a horrible day.

20

Homeward Bound

The next couple of days flew by in a flurry of zooms, writing at the desk overlooking the lake and spending nights with Charlie and Holly. Jen was doing well, and the hospital thought that she would be discharged on Friday and would be well enough to travel home on Saturday. Charlie had agreed to drive them both home, and Alice was preparing to drive home herself on Wednesday. It hadn't entirely been the relaxing week that they'd planned, but the relief of being reunited with Charlie had brought Alice such joy to her heart that she felt like she was floating out of her body every time they were together. The beautiful heart flutter every time she said her name Alice hoped would never fade.

On her final day in Bowness, after early visiting a calmer and friendlier Jen, Alice, Charlie and Holly had booked a table at Villa Roma before her long drive home. Alice had packed up her room and loaded her car, and Charlie had taken her things back to the centre. She felt a little deflated as they walked down to the restaurant. Charlie's hand and hers fitted perfectly into each other, giving a sense of security to them both. It had rained most of the day and the pavements looked glossy, the streetlights reflecting on the ground as though they were walking on ice.

As they entered the restaurant there was only their usual waiter and there was a glimpse of the chef going through the door to the kitchen. They took their seat at what had become their usual table but, on the table, next to theirs were two posters that said Closing Down in large red letters. The waiter approached.

'Good evening, can I take your order?' he asked.

The three of them gave orders of lasagne and garlic bread to share along with three lattes and Alice could see from the look on the waiters face that all really was not well.

After he returned with their drinks the manager entered and said a courtesy hello then picked up the posters.

'You're not closing permanently, are you?' asked Charlie.

'Yes, sadly so, our last day is Saturday, we just can't afford to keep going. After covid we just haven't been able to get back to where we were. We've had the restaurant for twenty years, but it's broken us' he explained.

'We've loved eating here this week, the food's amazing, I'm sorry that you're closing. What will you do next?' asked Alice.

'We don't know yet, it's all still so upsetting, my parents started the business, I do front of house and my brother does the cooking, they'd be so disappointed in us' he replied.

'It's been a tough few years for catering, no one could foresee what has happened so don't be so hard on yourselves,' said Charlie. 'Will you be open as usual until Saturday?'

'Yes, we will' he said 'I better put these up' he said and taking the posters went in search of blue tack.

'That's such a shame, there's nothing wrong with the food at all, the place is a little off putting from outside though' said Holly 'But once you've had the food you would definitely come back again'.

'It's probably used by the locals which is why they recommended it to me, but I am guessing that the area has a problem with second homeowners and there not being enough regular visitors. Of course, covid won't have helped either,' said Charlie.

Alice put her hand on Charlie's thigh under the table. She felt so proud of her. Their food arrived and was gratefully consumed in between discussions of Alice's drive home and Charlie's final few days at the centre.

'Dr Hanson has put me in touch with a therapist in York so I'll have support once I return home so it won't be like falling off a cliff with no safety net' smiled Charlie 'I can't wait to go home'.

'It'll be lovely to have you next door again' said Alice returning Charlie's smiles.

'Bless you both, you look so happy. I can't wait to get Jen home; it's been so strange without her. I can't tell you how happy I am that she's getting better. It really has reinforced just how much I love her' said Holly full of emotion.

Alice took her hand over the table 'We're both so relieved too, you've been through the wringer. Do you want to come and stay with me when you come back so we can both look after Jen as I guess you'll need to go back to work next week?'

'Can I think about it? That might not be a bad idea at all' replied Holly. 'It might really help, are you sure?'

'Totally' replied Alice. 'I work from home a lot in the week so I'll be around, and we can work around the times I'm not'.

'And I'm around too' said Charlie sympathetically. 'We can work it out'.

'Thank you both, let me sleep on it and I can talk to Jen tomorrow.'

After the meal they all walked back to the West Lodge and Holly hugged Alice goodbye and went to her room. Charlie walked her to the car.

'I'll miss you, but it's not long until Saturday, I can't wait to be next door to you again' said Charlie clearly tearful. She wrapped Alice in her arms holding her tightly. 'Drive carefully and will you let me know you got home ok?'

'Of course, I will, I should be home for 11 if you don't mind staying up' asked Alice not wanting to let go of her.

'I would stay up all night waiting for you' replied Charlie not releasing her either.

The chiming of a distant church clock broke the magic both realising that time was ticking on.

'Ok I better go; Love you' said Alice kissing her softly and gently. 'See you very soon'.

'Bye, love you too' said Charlie stepping forward to open the door for Alice.

Alice got into her car and Charlie bent to kiss her again, her heart fluttered, and the butterflies reappeared in her stomach. Charlie closed the door and stood back while she started the car and slowly drove away, waving as she went.

The journey back to York late at night was not as exciting as driving there, the roads were extremely dark, and the twists and turns were quite hairy, but once she got to Skipton it became easier and in no time, she was in Harrogate and a short time later back in York. Her house was in darkness and there was a light on at Charlie's, so she knew that Di was home. Unpacking the car, she approached her front door to find a large bouquet of flowers. Alice smiled, how lovely of Charlie she thought. Letting herself into the house and leaving her bags in the hall she instantly noticed how cold it was, so Alice boosted the heating then dialled Charlie's number.

'Are you home, ok?' she said anxiously.

'Yes, I'm back home, all's ok love. Thank you for the lovely flowers, that was so kind of you' said Alice looking at the beautiful roses in lilacs and cream.

'Flowers?' asked Charlie 'Sadly they aren't from me, is there a card?'

Alice checked the bouquet. 'No nothing, maybe Jen and Holly sent them, they are very pretty. I'm going to put these in water and then make myself a hot chocolate to warm up and then get into bed, shall I ring you when I'm done, or shall we just talk tomorrow?' asked Alice dragging her suitcase in front of the washing machine in preparation for the day afters domestic tasks.

'Yes ring when you're all snug to say a proper goodnight. I'm just writing in my journal and then I'll be in bed too,' said Charlie.

Alice put the flowers into a vase then loaded the washing machine, the first of many and set it going then put a pan of milk to heat on the range. She collected the post and giving it a brief scan left it on the worktop in the kitchen to deal with tomorrow. Even the mundane tasks were filled with joy knowing that she was going to be speaking to Charlie in moments.

Climbing the stairs to her room with her hot chocolate and phone, she switched off the lights, and reset the heating. Once in her bedroom she quickly changed into her pyjamas and climbed into bed, dialling Charlie as she did.

'I'm all snug now' said Alice 'I wish you were here with me'.

'So you can warm your feet on me?' laughed Charlie.

'Perhaps' replied Alice 'I know we only just said goodbye, but I can't wait to see you on Saturday'.

'Me neither, it will be strange going back, but I really want to be home, next door to you, I can't tell you how happy I am that we've sorted everything out' said Charlie softly.

'Me too, I'm so happy that we found each other' said Alice, she felt overwhelmed by the love that she felt in that moment. 'Let's not lose each other again'.

'I never want to lose you Alice, you're my world. I can even stand Jen not liking me at the minute, but I want to prove that I am genuinely here for you, both to you and your friends' said Charlie firmly. 'I know it'll take time though'.

'Try not to worry, she'll come round in time, she'll come to love you like I do. Well maybe not how I love you' said Alice cheekily.

'Well, I only have eyes for you Alice, I can't wait to show you how much I'm missing you' replied Charlie responding to Alice's flirting.

'Neither can I, god you make me feel so hot, and it's not all menopause!' said Alice.

'The feeling is mutual love' flirted Charlie 'But I'm not going to wind you up on the phone, you need to sleep for work tomorrow, and I have a meditation class at 8. Ring me in the morning if you get chance to beforehand, only if you've time'.

'Of course I will, alarm is set for 7 so I'll ring you before I get in the shower, night darling, sleep well,' said Alice.

'Night love' said Charlie as they both hung up.

Alice snuggled under the duvet and sleep didn't come easily, she looked at the empty side of the bed and it made her sad. She fell asleep willing the next two days away. Then remembering the flowers she fired off a quick text to Jen and Holly thanking them for the flowers, what a lovely gesture to come home to she thought as she drifted off.

The following day after her morning call with Charlie, Alice looked at her diary and realised that she'd her meeting with Kate on Saturday morning, she'd totally lost track of the time and knew she had to prepare something to go through with her but was unsure how to proceed with it. She'd written out the story of the two women, but Alice wondered if she should just approach it from a different angle, as a woman who had endured a violent and unsupportive husband. However, that was only part of the story and Kate, she felt, deserved the whole truth.

After her lecture on Thursday and admin work Alice went through the notes that she'd made, checking again with the letters and the dates where they had been written to build an accurate timeline for Hester and Charlotte. She wanted so badly for Kate to take the news well and give her permission to write the story to be published. There were so few lesbian stories prior to the 1950's, and those that existed were often so tortured that it did not give faith that there could have been positive love stories. Alice felt that this story gave hope that love could endure, that it could be alright in the end. Just as she hoped that her love story with Charlie would have a happy ending too.

Her phone was busy with calls and messages from Charlie and Holly and details that they would be arriving on Saturday at 2pm roughly so Alice knew it would give her a few hours with Kate if it was needed, and then be able to prepare for the arrival of Jen and Holly who had decided to stay with her. Charlie was going to drive them all back and had been going to visit Jen in hospital along with Holly each day. In preparation she booked an online food order for early Saturday morning with lots of healthy things for her guests, although she got bacon and cake for Jen, as it would be a telling sign her friend was well again if she asked for her bacon butty. Weirdly though Jen replied to her text to say that the flowers sadly weren't from them either so maybe they had been delivered in error.

Alice had gone round to talk to Di to tell her that Charlie was coming back on Saturday which she already knew about, and she said that she was planning on moving in above Valentine's into the managers flat on Sunday after Charlie returned home. She seemed really happy about this, both at having a permanent job, and having somewhere to live after losing her flat. It felt like a win win situation, but Alice feared what might happen once Charlie returned home, back to old haunts and potentially more women that were angry with her. Di also didn't know anything about the flowers as Alice thought they might have been for her instead. What a mystery.

Returning to her cosy, warm house Alice was hit by the sudden thought of what would happen to them when she came back. Charlie's return caused mixed feelings for Alice, and she resigned herself to talk to her about it, and perhaps go to the therapist jointly with her so she knew how she could help her. It didn't feel like a strain, it just felt like a hurdle they needed to face together.

Saturday morning arrived and the shopping was on time and put away before the arrival of Kate. At 10am promptly she rang the doorbell and Alice opened it to find a tall, attractive woman, dressed in a power suit, her grey hair cut short, who looked very stylish and definitely from money.

'Good morning are you Alice?' said Kate quizzically.

'Yes. Morning Kate, come on in,' said Alice leading the way into the living room where she'd placed the box on the coffee table and had printed out the short story she'd written about Charlotte and Hester.

'Wow it looks so different, but different is good Alice' said Kate walking into the living room and taking her time to look around smiling. 'You've made some changes, but you've kept the original features, I like that. I'm an architect, a rare sort these days who tries to keep the original or at least recreate it where I can'.

'Really, wow that's fascinating, as I said on the phone, I'm a historian and feel the same about old buildings, it is too easy to rip out the heart of them in the name of alleged progress' expressed Alice.

'It's amazing Alice, I think my mum would have liked what you've done. She did so little to it, she tried to hang onto the way the house had looked when her mum lived here' explained Kate 'It's nice to see it again'.

'I can understand that, although it must have been a hard decision. Before I tell you what I found, how much did you know about your grandmother Hester?' asked Alice gently.

'From what I understand she was married to my grandfather Peter who died suddenly and lived here until she died in the 1960's with her friend Charlotte. That was pretty much all that my mother told me. Have you found out more than that?' asked Kate 'My mother didn't like to talk about the past much, I brought some photographs of Hester and Charlotte from when they were younger, but I don't have anything else. What have you found out?'

'Ok, I've typed out a brief timeline and story of the lives of the two women, I'm afraid what I found out might come as a bit of a shock. Your grandfather was a violent man and he died in prison awaiting trial for attacking Hester' explained Alice gently.

'I knew there was something that my parents hadn't told me, they were very guarded about discussing Hester at all,' said Kate.

Alice then explained all about the box, the key and the contents and handed Kate the story that she'd put together from them.

'What I've written may come as a shock to you, so I'll go and make some tea and let you read it in peace. I'm sorry if you find it upsetting' said Alice going into the kitchen, heaving a sigh of relief that she'd let part of the story out. She busied herself making tea, taking it through a few minutes later where she found Kate still reading.

'My word, you weren't kidding when you said that it might be a shock. I had no idea at all. So, my grandmother was a lesbian like me. Amazing. How wonderful that she had Charlotte and love for all those years. I'd no idea how awful my grandfather was, I don't have any photos of him. I'm pleased about that now. Can I have a look at the letters?' asked Kate.

'Of course, the tin and the letters are on the table, and the lovely key and ribbon that my friend bought' explained Alice passing the box to Kate.

'Thank you' said Kate taking the letters out. 'Oh my goodness, the red ribbon! It's the same as the one on the key, do you think it was a ribbon that belonged to Charlotte or Hester?'

'I think so, it looks like Charlotte did it towards the end as the last letter she wrote after Hester died was in the box, it is incredibly sad but also filled with such hope, that their love lasted a lifetime' said Alice feeling emotional being able to talk about the letters and the wonderful lives the women had lived.

'Yes, it is rather moving isn't it' Kate was flicking through the letters, reading some and frowning. 'Would you be able to transcribe them for me, I'm struggling with the writing, I'll happily pay you to do it'.

'I wanted to talk to you about the letters, I'd really like your permission to turn their story into a book, I think it's so important that positive lesbian stories are told and not hidden, but if you don't want me to do that I totally understand' explained Alice.

'Would you be able to transcribe them, let me read it and then make a decision? I agree that it would be lovely to have their stories told but I'd like to know what's in them first if that's ok?' asked Kate.

'Of course, it may take me a while to do them all, but I can definitely do that for you,' said Alice.

Kate helped herself to the tea that Alice had brought through, and they spent a pleasant hour talking through the letters and she told her about her business and travels. She was married to a fellow architect and when she asked Alice about herself, she told her about Charlie. It felt so wonderful to sit and discuss their relationships and as Alice looked at the clock, she could see it was coming up to lunchtime and she knew she needed to crack on with preparation for Jen and Holly's arrival.

Kate saw Alice looking at the clock and looked taken aback.

'God is that the time? I must get back to the hotel for 12.30 so I better scoot, here's my business card with my email etc on it, drop me a line when you've managed to transcribe them if that's ok, and let's have a chat after that?' said Kate.

'Great, thanks for coming over, it's been lovely to talk about Hester and Charlotte.' Said Alice.

Alice showed Kate to the door then started making a quiche for when Charlie arrived with her friends, she wanted everything to be just perfect.

As the time ticked closer to 2, Alice put the kettle on and took the quiche out of the oven just as the doorbell rang. She rushed to the door, opened it wide, but the person stood there as not who she was expecting.

Sally was stood on the doorstep.

Stunned, Alice stood with her mouth open, shocked both by Sally being stood in front of her, but also Charlie parking the car behind her.

Sally turned and seeing Jen and Holly getting out of the car, she lunged towards Alice, pushing her into the house, kicking the door shut behind her. Alice, totally stunned to see her ex-wife shouted, 'What the fuck, get out Sally'.

Behind her she could hear voices approaching the door then 'Alice, Alice' as Charlie kicked the door as hard as she could. Fear rose inside her.

21

The Wanderers Return

Charlie waved Alice goodbye from the West Lodge and then turned and walked down the hill back to the rehab centre. She spoke to Toby briefly and went to the art room. Taking out her sketch book she flicked through the drawings that she'd done of Villa Roma and smiled. She planned to go back there tomorrow with a proposal for them which she hoped they would give serious thought to. Charlie smiled, she felt so hopeful about her potential ideas and her heart was full of intense feelings for Alice, she thought it would explode. She was even happier when Alice called to say she'd arrived home safely although she felt slightly puzzled when she mentioned the flowers and was also kicking herself for not having had that idea herself.

For the next couple of days, she'd had her final sessions with Dr Hanson, meditations and helping Holly get to and from the hospital to see Jen. She'd offered her the use of her Jeep, but Holly didn't feel confident enough to drive it, so Charlie offered to drive her instead. She popped in with her to see Jen a couple of times, but she was still frosty towards her, so she was polite but stepped away to leave Holly to visit. They both said they hadn't sent Alice flowers either, so the mystery deepened. Charlie felt slightly sick at the thought of Alice having a secret admirer.

On her final day she said goodbye to all the staff who had helped her so much since she'd arrived, and promised to continue with her therapy once she returned home. The previous evening, she'd collected Jen from hospital to spend a last night with Holly at the hotel, and although Jen was very cool with her, she was polite and thanked her for running around that week and taking care of Holly. So, when she collected them both on the Saturday lunchtime to drive them home, they were all in good spirits. Jen was feeling much better, and Holly, although very tired, was relieved to be going back to York and the support of her friends whilst Jen fully recovered.

The journey back was slow, the roads were packed whenever they came to a town which took some time to negotiate, but eventually they were on the A59 towards York and other than the queues to get onto the A1237 they were soon driving down Bootham towards home. She turned into the street, it felt like years since she'd last driven down it, but how differently she felt now from when she left. As she approached her house, she saw a car where she normally parked, so she reversed into the space in front of Alice's house where a woman was stood. As they got out of the car Charlie saw Alice stood at the door looking anxiously at her, then suddenly she disappeared from view as the woman lunged at her, pushing her into the house and the door slammed shut.

Charlie exited the car fast and rushed through Alice's gate, attempted to open the front door, but finding it locked she began kicking it, trying desperately to get in. Jen in her weakened state tried too, but to no avail, the door wouldn't budge.

Charlie shouted 'Let me in, let me in Alice' but at the same time Jen was shouting 'Sally open the fucking door'.

'Sally?' asked Charlie.

'Yep, the bitch is back' replied Jen, continuing to bang on the door.

Deciding that there was no way through the front, Charlie and Jen ran around the side of the house, through the back gate, and luckily found the back door unlocked. They went in, hearing shouting coming from the living room, so they both ran down the hall following the sound of Alice shouting.

'Get out Sally, get off me'.

Sally had Alice in a hug and was attempting to kiss her against one of the bookshelves.

Sally, who was red in the face, turned and screamed at Charlie 'Who the hell are you?' as Charlie grabbed her and frog marched her to the front door where Jen had already opened it.

'I just wanted to talk' she shouted. 'Can't we work something out? We used to be so happy Alice'.

'No bloody chance' said Alice loudly 'You broke my heart, why would I want you back?'

'Please, let's talk and see if we can sort things out'.

'Hasn't it worked out with Emily? Is that why you're here?'

'Alice please,' pleaded Sally.

Charlie could feel her heart beating out of her chest, she felt frozen and unable to process what was going on, she looked towards Alice, who from the look on her face was having a similar reaction.

Jen, unable to stand there any longer being quiet said 'Sally wind your neck in, you cheated on your wife and you threw it all away, you've no right to be here'.

'Sod off Jen, it's got nothing to do with you. We all know why you don't want me to get back with her. You've held a torch for her for years' said Sally spitefully.

Holly, who had stood there silently suddenly let out a gasp. Everyone turned to look at her.

'Stop talking bollocks Sally. You're shit stirring now and it won't work' said Holly with tears in her eyes.

Jen put her arm around Holly. 'You absolute bitch. How could you say that to Holly, what's she ever done to you, you're just a nasty shrivelled up bitch'.

'Alice, please, all I ask is a chance to talk to you alone, to make amends. Please, give me another chance' said Sally as she edged back towards her car with Charlie following her to make sure.

'Not a chance on this earth Sally. Don't ever contact me again' said Alice who turned and walked into the house, Charlie and her friends following, Jen slamming the door behind her.

'Are you ok love' said Charlie concerned.

'What the hell was that?' said Alice into the atmosphere. 'How dare she assume she can come back after all this time and pick up where she left off!'

'She always had the cheek of the sodding devil' said Holly 'And what's all that crap about Jen and you?'

'I've no fucking idea at all' said Jen angrily. 'We've only ever been mates; you know that love'.

'I know, but why say it?' asked Holly.

'Because she just wanted to shit stir, she gets off on drama' answered Jen. 'Honestly, there's never been anything between us'.

'No, not ever, we're friends, I'm sorry that she said that Holly, you do believe us don't you?' said Alice with deep emotion in her voice.

'Of course I do, I love you both and know you wouldn't do that to me, either of you' said Holly reassuringly.

'I'll go and make sure she's gone' said Charlie going out of the room, she felt slightly anxious at what Sally had said, Alice and Jen did get on very well. Was there more to it than they were saying she questioned in her head.

Sally's car had gone, then checking up and down the street and seeing the coast was clear, got their luggage from the car. Anxiety rose in Charlie, panic over whether Alice might still have old feelings towards Sally, and what she'd said about Jen. She couldn't bear to lose her, putting on a brave face she put the cases in the hall. Walking into the living room she saw everyone smiling, the atmosphere had lifted from the earlier tension, and her beloved Alice looked so happy.

'What on earth did I miss?' asked Charlie quizzically. 'I was only gone 5 minutes'.

'Jen's back! She's hungry again!' laughed Holly.

'Show me to the food' said Jen heading into the kitchen with Holly behind her.

'I told Jen I'd cooked; my old friend is back; she looks so much better than she did. Has Sally gone?' asked Alice.

'Yes, all clear love. Are you ok? Did she hurt you? I was so scared' said Charlie kneeling down and holding her hand.

'I'm ok, just shocked that she turned up. I just don't understand it?' said Alice frowning. 'What made her think she could just come like that. Oh, it was her that sent those flowers she said. Like a bunch of flowers could take away all that she did'.

'Is there anything I can do? Charlie asked. The anxiety continued to swirl inside her like a tornado, and the urge to run back next door to the safety of her own house, close the door and hide under her duvet was incredibly strong.

'No, I never want to hear from her ever again'.

Just then Jen and Holly came back into the living room with the quiche and salad. The visit from Kate and preparing lunch, already felt like the day before, so much had happened in such a short space of time.

'Come and sit-down and have something to eat,' smiled Holly handing Alice and Charlie two plates of food.

So they ate quietly in the living room, Alice with her feet up on Charlie, Jen and Holly in the armchairs. The quiche was a success as was the purchased cake and when they had finished Charlie stood up, cleared the plates and stacked them in the dishwasher.

She didn't want to leave Alice, but she needed to get next door and unpack, start her washing and set up her meetings for the following week, but knew she had company and would be in safe hands.

Returning to the living room Charlie announced that she was going next door for a couple of hours but to ring if she was needed.

Alice walked her to the door.

'Ring me if you need me or pop round if you like. Love you, I'm so glad to be home,' I could come back before bed if you wanted?' said Charlie, her breath catching in her throat, the anxiety and quiche feeling like it would spill out of her at any second.

'Yes, do come back, will you stay here tonight? I'd really like you to' asked Alice.

'Of course, it'll be lovely to be cosy in there again. I love your house, it's so you,' said Charlie.

'That's very sweet, it's good to be home and know you're here too' said Alice kissing Charlie goodbye.

As she went round the wall to her house Charlie looked up and down the street to make sure that the woman had really gone, then using her keys went into her house. Di, she knew would be at work and was moving out either that day or the next and she'd piled her post on the hall table. Charlie always liked walking into her house, the décor she loved, and it was the first place where she'd felt like it was home. Alice's house in contrast was plainer but had such heart. She loved them both. She smiled at the thought of Alice sat reading in her front room, she really did love her she thought.

Most of the stack of post was junk, a couple she could deal with in the week, and one was from the adoption agency as she recognised the postmark and envelope. She put that letter in her back pocket as she wanted company when she opened it, and the only person she wanted by her side was Alice.

Putting her washing in the machine she started it going and read a note from Di in the kitchen, that said that she was moving out into the flat above Valentine's the following day and not to wait up. Charlie wrote a note to Di telling her she was staying at Alice's that evening and would go round and see her in the morning.

Going up through the jungle into her bedroom Charlie for the first time noted the starkness of her room, how blank it was, totally devoid of any character. In the past she would have been the thing to look at in the room if she had a woman there, but now that was unimportant, she knew she needed to put some heart into it, and that heart was Alice.

After packing a bag with pyjamas and clothes for the following day, she opened up her laptop to check her emails and smiled at a couple of the replies she'd had from enquiries. Writing lengthy replies, Charlie smiled that the new plans looked as though they might just work, and then briefly checking the accounts from Valentine's Charlie could see that things were pretty much as she'd hoped. Di had done a good job as she knew she would.

Looking at the time Charlie packed up her laptop into the rucksack with her pj's then locked up and went back next door. Jen answered the Ring doorbell.

'Hey, come into the living room, Holly has set up the Monopoly, if you fancy joining and the pizza will be here in a minute. We were about to message you' she said.

'Sounds wonderful. But I must warn you I'm a bit of a shark at Monopoly' announced Charlie kissing Alice on the top of her head as she went by and sat on the floor in front of the coffee table where the board had been set up. 'How are you feeling now?'

'All's good, I'm starving though, salad never cuts it does it,' laughed Alice.

The pizza arrived and the four of them enjoyed a couple of hours eating, playing and laughing. It turned out that Alice was also a shark at the game too, and it became a battle between them as to who would win. Alice wiped out Jen and Holly quite early on, who then decided an early night was in order and went upstairs to the spare room. In the end Charlie beat Alice but it was a close call.

'Do you surrender to me Alice' asked Charlie provocatively.

'Always' replied Alice in a sultry voice, her eyes sparkling.

Charlie sat next to Alice and whispered in her ear 'Sit astride me, now' her voice firm but loving.

Alice pulled up her dress and sat astride Charlie, the house was silent except for their excited breathing as Alice waited in anticipation of what would happen next. Pulling Alice towards her, Charlie ran her fingers over Alice's face, touching her lips, then pulling her closer kissed her with such passion she could feel her quiver. Charlie's right hand began to work its magic, stroking Alice's inner thigh, her breathing getting louder as her fingers touched her underwear, this she repeated over and over, slowly moving her fingers over the fabric of Alice's pants and between her legs, she could feel how wet she was through the cotton. Slowly and gently pulling the elastic to the side, Charlie slid two fingers inside Alice and held them still. 'Slide on my fingers Alice' she ordered. Alice responded, her whole-body rippling with the pleasure that was building up inside her. Alice gripped Charlie's fingers which made her gasp too. 'Fuck you're so hot, faster'.

Alice slid up and down on Charlie's fingers who then moved her thumb onto her clit which made her arch her back and thrust deep onto her hand. She was so wet that Charlie could barely contain herself. 'I want to taste you, lie down'. Alice obeyed and Charlie took off her dress and pants as she did. Going down on Alice was like heaven, not just the beautiful taste, but also the amazing noises that she made, even tonight when she was trying to be quiet. Teasing her clit which had swollen to twice its normal size, Charlie slid her fingers back into Alice slowly, flicking her fingers inside her, which made her give out a small cry. Charlie applied more pressure with her tongue, moving it faster and faster, on and off, on and off, teasing her until she could see from the desperate look on her face that she had to come, right then, right there. Charlie stopped teasing her, focused all her attention on her clit which tipped her over the edge into heaven as she gave out a loud groan. She gripped Charlie's fingers so tightly in a climax which rolled on over and over, her body writhing as she came repeatedly, something that she had never made a woman do before. Alice gave out a final loud gasp and Charlie kissed her belly, her breasts which made her squeal and finally her neck. 'I love you, you're so bloody sexy'.

'I love you too, that was out of this world. I felt like I was floating above my body. I want to make you come too' said Alice who started to unbutton Charlie's shirt.

'No, let's go upstairs' said Charlie passing Alice her dress and underwear. Alice then led Charlie upstairs into her bedroom.

'What do you want me to do Charlie?' asked Alice stripping off and walking towards a very aroused Charlie.

Charlie took off her clothes in super-fast time, walked them both to the bed, then putting one leg up onto the bed, pulling Alice in close to hold her, she took Alice's hand and put it between her legs. 'Please do me fast, I'm so close already, I just need to feel your fingers on me, in me, everywhere. Please Alice'

Alice did as she was told, moving her fingers in the silky wetness as Charlie held onto her tight as she felt her knees buckling as she came very quickly. Alice kissed Charlie gently as they looked into each other eyes.

'Just when I thought it couldn't get any more exciting' said Alice 'That was just mind blowing. Do you think Jen and Holly heard us?'

'You were quite loud Alice; we'll find out tomorrow won't we' giggled Charlie as they both got into bed and cuddled for a short while until their body heat made them both move away. 'Goodnight beautiful, I'm so pleased to be home'.

22

What the hell?

The following day Alice was the first one up, so she went downstairs to make a pot of coffee and to put a tray of bacon and sausages into the oven. As she came down the stairs, she saw a note on the doormat. She instantly knew who it was from.

She unfolded it cautiously, and sure enough it was from Sally.

Dearest Alice

I'm so very sorry about yesterday; I didn't mean for it all to get so out of hand. I've been trying to ring you, but you've blocked me I presume, which I totally understand because of what I did to you. But please understand this, I've never stopped loving you, or thinking about you in all this time. I'm so very sorry for what I did to you, Emily was an enormous mistake and one I'd never repeat again. I am staying at The Churchill at the top of your road, please call me or come and meet me for dinner tonight so we can talk and sort this out.

Please believe that I'm so very sorry for what I did to you.

Love always.

Sally

Alice shook her head and put the note into her dressing gown pocket and went into the kitchen. She heard movement above of someone getting up, so putting the oven on, she prepared the breakfast ready to go into it. She knew that Jen would definitely want her bacon. She felt too happy to think about the stupid note from Sally or what she could possibly want from her.

The kettle had just boiled when Holly appeared in the kitchen.

'Morning, did you sleep well' asked Alice 'I've made a start on breakfast?' said Alice putting the tray in the oven.

'Morning Alice' replied Holly smirking at Alice 'Have a good night did we?'

Alice blushed, plunging the cafetiere down, chuckling. 'Yes thanks' she said embarrassed.

'I think it's lovely. After yesterday Jen is warming to Charlie very well' said Holly hugging Alice.

Jen walked into the kitchen smirking. 'What a racket woman, should have given us ear plugs you noisy bugger?' she said laughing.

Alice went scarlet again laughing. 'Shit. Can I make it up to you by making you a full English?'

'Ey that sounds proper grand!' smiled Jen putting the coffee and cups onto a tray and taking it into the dining room as Charlie came downstairs.

'Blimey, you've been productive, I'll have to get you all working at my new venture?' said Charlie in an amused voice.

'New venture?' said Alice giving Charlie a kiss good morning.

'I'm going to revamp Villa Roma in Bowness and become part owner' smiled Charlie. 'I've just checked my emails and the family have agreed to let me invest'.

'Wow that's amazing news, I'm so pleased, I'd no idea that you were going to do that' said Alice smiling.

'I talked with them last week and they sent me the accounts last night, I think it's salvageable with a few more business ideas and a bit of financial input,' said Charlie. 'Anyway it's breakfast time and I don't want to hog your Sunday, but I could do with a quick chat with Alice if that's ok?'

'Is everything ok' asked Alice concerned.

'Yeah nothing serious, don't worry, how long before breakfast as it can wait until after' asked Charlie.

'Don't worry we'll sort breakfast; I think Jen got up as she heard you opening the bacon,' laughed Holly.

'Thanks' said Charlie taking Alice's hand and they went into the living room.

Once inside Charlie closed the door and took out the letter from the adoption agency. 'I got this in the post yesterday but haven't opened it. I wanted us to do it together if that's ok?'

'If you're sure' said Alice, knowing that she'd a note of her own in her bathrobe.

They both sat on the sofa, and Charlie tore open the envelope and took out the letter, holding it in front of them both so they could read it jointly.

Dear Ms Lowther

Apologies for the delay in getting back to you. I am writing to let you know that we have found your birth mother who has agreed to have contact with you if you're still willing to do so.

If this is still something that you wish for, then please can you contact me as soon as possible, so that we can facilitate the introduction in a safe, and supportive environment.

Yours sincerely

Judith Pearson

'Wow Charlie, how do you feel?' asked Alice.

'I'm stunned, after the last letter I didn't think they'd find her' looking at the envelope Charlie said 'It was posted a month ago, well that's the first thing to do tomorrow isn't it' she said smiling. 'My mum wants to meet me!'

'That's bloody amazing, I'm so happy for you, I'll be there right by your side if you want me to be,' said Alice, holding her hand.

'I'll always want you to be by my side' replied Charlie putting her arm around Alice, holding her close. 'It's all coming together; I can't believe it!'

'You really deserve good things Charlie, you honestly do' whispered Alice. 'Before we go into breakfast, I wanted to show you something that was on the doormat this morning' said Alice getting out the note and passing it to Charlie.

Charlie read the brief note. 'What the fuck! How dare she come back here. Who the hell does she think she is?' exclaimed Charlie as Jen came into the living room.

'Breakfast. What's up?' said Jen, her hackles clearly up, her face looking stern.

'Just a stupid note from Sally I found this morning when I came down' Alice said passing Jen the note.

She read it and burst out laughing. 'Who the hell does she think she is?'

'That's exactly what I said' replied Charlie.

'Are you coming through before it gets cold' said Holly going into the living room.

'Have a read of this' said Jen passing the note to her.

'She's some nerve coming back at all, what makes her think you'd ever take her back?' said Holly.

'I honestly don't know, and I don't care' said Alice taking back the note and ripping it into pieces and putting it into the wood burner. 'Best place for it'.

Jen smiled, 'Always was full of herself' heading into the dining room followed by the others. The breakfast laid out by the duo looked very appetising.

'You're looking so much better, how're you feeling?' asked Alice.

'Better than I was, breathing's still off, and I feel knackered all the time, but it's so good to be home. Thanks for letting us stay but I think I'll be ok to go home in a day or so?' said Jen.

'Of course, just make yourself at home. What's everyone doing today?' asked Alice.

'I'll go see Di in a bit before she moves out and have a chat about work stuff, do you want to come?' asked Charlie looking at Alice.

'If you'd like me to yes, I've emails to sort for tomorrow, but other than that nothing else, what about you guys, any plans?' said Alice.

'I think we'll just hang out here if that's ok, I'll cook dinner if you like' offered Holly.

'That'd be lovely, thanks. said Alice smiling. Right, I'm going to jump in the shower and get dressed, are you coming Charlie?'

'I'll be right up, just going to stack the dishwasher' said Charlie clearing the table.

'They're at it again' laughed Jen 'Better get the earplugs out'.

Alice blushed again and smiling to her friends said, 'Well it's good to conserve water isn't it?'

Alice went upstairs to get ready shortly followed by Charlie, and although they shared the shower, they were well behaved, although Alice found it very hard not to start something, so spent most of the shower biting her lip and being quiet. As she was getting out of the shower Charlie wrapped her in a towel and kissed her, her knees going wobbly. 'Bloody hell you just melt me, I wish we could have a day in bed'.

'Well let's book something love, that would be divine' said Charlie squeezing Alice' bottom as she exited the bathroom.

Alice squealed just as Jen was coming up the stairs. 'Shall I go back downstairs again' she laughed.

Alice and Charlie went into the bedroom giggling, dressing quickly and were back downstairs in no time at all. The temptation just to lay next to each other was huge but she knew that Charlie had things to do next door.

After showing Jen where the tv remotes were, they both went next door to see Di. Walking back into the jungle, Alice realised how much she'd missed seeing the feast for the eyes that was Charlie's house.

Charlie shouted up to Di who responded that she was just finishing off her packing, so Alice went and took a seat in the living room whilst Charlie set about tackling the pile of post and checking her emails.

There was a thudding as Di came down the stairs carrying her suitcase and bags then leaving them in the hall came into the living room. Charlie went over and gave her a hug.

'Bloody hell Charlie, you look so good, the break really has done you well. Hi Alice, how are you? Glad to see you two sorted things out' said Di flopping into an armchair.

'Ta Di never felt so good to be fair, it was hard work but amazing, so glad I went. I need to talk a couple of things over with you. Whilst I was away, I bought into a restaurant in Bowness, and I will be focusing on design work from now on' explained Charlie.

'Are you selling Valentine's? Am I out of a job and house again?' said Di crossly.

'God no, I just won't be involved with it much, you're the manager and you can carry on running it as you've been, I will just help out with accounts, I just don't want to be in there anymore' explained Charlie. 'But I can see you're doing a grand job with it, so keep doing that and it'll be perfect'.

'Yeah, I get it. Lots of LGBT groups are using it and doing events now, the words getting out. Can only be a good thing' said Di smiling with relief. 'So what are your plans you two?'

'No plans, just taking it slowly, but it feels so right now I have started sorting my head out.' said Charlie squeezing Alice's thigh. Alice smiled at her.

'So what's this restaurant?' asked Di 'What are you going to do with it'.

'I'm going to put some heart into it and bring it into this century, it's very 1980's, but the food is stunning, so the roots are there. I'm also looking into expanding it into mail order Italian food. It'd be amazing doing that' explained Charlie.

'Interesting idea, if the foods that good then it could work, maybe we could change the menu here? I was thinking about that, too many places with similar menus to ours, think we need a revamp on that, theme nights or something?' suggested Di.

Charlie smiled, 'Now that would be a cool thing to do, we could have Italian, French or old-fashioned English food nights, proper themed events. That would be great, stop aiming everything at 20-year-olds and give us oldies something to come out to'.

Alice smiled, it was wonderful to see Charlie so animated and happy, but she had to admit that she was relieved that she wouldn't be going to Valentine's anytime soon. She wasn't sure she could face it again after what had happened the last time, but she knew that one day she would have to face up to it again.

'Sounds perfect, we can talk more about that in a few weeks once I know more but it really could work,' said Charlie. 'Thanks for looking after the house for me, it really helped knowing everything was ticking over here while I was away'.

'Cool no worries. Thanks for letting me stay here Charlie, but I have to get going, I want to do a few things before we open at lunchtime, good to see you again Alice' said Di heading to the hall and taking her things and went out through the front door.

'That was brilliant love. What a brain you've got. Very impressive. Your head is full of wonderful ideas' said Alice feeling tongue tied. 'It's very hot'.

'Well, if you find that hot, what will you be like when I'm doing my accounts?' said Charlie jokingly.

'Orgasmic at all times' smiled Alice.

'Oh, I do hope so. What do you fancy doing now? Go back to yours or hang out here til dinner?' asked Charlie.

'I could get my laptop and we can do what we need to do before dinner? Then the evenings our own,' said Alice.

'Perfect, ask when dinner will be ready, so we know what time we need to be back for,' said Charlie.

'Shall do, back in a minute' shouted Alice as she headed out of the front door, then having retrieved her work things, she went back to Charlie's.

'Hi, I'm back, where are you, Holly said dinner will be ready in a couple of hours' shouted Alice seeing that she wasn't in the living room or kitchen.

'I'm upstairs in my office, come up and have a look if you like, I might have a surprise for you,' said Charlie.

Alice went upstairs and saw the small bedroom door was ajar ahead of her, she pushed the door open to find Charlie sat wearing the blue suit that she'd worn on their date to the Fairfax Arms

'Now that is rather a lovely surprise!' Alice exclaimed she walked over to Charlie and kissed her. 'You look amazing'.

'I thought I'd make an effort for dinner, I've texted Holly and they're dressing up too, there's a surprise for you in my bedroom' said Charlie, taking her hand and leading her into the bedroom where the blinds were down, and across the white duvet was the cornflower blue dress that was ruined the night she saw Charlie had cheated on her.

'What? Er I can't Charlie, I just can't' said Alice, tears appearing in her eyes. 'That night was the worst of my life, I don't want to remember it, I'm sorry Charlie I just can't'.

'Oh god, Holly said how upset you were at the dress being ruined I thought that if I got you another it'd go in some way to say how sorry I am' said Charlie apologetically 'I've read this totally wrong haven't I, I'm so sorry. Look I'll send it back' said Charlie picking up the dress and folding it put it back in a bag that was on the floor.

'It was a lovely idea Charlie, sorry I sound so ungrateful, I just don't want to remember what happened' said Alice sitting down on the bed.

'I know you don't want to remember, but it isn't healthy to never talk about it again, it'll eat you up. Sorry love, what can I do to make it up to you? I'll do anything' said Charlie sitting next to Alice putting her arm around her.

'I just don't want to go over things again yet, we're getting on so well now, I don't want to ruin it' said Alice looking into Charlie's concerned eyes.

'You wouldn't ruin anything love, you and I are on a better footing now, we can talk about anything and get through it. I'm really not that person anymore, I want only you, only you forever' said Charlie with such love in her eyes that Alice melted, then slowly she slid off the bed and down onto one knee 'Will you marry me Alice?'

23

With a Sparkle and a Smash

Alice was stunned. 'Oh my god I don't know what to say. I thought you wanted to take things slowly?'

'I do, but I'm more sure of this than of anything I've ever done or said in my whole life,' Charlie asked again. 'I'm not suggesting that we elope or anything, I just wanted to show you how serious I am about us. Will you marry me?'

'Yes, yes I will marry you, I love you so much sweetheart' replied Alice pulling Charlie back up onto the bed, kissing her and hugging her tightly. 'Wow, you've taken my breath away, wow'.

'I wanted to do it in Bowness, but I didn't know how you'd react, but I can't tell you how happy you've made me. You're my one. My life. I want to spend every day making you happy,' said Charlie. 'I bought you a ring which I know was presumptuous of me, but I saw it in an antique shop in Windermere and thought it was almost as beautiful as you'.

Charlie went to her chest of drawers and took out the ring box, opened it and went towards Alice with the very delicate three diamond ring on a simple gold band. She slipped the ring onto her finger, and it was almost a perfect fit.

'Charlie it's absolutely gorgeous, if I were to choose any ring at all it would have been this one, it's beautiful, I feel like I'm dreaming' exclaimed Alice.

'No, you're not dreaming, this is totally real. I want to make you happy. Do you want to tell people or keep it quiet?' asked Charlie.

'God no! I want to shout it from the rooftops. Take an advert out in The Guardian, put up a Facebook alert, the whole works!' said Alice jumping with glee around the bedroom.

Charlie began jumping around too, until they both almost collided with each other, then collapsed laughing on the bed. Alice felt elated, staring at the ring on her finger which sparkled in the lamp light. She felt like fireworks were going off in her belly and her heart sang with joy.

Alice rolled on her side to face Charlie, linking their hands together. 'I want to be with you for as long as you can put up with me, I know I'm not an easy person to be with'.

'You're so easy to be with, you think yourself to be this messed up person, but really you're not. You've had issues, but who hasn't at our age. I want to make you happy every day of your life' said Alice stroking Charlie's face.

'Do you want to go and tell Jen and Holly now, I don't mind, I can see how excited you are,' said Charlie anxiously.

'No, I just want to lie here in your arms and talk for a while, I'm so happy you asked me. You've made my year, my life complete' said Alice with joyful tears in her eyes. 'I never thought you'd want to get married?'

'To be fair it wasn't something that was high on my list but being with you has made me realise how much I really want all those things with you' said Charlie smiling broadly, holding Alice close. 'As much as

I would love to undress you right now and show you just how much I love you we really do have work to do for tomorrow don't we. Does that sound dull?'

'Sounds like lesbian bed death to me already' laughed Alice nudging Charlie. 'There's plenty of time for that sweetheart but here is a small taster' said Charlie pulling Alice on top of her and kissing her softly, her teeth gently nibbling Alice's bottom lip. She could feel Alice's heart beating through her top and she let out a loud moan.

'You're such a temptation' said Alice laughing 'Come on let's be good'.

They both went back to Charlie's office and Alice set up her laptop next to hers and they both set about working through emails, and Alice dived into a research paper that had just been published by one of her colleagues on Viking combs and their use in everyday society. It was sometime later that she caught sight of Charlie out of the corner of her eye smiling.

'What? Have I got something on my face' said Alice wiping away imaginary crumbs.

'No, I was just smiling as you look so adorable frowning and smiling at your screen, is it interesting?' asked Charlie.

'Mmm not my field but they certainly have some interesting theories on why Vikings in York combed their hair. Do you want to read it?' asked Alice.

'Er maybe later, shall we go and see how they're getting on with dinner?' said Charlie smiling 'Not really my cup of tea, but you could give me a brief outline sometime'.

'Ok, sorry about the dress Charlie' said Alice packing away her laptop and papers.

'Don't worry about it, it's fine' said Charlie offering her hand to Alice and they both left the house ready for dinner.

The glorious smell of a roast dinner greeted their noses as they walked in, candles had been lit in the dining and living room giving it an added elegance as the lights danced off the glasses and cutlery on the table.

'Wow it all looks amazing guys, let me just go and get changed, won't be long' said Alice running upstairs.

'Didn't Alice like the dress?' asked Jen.

'No, it freaked her out, I should have realised that it would,' said Charlie.

'Oh hell, I didn't think either' said Holly pouring the gravy into a large jug.

'Hopefully no harm done' said Jen 'Let's take these through'.

The three of them carried tureens of vegetables and a platter with roast beef and potatoes, followed by 12 of the largest Yorkshire Puddings that Charlie had ever seen.

'Wow, who made these' she asked.

'All Jen's creation, she's a knack getting them to rise,' said Holly.

'It's all in the hand action' said Jen grinning at Holly.

'Cheeky!' said Holly laughing.

Alice came into the dining room wearing a turquoise blue dress with matching necklace and earrings. Charlie went over and gave her a kiss and whispered in her ear 'You look amazing, shall we tell them?'

Alice smiled and nodded.

They all took a seat around the ladened table as Holly began carving the beef and Jen passed round the vegetables and Yorkshire puddings. Once their plates were full and the gravy had been poured Charlie cleared her throat in an obvious fashion.

'Alice has something she'd like to tell you,' she said smiling.

Jen and Holly looked up smiling. 'You're getting a cat?' said Jen.

'No' laughed Alice 'I'm really not a cat person. I wanted you two, my best friends in the whole world to be the first to know, Charlie has asked me to marry her' Alice put out her left hand towards her friends, the diamond ring sparkling in the candlelight.

'Oh wow, that's amazing, congratulations to you both' said Holly standing up and going around the table gave them both a large hug. 'Let me see that ring' she said taking Alice's hand. 'Stunning'.

Charlie was aware first of the silence from across the table. Jen was immobile and her face did not show the same happiness that the others had in the room.

'Are you serious?' said Jen crossly. 'Are you mad?'

'Jen!' said Holly 'What's the matter?'

'For fucks sake! You can't have said yes! How can you be getting married; you've only just met! Look what she did to you, literally 5 minutes ago, what if she cheats on you again?' said Jen angrily.

'I thought that we'd gone over all that, it's ok Jen, I know what I'm doing,' said Alice. 'We aren't getting married right now, it's simply a promise that we will. We both know we've a long way to go, but it's so lovely to know that Charlie loves and wants me in her life. Please Jen, don't be angry'.

Alice sat down next to Jen and attempted to hug her, but she was as stiff as a board.

'I promise you Jen, I will never knowingly hurt Alice again, I truly love her,' said Charlie. 'Let's talk about it, let's not spoil this lovely meal you've made for us'.

Alice returned to sit next to Charlie looking dejected. Charlie squeezed her hand and gave her a brief smile.

'It'll be ok Jen, we aren't running down the aisle, we're both aware we have a lot to work through. Please give us a chance,' said Alice.

'Well, I think it's wonderful, I wish you years of happiness' said Holly raising her glass, firstly smiling across the table, then frowning at Jen.

'Thanks Holly' said Charlie suddenly realising that she was holding a glass of wine in her hand. She froze, staring at her hand. She put it slowly down on the table.

'Oh god Charlie, I forgot. Look let me get you something else' said Holly reaching over and taking the glass of wine.

'Don't worry it's ok. Easy mistake to make, I'll just get something else' said Charlie going into the kitchen. She went to the sink and turned on the tap, splashing cold water on her face and took some deep breaths. She'd come so close to drinking the wine, thank God she'd realised. Drying her face, she took out a bottle of water from the fridge and went back into the dining room where the atmosphere hadn't improved. Jen still looked cross, and Alice looked sad. This wasn't how she'd wanted the night to go at all.

Sitting down she raised her bottle of water 'To Jen and Holly, thank you for making this lovely meal for us, let's tuck in before it gets cold'.

The four of them ate in semi silence, occasionally passing a comment as to the size of the puddings or the texture of the meat, but it was all superficial and forced. After they'd finished Alice and Charlie cleared the dishes and plates and stacked the dishwasher and washed up the pans, Holly noticeably took Jen into the living room and closed the door.

'God I wasn't expecting that reaction, I thought that she'd softened to you, I'm sorry love,' said Alice.

'You don't need to apologise and neither does Jen, it'll take time to get over what happened, as it will for you too. We can take as much time as you need love' said Charlie cautiously.

'It'll be ok won't it?' said Alice putting the tea towels into the washing machine and putting the last pan and tureen away in the cupboard.

'Yes of course it will darling, just give her time' said Charlie softly.

Alice smiled at Charlie, the love for her felt like it would overflow.

'Do you fancy going out for a walk? We could go and have a walk around town and see if they have put up the Christmas lights yet?' asked Alice

'Ok sounds good to me, I'll go and get my coat, meet you outside in 10 minutes' said Charlie getting her keys out of her pocket and leaving Alice's house.

Alice went into the living room where a moody Jen was sat staring into the log burner which had been lit.

'Charlie and I are heading out for a walk round York, sorry if that was all a bit much,' said Alice.

'Just think it's too soon, don't want you getting hurt again' said Jen still looking into the flames in the log burner, but Alice could see her eyes were teary.

'Don't worry, we just want the best for you. Charlie's lovely and obviously cares about you, but please take your time, won't you?' said Holly. 'But have a nice walk, are you coming back here or staying at Charlie's?'

'I'm not sure, I'll take my keys just in case. Just lock up if you like, I can stay with Charlie if she's up for that' said Alice getting her keys from the bowl on the bookshelf. 'We aren't in any rush guys; it'll be ok. See you both tomorrow', and with that Alice got her coat, gloves and hat from the hall stand and left the house, making sure that the door was locked as she closed it.

Charlie was just coming out of her house as Alice closed her gate.

'That was good timing love. Where do you fancy going?' asked Charlie, putting on a pair of black leather gloves.

'God, you look hot putting those on' smiled Alice, she took Charlie's gloved hand, and they walked up the street towards Bootham.

'How about you take me on a guided tour of Charlotte and Hester? Didn't you say that Charlotte lived near here growing up?'

'Yes, she did on St Leonards, the same house where I collapsed outside' said Alice sadly.

'Seriously? Now that's weird, are you sure you want to go back there? Maybe we should do something else' suggested Charlie.

'No, it's fine honestly, I went there a few weeks ago and met the owner, it was lovely to go in through the lovely black door,' said Alice. The evening was autumnal, a light breeze but warmer than they had expected, so much so that they removed their gloves and undid buttons on coats.

After a brief walk, they both arrived outside the Theatre Royal on St Leonards Place. Alice pointed across the road to No 2 which had its living room lights on and the light above the front door.

'Charlotte's parents leased this house for a long time, and this is where she and Hester fell in love as teenagers. Isn't it a dream of a house to look at' said Alice beaming.

'It really is, mind you when they lived there the road would have been quieter than it is today! The noise would drive me nuts,' said Charlie.

'It would me too, but it's rather gorgeous, wish I could afford something like that one day, but maybe somewhere quieter' said Alice with a dreamy look in her eyes.

'Well, who knows what the future holds' said Charlie smiling at her.

Alice smiled back. 'When I win the lottery maybe' she laughed.

'Where else did they go from what the letters said?' asked Charlie.

'Just up here' said Alice taking Charlie's hand as they crossed the road into Blake Street. 'The Assembly Rooms was the place to go and be seen, so their parents would more than likely have used it for social events, and what is now a house on the corner behind us was once a Gentleman's club so lots of affluent families lived around here. It was THE place to be, now it's the place to get Italian food'.

Charlie smiled at Alice. 'You look so sexy when you're excited, intelligence is a very attractive quality'.

'Yes it is, that's one of the reasons why I love you' said Alice hugging Charlie, putting her hands into the pockets of her coat and letting out a shiver.

'Shall we go find somewhere for a drink or keep on walking? How about we call into Valentine's?' said Charlie.

Alice stopped smiling. 'I don't think I'm ready to go back in there yet, is that ok, does it sound daft?'

'No of course not, I shouldn't have mentioned it. Does Betty's stay open on an evening?' asked Charlie.

'No, I think it closes at 6, Café Nero is usually open til later, shall we go there? I love their hot chocolates,' said Alice.

'Great sounds like a good plan' said Charlie taking Alice's hand and walking towards Coppergate. 'How good is your Viking history if we are going near Jorvic?'

'Sadly, only very basic! In my younger years I did volunteer for the York Archaeological Trust and helped repackage some of the finds from the dig there. Leather shoes and combs and things. Have you heard about the Viking Poo?' said Alice giggling.

'Er no.' laughed Charlie 'Are you winding me up?'

'Not at all, it was a large poo that they found during the excavation, huge! I can take you to see it one day if you like. The information they got from it really helped shape more of the story of life a Viking in York back then. Fascinating stuff' said Alice animatedly.

'I never thought I would enjoy hearing about someone else's poo!' said Charlie. 'God knows what they'd think if they analysed mine, too much caffeine and my addiction to pastry'.

'That's funny. Doesn't York look lovely at night, when it's quiet and no traffic' said Alice looking up at the lights in the trees on Parliament Street. 'The street will soon be full of those cabins for the Christmas Market, it's all a bit busy and rammed for me, but I guess it must be good for your business?'.

'This is the first full year for Valentine's so I'm hoping that we can benefit from it yes, but I understand that it isn't for everyone. It's been a rough couple of years because of covid, I hope that it does bring in a lot of trade,' said Charlie. 'I promise I won't ask you to come shopping with me'.

'And for that I am extremely thankful Charlie' replied Alice with a grin.

At Café Nero they both ordered hot chocolates and sat in the window looking out onto Coppergate. There were a few people around for a Sunday night, but it wasn't as busy as it would have been on stag and hen night hell on a Saturday. As they sipped their drinks and chatted Alice realised how different Charlie was from her ex-wife Sally.

Charlie was attentive, cared about her, and always asked things about her life, whereas Sally only talked about herself and rarely seemed interested in anything that Alice did. Alice realised how much of herself had been lost in that relationship, she'd loved and cared about Sally but exhausted herself always trying to please her. That was a massive realisation. Charlie totally gave all of herself, but Sally was closed off and self-obsessed. How had she not realised this? Why had she ignored all the red flags? Did she have any red flags now?

'Penny for your thoughts' said Charlie seeing that Alice was miles away.

'Sorry love I was just deep in thought about something, shall we head back after this, I'm knackered?' replied Alice.

'Ok love, it's been nice to get out of the house, it's hardly the quiet of Windermere but it's still beautiful isn't it' said Charlie finishing her drink, dribbling hot chocolate down her chin.

'Mucky pup' said Alice laughing and passing a napkin to Charlie who cleaned herself up.

'Can't take me anywhere unsupervised can you' she replied mopping up the spillage on the table too.

They were both so engrossed laughing they didn't notice that they were being watched. Suddenly there was a loud bang as something hit the café window. Alice and Charlie threw themselves onto the floor hastily.

24

Grab and Run

Aware of screams around her, Charlie lifted her head, anxiously looking over at Alice who was laid on her side in the foetal position, her arms wrapped around her head, reaching out to her she took hold of one of her hands.

'Are you ok?' Charlie asked looking at the window and saw that the glass was all crazed.

The barista, who had run out of the café came over to them and helped them both up to their feet.

'Are you both ok?' he asked, 'Did you see anything?'

'Nothing at all, what hit the window?' asked Alice dusting herself down, looking over at Charlie whose suit was covered in hot chocolate residue and her hand was bleeding.

'There's a brick on the floor outside but I didn't see anyone, I'll call the police and check the CCTV, we've never had problems before' he said getting out his phone and walking back behind the counter.

Alice grabbed a handful of napkins from the counter and handed them to Charlie who wrapped them around her hand. 'Is it deep?'

'No I think it's ok, don't worry. Are you ok?' asked Charlie putting on a brave face because it bloody hurt.

'Yes I'm ok love, what should we do, wait here or what?' asked Alice puzzling over whether they could go or not.

The barista came back over to them 'The police are on their way, can you hang around until they've been as may want to take a statement, can I get you both another drink?'

'Can I have a bottle of water?' asked Alice.

'A latte please; think I need some caffeine' replied Charlie feeling a little bit jittery already but deciding that a coffee really couldn't make her feel worse than she did. 'Any chance we could have a look at the CCTV?'

'Sure let me get your drinks then come through the back and I'll show you, was probably just kids' he said making Charlie's latte and Alice took a bottle from the fridge. She got out her card to pay but the barista said they were on the house after the shock they'd just had.

The café door opened, and a female police officer came in with her male colleague. The barista went over to explain what had happened, then they asked Charlie and Alice if they'd seen anything to which they replied a resounding no.

'Ok let's go and look at the CCTV so I can radio in a description, they might still be in the area'.

They all filed into the back office of the café to where there was a computer which the barista clicked onto the CCTV and saving it down to the computer then rewinding it until a couple of minutes before the brick hit the window. The screen showed what appeared to be an empty walkway with the lights from the shop opposite, then slowly out of the shadow of the shop doorway a woman walked slowly but purposely toward the café, a brick clearly visible in her hand. There was no mistaking who it was. Alice gasped.

'Do you know who that is?' asked the PC.

'Yes, it's my ex-wife Sally Twist. She turned up out of the blue yesterday. She must have followed us,' said Alice stunned realising just what had transpired. 'She wrote me a letter and it said she was staying at The Churchill on Bootham'.

The PC got onto her radio and gave the information through to the control room, giving them a description of Sally and where she was staying. 'Can we come and take a statement from you in the next couple of days? If I could just take your details' she said getting out her notepad and wrote down their addresses and phone numbers.

'Are we ok to go now, or should we not risk walking back, it's obvious that we were targeted' said Charlie putting her arm around Alice protectively.

'I'd suggest getting a taxi home, but I would imagine that she's gone back to her hotel, there's a car on the way there now' she said.

Charlie got out her phone and rang a taxi firm, luckily being a Sunday evening, they were able to send a car straight away to meet them at the top of Coppergate. The male PC followed them up the pavement to where it joined the road and the taxi was there within minutes, whisking them away home.

Alice called Jen and Holly to let them know what had happened and to warn them of anyone hanging around and they said they'd make sure they kept an eye out for them until they got back, it all felt very scary and surreal.

'Do you think we should go and stay elsewhere tonight? Just in case?' said Alice to Charlie, puzzling in her head what was the best thing to do.

Charlie nodded. 'Yes, that's a good idea love'.

'What about my friends in Askham Bryan Lou and Henry?' asked Alice looking at Charlie for reassurance.

'There's no harm in asking' said Charlie.

'Ok, I'll go and give them a call' said Alice going out into the hall and dialling Lou's number.

The phone was answered by Henry, and after a brief hello he passed the phone onto Lou. Alice explained the situation and asked if there was any chance that they could all go and stay at their house for a few days potentially.

Lou of course was amenable and agreed to it readily but explained that Grace and Harriet were there that evening as they were there for dinner, but they'd all be very welcome.

Alice returned to the living room and nodded.

Charlie kissed Alice then went next door to get a few things together, clean and dress her hand and to take a few long deep breaths. 'Maybe we should have all stayed in the lakes' she thought as she went around the wall. She was anxious to get changed too as her suit was dirty from the café floor and the spilt hot chocolate.

Alice, Holly and Jen went upstairs and gathered their belongings, returning to the living room with rucksacks, small suitcases and laptop bags.

'I've called my practice partner as I'm due back tomorrow, but we've agreed I'll work remotely for a few days, I need it to be honest as still not back to full strength myself. I'm not quite ready to leave Jen either really, country air will do us all the world of good'. Holly explained.

'This is so understanding of you, god what a week it's been, feel I need a month on a beach to get over all this,' said Alice.

'You don't like the sun though remember; you turn into a lobster,' laughed Jen.

'True, ok a week in an air con room somewhere quiet and a bit warmer than here' Alice conceded.

They were all laughing when Charlie returned with her bags wearing jeans and a big warm jumper and puffa jacket.

'What did I miss?' she asked quizzically.

'I was just saying how I want to go on holiday when all this is over, it's been a rough few weeks hasn't it, but Jen pointed out I hate the sun' smiled Alice 'I turn into a lobster at the smallest of rays'.

'Well, we'll have to find you somewhere shady then won't we. It does sound a lovely plan' said Charlie smiling.

The four women got into Charlie's Jeep and set off. It was dark and beginning to rain as they got onto the outer ring road, and at one point the road was awash with rainwater making the going difficult and slow. Charlie was a good driver and negotiated the roads, with Alice giving directions towards Askham Bryan as they drove. Jen and Holly were very quiet, it'd been an awful couple of days, in a week that had been stressful and full on, yet here they were displaced from Alice's house, when all they wanted to do was to rest and take it easy for a while. What the hell had driven Sally to do these things was the question in every person head, but they just weren't voicing it so as not to unsettle each other more than they were already.

Charlie pulled into the lane and slowly made it down towards Lou and Henry's house which was lit up like a Christmas tree. Lou came out to join to meet them, closely followed by Henry.

Alice made the introductions as they unloaded the car.

'I can't thank you enough for letting us come and stay, it's all a bit mad' said Alice as they all grabbed their various bags and headed into the house.

'Don't worry, come in and tell us everything,' said Henry. 'Would you like tea, coffee, wine?

'I'd love a cup of tea' said Alice and there were other murmurs of agreement.

Grace and Harriet were in the living room and Lou made the introductions as they all took a seat on the various sofas and chairs.

'Lovely to see you again Alice' said Grace, 'Sorry I meant to call but work got in the way, hope you're keeping well, and Holly it's been ages, and you must be Jen, lovely to meet you'.

'Yes I'm good thanks. This is my girlfriend, no fiancée Charlie, we got engaged today, God was that really just today? It feels a week ago already, it's been quite a day,' said Alice.

Charlie smiled. 'Hi Grace, and you must be Harriet. Nice to meet you both'.

Henry came in carrying a tray with a teapot, cups and a jug of milk, putting it onto the coffee table. Lou poured out 4 cups of tea, and Henry brought in a bottle of wine and glasses in case anyone wanted something a bit stronger.

'So what on earth has been going on?' asked Lou 'All sounds so scary'.

'Yes it's been barking the past few day' said Alice, who then explained what had happened since they arrived back from Windermere.

'I wonder why she's come back. Didn't she leave you for someone else?' asked Lou gently.

'Yes she did, but they broke up, but it's been well over a year of no contact, and way too late to rekindle anything with me. I don't understand how she could just turn up like that and expect me to welcome her with open arms,' explained Alice.

'I bet it has. You can all stay as long as you need to, our door is always open you know that Alice' said Lou 'Do you fancy a ride tomorrow? I'm sure we can find rides for you all'.

'I'd love to' smiled Alice, Charlie she could see grimace out of the corner of her eye, turning to look at her she giggled. 'Not for you I guess love?'

'Er no if that's ok, I like both feet firmly planted on the floor, but I will happily give you a leg up' she laughed.

Everyone laughed.

'I'm working tomorrow and have never ridden, what about you Jen?' asked Holly.

'I'm afraid I agree with Charlie, now there's a first, horses are not for me I'm afraid' Jen replied.

'Well you could borrow Max again if you wanted' offered Harriet 'We're still looking for a house and Lou has kindly let us stay on for a bit longer'.

'That is so kind of you both, I can't wait' said Alice, whose face had lit up. 'What time are you setting out?'

'About 8.30 if that's ok? Are you working this week?' asked Lou.

'Yes, but I'm working from home most of the week, I won't have to go in until Thursday, hopefully we won't have to stay that long' replied Alice yawning. 'Sorry I'm bushed would you mind if I turned in?'

Charlie, Jen and Holly all concurred.

'Bless you, you must all be exhausted. I've put you and Charlie in the room you stayed in before Alice if that's ok, and Holly and Jen, I have put you in the one next door, let me help you with your bags'.

They all said goodnight and followed Lou upstairs. The room was just as Alice remembered it and after a swift goodnight to everyone Charlie closed the door.

'Omg Charlie what a horrible night, I'm so sorry you've been dragged into this, they'll find her won't they?' said Alice undressing and putting on pyjamas that she retrieved from her bag.

'I'm sure they will, she hasn't really got anywhere to go, it'll be ok love' said Charlie who had already dived under the duvet. 'Now get in here and let's get warm' she said throwing back the duvet.

Pretty soon they were both fast asleep, the outside world was silent except for the occasional owl hooting.

The following morning Charlie was already in the shower when Alice awoke to a light knock on the door.

'Come in' said Alice sitting up and rubbing her eyes.

Lou came in with two coffees and jodhpurs hooked over her arm. 'I thought I'd bring these up for you sleepy head. It's after 8'

'Really wow, I didn't realise the time, I'll be down soon, sorry to hold you up' said Alice apologetically.

'You aren't at all; Holly and Jen are down already having breakfast if you'd like some before we head out?' said Lou turning to head out of the room 'See you soon but don't rush'.

Charlie came out of the shower just as the bedroom door closed. 'Sorry I should have woken you, but you looked so peaceful and comfy. Let me throw some clothes on and I'll be ready' she said going into her bag and retrieving some clean underwear and a t-shirt.

Alice ducked into the bathroom with the jodhpurs and underwear and emerged shortly afterwards.

'Now that's a lovely sight' said Charlie 'Are you intending on riding in your bra lovely? Might be a tad nippy on the nipples'.

'Ha ha' said Alice diving into her bag the put on her sweatshirt and top 'What do you think?' giving a small twirl.

'Sexy as sexy could be, don't you feel nervous?' asked Charlie.

'Not at all, I've really missed it' Alice replied. 'Some of my favourite childhood memories all involve horses'.

'Then you should do it more often lovely. Especially if it makes you smile like you are now' said Charlie looking proudly at Alice, her eyes sparkling.

'I'd like that,' squealed Alice as they headed out of the bedroom and downstairs joining everyone in the kitchen.

'Morning' said Henry who was wearing Lou's apron and was stirring a pan of porridge.

Jen and Holly were sat at the kitchen island drinking tea and toast, Holly already had her laptop open ready to start work.

'Morning everyone, are you working already?' asked Alice.

'Yes, up with the lark this morning to crack on with my emails. You look the part this morning Alice' said Holly taking a bite of toast.

Alice did a small curtsey 'I'm so excited, thanks again Lou for offering'.

'It's a pleasure. Now help yourself to tea and toast, or porridge if it's ready. Henry?'

'Yes, all ready now' said Henry putting the pan on a skillet on the kitchen island next to a stack of bowls. 'There's fruit and honey to add if you wanted too, it's cold out there today'.

Alice helped herself to some porridge and blueberries, stirring them in so they turned the mixture a lovely blue, then scooping a delicious spoonful blew frantically to cool it down so as not to remove the roof of her mouth. Everyone followed suit and there was general silence interspersed with the thorough blowing of boiling oats. Lou caught Charlie's eye as they did the same and they burst out laughing.

'What do we look like, anyone outside listening in would think there was some kind of orgy going on,' said Lou.

Henry burst out laughing 'Now that'd get tongues wagging in the village'.

'It certainly would' said Charlie 'I'm going out to explore if that's ok, I fancy stretching my legs, any points of interest?'

'Well, there's the rather nice church and the pond if you turn left out of the drive, or if you turn right there are some public footpaths that are pretty and quite flat, depends on how far you want to go' answered Henry, 'I'm here all day so come and go as you please'.

'Wonderful thanks, am I ok to work upstairs as I have some confidential calls to make?' asked Holly.

'Yes of course or you could use my office as I don't need to be in there today, it's up in the loft so out of the way and has a good booster signal' replied Henry.

'Thanks Henry. What are you going to do today Jen? I feel bad abandoning you while I work,' said Holly.

'It's fine, as long as there's a working tv and a remote, not sure I'm up for a walk' replied Jen.

'Ok love, I'll check up on you at lunchtime, but text me if you need anything' said Holly packing up her laptop and work phone and set off upstairs to find the office with Henry.

'Right are you ready Alice, let's go ride!' asked Lou passing Alice a riding hat and jodhpur boots.

'Yes, I'm good to go thanks, are you coming to meet the horses Jen? Charlie?' asked Alice.

'Er ok, I'm not very good with them though' warned Charlie.

'You'll be fine love. Jen?' asked Alice.

'Think I'll stay where my toes are safe ta' replied Jen 'Going to find something on the telly' and she headed off down the hall.

Waving Henry goodbye whilst he stacked the dishwasher, the three women headed out to the stables.

25

Banged to Rights

Growing up in Leeds Charlie had only ever seen horses from a distance on school trips, or when on holiday pulling a carriage or rickshaw, so being up close and personal with these half ton animals was not something that came naturally. Rather than going up to the horses in the stables, she stood well back as though if she got too close, they would miraculously escape, and trample her to death. Horses of course are very inquisitive and immediately had their eyes on her, staring and snorting, picking up her nervous energy that poured out of her.

'Relax Charlie you're totally safe' said Lou 'They can't get you'.

Charlie laughed nervously, watching as Alice approached a stable door with a saddle and bridle hooked over her arm. Then like a pro negotiated opening the door with her hand and foot and went inside where the big brown horse towered above her. Then expertly she put all the equipment on the horse as though she did it every day of her life.

'Wow, you really know what you're doing. Very impressive' said Charlie inching towards the stable door now the wild beast appeared to be under control, although it kept snorting at her, with eyes on stalks. When Alice unbolted the door and led the horse out, she stood well back again.

Alice led the horse over to a large block, then fiddling with things on the saddle she stepped up, put her foot in the stirrup and up she went in one swift, easy movement. God that was quite hot thought Charlie, or it would have been if she hadn't been so terrified.

Lou repeated what Alice had done, followed by Harriet who appeared from one of the other stables.

'Morning all, Monty is rather keen today, this could be a fun outing' she said mounting the horse which appeared to be doing some sort of ballet movement on the concrete yard. 'Off we go, catch you later Charlie'.

And with that the three women set off at a fast walk down the lane, Alice waving goodbye as they rounded the end of the stables.

Charlie looked at her watch, it was nearly 9 o'clock and she knew the first job of the day was to ring the adoption agency and let them know that she was very keen to hear from her birth mother. Sitting down on a bale of straw in the small barn, Charlie watched the second hand on her phone tick round until it hit 9, then getting the letter out of her pocket, she dialled the number at the top. It was answered swiftly.

'Good morning can I speak to Judith Pearson please, she's the case worker for my adoption query' said Charlie with a slightly shaky voice.

With a couple of clicks and a little answerphone music she was connected.

'Morning, this is Charlie Lowther, you wrote to me some time ago in regard to my adoptive mother getting in touch. I'm sorry I've been away and only just received your letter. I'd be interested to be put in touch with my mother if that's still possible?' said Charlie rambling a little with nerves.

'Lovely to hear from you Charlie, yes we've had contact a couple of times with your birth mother and she's very keen to meet you. I'd like to arrange for you to come into the office so we can pass on her full details and then we can arrange for you both to meet. How does that sound?' said Ms Pearson.

'That sounds perfect thank you, and she definitely wants to meet me?' asked Charlie anxiously.

'Yes she's very keen, our offices are in Meanwood in Leeds, can you possibly come in on Friday about 10.30?' she asked.

'Absolutely, is it the address on the letter?' asked Charlie, knowing it must be, but she was so nervous she asked anyway.

'Yes it is, and if you've any questions we can help you either before or after the appointment just give me a call. This is great news Charlie; you can relax now' she said.

'Thanks, can I bring my partner with me?' Charlie asked.

'Yes of course, we'd want you to have someone with you, I look forward to meeting you on Friday, bye for now' and with that she rang off.

Charlie stood in the concrete stable yard feeling a bit trembly, she was actually going to meet her mother, after all these years. It'd been quite the journey to get to this point. She wished that she'd waited for Alice to come back before she made the call. After a few deep breaths she regained the use of her legs and decided to walk to the church. Having been raised by religious parents' churches held a reverence to her, but she also knew how she was ostracised for being a lesbian, and that she would probably never get married in one. Not that she was religious anymore, it was a strange sort of pull, the silence was grounding without the prayers and the vicar's input.

It was a short walk to St Nicholas's church and going through the lychgate Charlie approached the rather magnificent building, however the door was locked so she couldn't go in to sit in the quiet. Instead, she took a seat on the bench outside and breathed in the fresh country air.

The quiet was beautiful, she could hear herself think for the first time since leaving the lakes, this is what she wanted in her life, to open her door and not hear traffic and other people's lives being played out around her. She began to daydream about her and Alice selling their respective houses and buying something here. Waking up every morning to coffee on the terrace listening to the birds and Alice's beautiful voice. However, Charlie knew that was a long way off, but what a delightful dream. She realised that she wanted her lesbian happy ending. Taking her phone out of her pocket she checked the time wondering where the last hour had gone, she must have been sat there far too long and getting up headed back to Lou and Henry's. Ahead she could see three horses and riders coming along the lane and she waved and increased her stride to meet them at the top of the house driveway.

'Did you have a nice ride?' asked Charlie keeping well back.

'It was great fun' said Alice whose cheeks were rosy red, and her eyes were sparkling.

The three riders led the way down the drive, Charlie walking a fair distance behind away from any potential hooves. They turned into the yard and Alice did the reverse of what she'd done earlier, heaving the saddle onto the door, closely followed by a bridle. The wild beast seemed much calmer now and was no longer staring at her but was focused on some hay in a net at the back of the stable.

Alice came out and hugged Charlie. 'That was so much fun, we did a fairly quick lap because Monty was a bit fresh today, I haven't galloped in years. And the bonus is I didn't fall off or make an idiot of myself'.

'You looked magnificent riding Alice, very hot in fact' said Charlie quietly.

Alice blushed, then smiling took Charlie's hand and took her into a stable that had lots of metal and plastic bins in it, and what she presumed were feed buckets. On the wall there was a list of what each horse had and when and expertly Alice negotiated all the different containers, partially filling one of the buckets, then hooking it over her arm she took it to Max's stable putting it onto the door. Removing the saddle and bridle from the door, she took them into another shed and put them on a metal rack.

'What've you been up to? Did you enjoy exploring?' asked Alice taking Charlie's hand as they went back into the yard. Harriet and Lou were both repeating what Alice had just done and once the feed buckets were hooked onto their doors, they joined them, and they all returned to the house.

Jen was in the kitchen making tea when they went in as they took off coats and boots.

'Hey, it's John Wayne' Jen said looking at Alice.

'Yes, I'll be walking funny tomorrow for definite. Certainly makes you realise how unfit you are' said Alice rubbing her thighs 'I forgot that I'd muscles there, think I might go for a bath if that's ok Lou?'

'Yes of course, help yourself, I'm going to pop and see Grace for a bit, but I'll be back around 1 and we can have lunch' replied Lou, then putting on some trainers she went out of the back door.

Grabbing a banana from the fruit bowl Alice again took Charlie's hand and they went upstairs to their bedroom leaving Jen looking rather miffed.

Inside the bedroom Charlie got out the adoption letter. 'I rang the agency whilst you were riding and I have an appointment on Friday morning to discuss the next steps in meeting my mum, can you come with me?'

'Yes of course, where's the meeting?' asked Alice getting out her phone and checking her diary.

'Leeds love, but not the town centre, north Leeds so we can be there in 40 minutes, is that ok, sorry to put you out if you're working?' said Charlie.

'Well, there's nothing I can't move around a bit, don't worry, I'm so excited for you Charlie, I want to be there with you' replied Alice taking off her top and jodhpurs, her thighs were still red from the coldness of the morning ride.

'Do you want me to warm you up a bit, you look terribly cold stood there' said Charlie cheekily.

'I thought you'd never ask' said Alice taking off her underwear.

Charlie stripped off, her desire rising within her. Looking at Alice, who she thought was beautiful inside and out, stood in front of her so radiant, so tempting, biting her lip, teasing her from the other side of the room. They met in the middle, eyes locked in desire, knowing from just that look that they wanted each other quickly, quietly and exquisitely. They both knew that no foreplay was needed as Charlie took Alice into the en suite and closed the door.

Gently pushing Alice back onto the door their desire for each other overcame them, the kissing went instantaneously from gentle to frantic, hands moved swiftly and gently between each other's legs, with mutual gasps and sighs, stifled by the increasing intensity of lips on lips, gently biting, with tongues flicking in and out of parted mouths.

Charlie, unable to contain herself came first, her nails digging into Alice's back, her body exploding in bursts of pleasure. Alice followed so overcome that she bit Charlie hard on the neck, Charlie squealed loudly, partially in ecstasy, partly in pain.

'God, sorry' said Alice pulling away and seeing teeth marks on her neck. 'I couldn't contain myself, did I hurt you?'

'Yeah, a bit' said Charlie jokily rubbing her neck 'Are you feeling a bit hungry by any chance or are you a vampire?'

Alice laughed 'I am a bit, sorry, that was so hot Charlie, I hope no one heard us, I tried to be as quiet as I could, are we bad for having sex in Lou's bathroom?'

Charlie smiled at her then walking into the shower turned it on 'Nah, it's extra exciting having sex when you know you really shouldn't. Come in here and I will show you how much I enjoyed it'.

'Again?' asked Alice puzzled. 'Not sure I've got much left in me'.

'Well, I'll give it a try if you do too' said Charlie 'I want to show my fiancée how much I love her'.

'Well, when you put it like that, then let's get more wet' said Alice following Charlie into the walk-in shower where the noise from the water drowned out the noise as she made Alice come again and again.

Afterwards, wrapped in dressing gowns and towels, laid on top of the bed, Alice's head nestling into Charlie's armpit, she felt that she'd never been as happy as in that moment in the whole of her life. Despite everything that was going on she knew that this was the person she was meant to be with, the One. That lesbian dream of finding your perfect match, someone who had your back always, who would share your life's hopes and dreams. She felt thoroughly blessed.

Footsteps in the hallway broke them out of their reverie. From the depths of the ground floor Henry shouted that lunch was ready so they both swiftly retrieved clothes from their bags and dressed hurriedly.

As they descended the stairs they were greeted by the delicious aroma of garlic. In the kitchen everyone was already seated around the dining table and were smiling in their direction.

Charlie and Alice blushed.

'Ah there you are, we wondered what'd happened to you, thought you might have been sucked down the plughole' said Lou smiling.

'Sorry I had a shower instead and a rest, it takes it out of you horse riding' smiled Alice.

'I know' said Lou 'Henry has been an absolute darling and has made us all lasagne and garlic bread for lunch. Help yourselves'.

They took a seat and spooned the delicious pasta and garlic bread onto their plates, it looked absolutely delicious.

'Oh wow this is amazing thank you' said Holly 'Your home is lovely; we feel very spoilt'.

'My pleasure, I know from last time that Alice said that she's a carb queen so knew that I couldn't go far wrong with pasta' said Henry taking another piece of garlic bread.

'Very true' Alice replied, 'You've both been so kind, thank you'.

'Have you heard anything from the police?' asked Lou.

'Nothing at all, I think I'll give them a call after lunch' said Alice.

'Wonder if they've caught her yet?' said Charlie.

'I can't imagine they have, she worked in York so she could have just gone to a friend or maybe got a train as far away as she could,' said Alice.

'Call them now if you wanted?' asked Lou.

Alice took out her phone and dialled 101. It rang for a while before being answered.

Alice gave the switchboard her incident number and waited whilst she was connected to another department. 'Hi, I wondered if there's any update on if Sally had been found?' she asked anxiously.

'Hi Alice, no not yet but I haven't checked the system for a couple of hours. Give me a minute' in the background Alice could hear the hum of voices and typing on a keyboard. There was a slight pause then the officer said 'Ok so it looks as though she used her card at a cash machine about an hour after she broke the window in Haxby. Do you know if she knew anyone who lives there?'

'Er I'm not sure, I don't know where Emily lived in York, maybe she did?' replied Alice.

'Ok we can check that out and get back to you' they replied.

'Do you think we should stay here or is it ok to come back?'

'No stay there for a bit longer, it can't hurt if you're enjoying yourselves and your friends don't mind having the extra guests. We'll check out Emily and get back to you' they replied.

'Ok thanks,' said Alice 'Bye for now'.

Everyone was looking at Alice quizzically as she hung up and put her phone down on the table.

'Sorry, no news' she said, then repeated what they had said. 'Sorry to put you out but can we stay another night possibly?

'Of course that's fine, but we'll need to head out for supplies I think, do you fancy coming shopping with me anyone?' asked Lou.

'I'll come with you Lou' said Charlie 'Anyone else fancy it?'

'I need to be on a work call this afternoon sorry' said Alice 'Are you working too Holly?'

'Yes sorry, what about you Jen?' asked Holly.

'Yeah, why not, I can sit in the trolley, and you can push me round if I get tired' she laughed.

'I can just imagine us having to get the fire brigade if you got your legs stuck in the seat holes. You're funny Jen' said Lou 'Are you both ok to go shortly, I've a few errands to run too'.

'Perfect with me' said Charlie finishing off her lasagne and mopping up the sauce with the last piece of her garlic bread. 'That was delicious thanks'.

'Glad you enjoyed it' he replied taking his plate and opened the dishwasher.

Between them they finished their food and then helped stack the pots away until it was all cleared and wiped down.

Charlie grabbed her coat and put on her shoes, then kissing Alice goodbye followed Lou and Jen out of the back door.

Within a minute of their leaving Alice's phone rang. It was the police.

Alice headed outside hoping to catch Charlie.

'It's ok we've got her, and she's on her way to the station. She was at Emily's flat in Haxby, looks like she'd a key. Anyway, we'll interview her, and she will be charged with criminal damage. Could mean the end of her career' explained the officer.

'Really? I hadn't thought of that' said Alice rounding the corner of the house but Lou's car had gone. So turning on her heel she headed back inside after saying goodbye to the police.

A phone rang on the table. Charlie had left her phone behind. Alice rolled her eyes then dialled Jen. Again, there was a ringtone but this time from the hall where Jen's coat was hung up.

'OMG why can't people check they have their phones' said Alice out loud. The kitchen was empty so there was no reply. 'Thank god they found Sally'.

Shaking her head Alice went upstairs to her find her laptop and log onto her meeting, blurring the background so her students wouldn't see the bedroom. She could faintly hear Holly talking on her meeting down the hall and a dull murmur of Henry's voice too. All three of them being productive as the afternoon ticked by.

26

The Day of the Overthinker

Lou negotiated the country lanes at speed, her Range Rover taking corners and junctions so quickly that Charlie felt quite car sick. Her right leg hitting the imaginary brake on her side of the footwell. Speeding seemed to be Lou's forte, and Charlie wished that a police car would appear to make her slow down. She took the corner into Morrisons car park, the wheels squealing on the tarmac, practically throwing the car in between two car parking spaces.

Getting out Charlie rubbed her right leg, hitting the brake had given her cramp and she took some deep breaths to try and alleviate the nausea. Jen got out of the door behind hers and making eye contact she could tell that she felt exactly the same, she mouthed 'Wow'.

The three of them walked up into Acomb, Lou talking ten to the dozen about pretty much nothing, Jen was lagging behind, disinterested in Lou, and the atmosphere towards Charlie was noticeable. They trekked past the supermarket and numerous small shops, takeaways and charity shops, and then entered an old-fashioned greengrocer which looked pretty, but out of place amongst all the discount shops. The shelves were ladened with fresh produce and grabbing a wicker basket Lou filled it with paper bags of assorted vegetables. Charlie and Jen stood at the entrance waiting for Lou to finish, there was an air of anger around them.

Charlie broke the ice 'Come on Jen, what's up? I don't like atmospheres; Do we need to talk?'

'I'm not happy. All this marriage bollocks is happening too soon. Alice thinks she loves you, and I know you've been trying hard, but you nearly broke her. Please don't hurt my friend. Slow down for fucks sake' said Jen looking sternly at Charlie.

'I never wanted to hurt her, but I'm a different person now, I am trying really hard,' said Charlie.

'If you love her you shouldn't have to 'try' said Jen in a quiet but firm voice.

'Give me a break Jen, that's all I ask. Give us a break and let us try and make this work' Charlie pleaded.

'Right that's the veg sorted, now let's go to the butchers, any special requests or can I make a cottage pie tonight?' asked Lou, unaware of the atmosphere.

Charlie and Jen followed behind her, resisting the smell from the bakeries and the delicious smell of sausage rolls fresh from the oven.

Lou was totally oblivious of the spat that she'd just missed, and the cloud that followed behind her. She went into Acorn butchers and got mince, bacon, chops and burgers and a whole chicken, Charlie was stood well apart from Jen, she just didn't want to get into a full-on argument with her in front of Lou.

After the butchers they took a trolley around Morrisons and filled it to the top, Charlie wasn't sure how long she thought they were staying but Lou was buying enough to feed the whole village. Both Charlie and Jen offered to pay for the shopping, but she wouldn't hear a word of it, so they all bagged up frantically at the checkout and hauled the food to the 4x4.

The journey back was slower. They luckily encountered a couple of learner drivers doing the actual speed limit and therefore Lou had no option but to slow down and follow them out through Acomb, onto the A1237 and back down into the village. From the tapping of fingers on the steering wheel it was clear to see how frustrated she was at this slower pace, but at least when they all arrived back at the house their stomachs didn't feel as though they had gone through a spin cycle.

With the three of them, the unloading of the car was swift, they piled all the bags onto the island and Lou began putting things away with the aid of Jen and hearing Alice' voice faintly from upstairs she excused herself and headed upstairs.

Knocking on their bedroom door she heard Alice say come in softly.

'Hi love, god that was a bit of an experience, Lou's a mad driver, I feel a bit queasy, have you got any Rennie's?' asked Charlie going over and giving Alice a kiss on the forehead, then anxiously looking at the screen she saw 4 faces staring back at her. 'Oh hell sorry'

'It's ok my camera's off and I'm muted, they're just in a breakout room discussing the Assembly Rooms. Was it really hideous? There's some tablets in my laptop bag' replied Alice pointing at the bag in the corner of the room.

'Thanks love. I had a run in with Jen again, she really won't let it drop, I understand that she wants to protect you, but the woman's like a dog with a bone. Do you want me to leave, or can I work from the bed?' asked Charlie.

'No the background is blurred out anyway and there's only 10 minutes left now so do stay' said Alice turning around and switching on her camera and microphone again.

Charlie popped two tablets into her mouth then finding her laptop she settled down on the bed to look at her emails. However, she quickly became distracted with watching Alice working, listening intently as she guided her students through the rest of the session. Her knowledge was incredible, and Charlie could see how the students were listening to her every word, some just watching and others writing frantic notes. It was noticeable how many were enthralled by how Alice was describing how the building had been used in the 19th Century and hearing how important socialising and going out to be seen was important in upper class societies. Nowadays, on a Saturday York was still a place to go out to parade and be seen,   Charlie thought about the contrast, not only in the fashions but also in the social etiquette, something she'd witnessed in her bar in Stonegate.

She heard Alice saying goodbye to her students and she logged off zoom then wrote a few things down in her diary.

'Ok now I can give you my full attention' she said standing up and joining Charlie on the bed. 'They've caught Sally, the police rang a couple of minutes after you left, I called to tell you, but you'd left your phone here'.

'Oh crap sorry, I didn't realise, where is it?' asked Charlie looking around the room for it.

'It's in the kitchen, sorry I left it down there,' said Alice.

'What happens next? How long will they keep her for?' asked Charlie, the relief was palpable, but she knew it was far from over.

'I don't know, I guess we'll find out more later today maybe. She was at Emily's flat in Haxby apparently, so she obviously had her keys or something. I'd presumed that she would have sold up. Maybe it wasn't all rosy in her world after all' replied Alice frowning.

'What do you think happened between them' asked Charlie concerned, her brain started firing and she knew that she was beginning to overthink massively. 'Do you think she really wants you back?'

'I've no idea Charlie, why would she?' said Alice.

'Do you want her back?' said Charlie anxiously.

'What makes you say that? She blew it, I don't want to see her ever again. You can't seriously think I would?' Alice had raised her voice and looked cross.

'I'm sorry Alice, I don't want to lose you' said Charlie 'It's all making me really nervous'.

'Don't you trust me? When have I ever given you reason not to trust me? If the tables were turned Charlie, you wouldn't be coming up covered in roses would you. Let's face it, you've more form on that front than me' Alice said trying not to talk too loudly, but Charlie could see the anger in her face.

Charlie crumpled, holding her head in her hands and began to rock back and forth. She was totally silent, Alice didn't know what to do, she was so cross to be accused, but her heart also went out to the pain she'd just inflicted on her.

'I need to get some fresh air, let's get out of the house and go down the lane to the fields whilst it's still light. It feels awkward to have this conversation in Lou's house, with Jen ready to pounce every time she hears us argue' said Alice getting her jumper out of her bag and her boots. 'Charlie?'

Charlie looked up, 'I really don't want to if that's ok, you go and have a walk'.

'Come on Charlie, this is hard enough as it is, don't shut down' pleaded Alice.

'Look this isn't the time nor the place for this. You go for your walk, I'm ok' said Charlie, folding her arms, her face frozen with a glazed expression in her eyes.

'Ok, you stay here then' said Alice leaving the room and stomped down the stairs.

Charlie waited until she heard the back door close before she grabbed her keys, coat and shoes. Putting them on she went downstairs, taking her phone from the kitchen island and went out of the front door to her car and set off at speed down the lane. Not looking in her rear-view mirror where if she had, she would have seen Alice running frantically behind her waving her arms. Instead, she turned off and sped away towards York.

At the first opportunity Charlie pulled her car into a layby and got out her phone, ignoring the one missed call from Alice already registered on her screen. Searching she typed in AA meetings and seeing that there was one in the next couple of hours she headed to her house to wait.

By the time she arrived home there were more missed calls, both from Alice and an unknown number, she dialled Alice pacing the floor of her living room. The heating had come on but despite that Charlie felt freezing cold.

Alice answered quickly 'Charlie, what are you doing? Where are you?'

'Sorry Alice I had to come and find a meeting, I panicked and needed to get out, sorry for worrying you. 'I just needed to get out' said Charlie, her teeth chattering.

'Where are you now? Shall I get Lou to come and bring me? Are you ok?' said Alice anxiously.

'I just need to be alone for a bit and go to an AA meeting. I might stay here this evening depends on how I feel afterwards. I better go as it's in the centre of York and I'm walking' said Charlie firmly 'I'll message you later'.

And with that she hung up and put her phone on silent.

Sitting down in her armchair she burst into tears. She could feel all the old emotions and reactions coming back, the urge to go and get hammered, the need for oblivion. She knew that she was punishing herself but more than that she was doing the same and more to Alice, but she felt in a spiral and her head was simply out of control.

Leaving the house, she walked the 20 minutes to where the meeting was being held, arriving slightly early, she poured herself a cup of coffee and took a seat in the circle. People slowly filed in, repeating what Charlie had done either nodding or saying hello as they took a seat. The meeting got underway with a few words from one of the women who had come in last, then everyone was encouraged to talk if they wanted to. Charlie let someone else go first and listened to a harrowing story of loss and alcohol fuelled years and wasted opportunities. Charlie then raised her hand and began to talk.

She explained what had happened in the past few months, where she felt at the minute and why she'd come to the meeting that evening. Everyone was very supportive, and she knew that she'd made the right decision in coming, so when she left a couple of hours later her head felt clearer.

Once home she called Alice again. The phone rang and rang, and she panicked thinking that she was blanking her because she was angry. The feeling of vomit rising in her throat, her heart pounding.

Then she answered.

'Charlie thank god, are you ok? You hung up on me, I've been so worried. Where are you now?' asked Alice, her voice concerned.

'I've just got back home from my meeting, I'm fine and it really helped but I think I'll stay here tonight, I just feel a bit overwhelmed with everything going on' said Charlie not giving Alice an option of saying what she felt.

'Oh ok Charlie, if that's what you want. Are you sure you don't want me to come back?' asked Alice.

'No, I'm ok I just want to have an early night and do some writing if you don't mind. You enjoy your time with everyone, I'll come back tomorrow after breakfast' said Charlie walking up through the jungle into her office. The place where only the day before she'd been so happy. 'Have a nice evening, night'.

Charlie turned off her phone and took out her journal and spent a couple of hours writing down all that was going on in her head, trying through words to find her way out of the feeling of being out of control. It helped a little, the words flowing out of her, trying to find some level of why she felt this bad over such a small disagreement. Turning on her phone, ignoring the WhatsApp pings, she looked at her contacts and found the number for Dr Hanson. She knew it was late but hoped to leave a message to talk first thing the following day, but she answered.

'Hi Dr Hanson, I'm really sorry to call so late, I was just going to leave a message. I haven't had a chance to make an appointment with anyone and I've hit a snag already, I wondered if we could do a therapy session on zoom or call?' explained Charlie, her words rambling.

'Hi Charlie, I'm still at the centre as we had an emergency, we could have a talk now if you wanted, what's happened? You've only been gone a couple of days' asked Dr Hanson.

Charlie explained all that had gone on since they had arrived back on Saturday, it was only a couple of days, but it felt like weeks already of high stress and emotion.

'That's a lot to deal with I agree. What techniques have you tried? Have you meditated since you got back?' she asked.

'No, I've not had the time or the head space, it's been one thing after another. Sally coming back has really messed with my head, I'm so scared of losing Alice, but I know from my reaction today that it's all got too much. I just don't know what to do. I got so excited about being back that I proposed to her. I really wanted to, it is something I've been thinking about for a while, but her friend thinks I am making a big mistake and now I'm wondering if they're right' said Charlie, her voice quaking as she spoke.

'I think the first thing you should do is meditate. I can send you a link to an app to use that will help, but maybe you need to take a step back. Have you done any writing?' Dr Hanson asked.

'I've done some writing today in my journal and I've been to an AA meeting but it's this foreboding feeling I have inside, one that before I would have just got drunk and done something stupid, but today I recognised it and tried to stop it, but it just isn't stopping, my head is spinning. I feel out of control' cried Charlie, her emotions taking over.

'Ok, are you sitting somewhere comfy, or can you get somewhere where you can? She asked.

'Yes I can,' said Charlie standing and going into the bedroom and laid down, putting her phone onto speaker phone.

Dr Hanson then guided Charlie through a Letting Go meditation for the next thirty minutes, her breathing going from fast to slow, bringing down her heart rate and calming her brain. As it drew to a close Charlie opened her eyes and sat up.

'That was relaxing, sorry to have bothered you with this, I just didn't know what else to do' said Charlie apologetically.

'It's fine, you did the right thing, but tomorrow, first thing try those numbers I gave you and get something set up, you did right going to a meeting too. You've got this Charlie. Are you going back to Alice tonight?' asked Dr Hanson.

'No I thought I'd stay here' replied Charlie.

'I think I'd be inclined to go back; you shouldn't leave it as it is, because if I know you, and I think I do now, you'll start over thinking and you'll be wracked with guilt by 2am. Just get in your car and go back. I'm sure that Alice would appreciate it too' she said.

'If you think so, I just thought staying here would be better, shows how much I know! You know me better than I know myself' said Charlie sadly.

'You know yourself better than you think, now go back to Alice and I'll ring you later in the week. It'll be ok Charlie' and with that she said goodnight and hung up.

Charlie tried Alice's number, but it went straight to voicemail, so she sent a text saying she was on her way back and locking up, got back in her car and went back to Askham Bryan.

Pulling into the parking space outside Lou and Henry the house was in darkness except for a light coming from the kitchen at the back. Charlie went to the back door and knocked. A few seconds later Henry answered the door. He had a glass of red wine in his hand and was clearly inebriated.

'We weren't expecting you back Charlie, are you ok, you had us really worried. Come in, come in' said Henry slurring his words.

'Sorry to worry you all, I just needed some time out. Is Alice in bed?' asked Charlie.

'No the girls went to the Nags Head up the road, why don't you go and join them? Oh god sorry Charlie I forgot' apologised Henry.

'It's ok but I wouldn't say no to a cup of tea. I'll make it. I'm sorry to put you through all this on top of us invading you' said Charlie putting the kettle on and setting out a cup and teabag. 'Would you like a cup?' asked Charlie thinking he really needed something to sober him up.

'No I've got my wine already; I was just finishing off an application' said Henry returning to his laptop on the kitchen island.

'What are you applying for? Something local or further afield?' asked Charlie.

'I'm applying for a business grant as I want to set myself up as an independent financial adviser. I don't want to go back to London, and I need something to keep my brain busy, I'm getting under Lou's feet and pissing her off I think' he said.

'I'm sure that's not true. Lou should get a job as a racing driver; she is rather wild behind the wheel,' laughed Charlie.

'Yes she's rather erratic, I worry about her driving, but she seems to get crazier as the years go on. I'd hoped moving here she would feel more settled, but she really isn't. I don't think she's happy with me at all anymore. I don't know how to put it right Charlie' he said coming over to where she'd sat down at the kitchen table.

Charlie felt uncomfortable, she'd enough of her own crap going round her head and being around a drunk Henry was not helping.

'I'm sure she's fine Henry, she looks very at home here with the house and the horses, it must have been a big adjustment moving here after the excitement of London' she said trying to defuse the situation.

'She spends more time with the horses than me. And then she's in the art studio, I don't know what to do with myself' he said taking a big slug of wine.

'It takes time to settle into a new routine, maybe you just need to find a hobby too?' suggested Charlie.

'Perhaps, golf seems to be the thing all my London mates do. It's never really interested me. I feel such a loser. It's my fault we couldn't have children and she probably resents me but is too polite to say' Henry said wobbling about, his glass tipping over onto the table.

Charlie grabbed the kitchen roll and began mopping up the wine which had also dripped onto the floor. She was just holding the wine glass and the soggy paper when the door opened and Alice, Lou, Jen and Holly came in. Alice looked momentarily happy at seeing Charlie, but then her eyes fell onto the wine glass.

Jen, unable to contain herself pointed 'See told you the bitch would let you down'.

27

When Love Breaks Down

The kitchen fell into silence. Everyone was staring at Charlie with the empty wine glass, and you could have cut the air with a knife. The silence was broken by Alice.

'Have you been drinking?' she asked.

'No of course not, Henry spilt his drink, and I was just cleaning up. I haven't touched a drop, smell my breath, ask Henry!' said Charlie infuriated that Alice had believed Jen's accusation.

'Henry?' Lou questioned 'Is it true?'

'No it's all me, I knocked my drink over, Charlie's only just arrived' said Henry sobering up fast.

Sensing that there was about to be a major explosion in her kitchen Lou tried to defuse the situation.

'Can I get anyone anything? Tea, coffee? She asked.

No one answered. Holly ushered Jen out of the kitchen and upstairs and Lou and Henry sensing that their presence really wasn't wanted either followed suit.

'Alice, you can't seriously think that I would start drinking. I'm sorry for worrying you earlier but I just needed to get out to a meeting and to talk to someone, my head felt like it was going to implode. I came back to talk to you, but you jumped down my throat straight away' her voice raised and clearly angry.

'Yes but you'd have thought the same if you'd just seen what we did' explained Alice.

'No I wouldn't, because I've told you I wouldn't drink again, I promised you. So basically, you don't believe what I've told you,' Shouted Charlie.

'Charlie please don't shout' pleaded Alice. 'I can't bear shouting'.

'Then don't accuse me of something I haven't done! I came back to sort things out, but I think I'd better go, this isn't helping anyone' said Charlie sadly. 'I'll just get my things'.

'Charlie please don't go, let's talk about it. It was a misunderstanding, I'm so sorry, let's sort it out. Please don't go' said Alice tears appearing in her eyes.

'Sorry Alice, I just need to be away from this' Charlie said heading upstairs, packed her bag then returned to the kitchen where Alice was sobbing.

'Charlie please, things were so good, I don't know what's going on. Please talk to me or take me back with you and we can talk there. Please' she pleaded.

'I just want to be on my own. I'll call you tomorrow' and with that she left.

Turning to go up the hall she saw Holly at the bottom of the stairs waiting to give her a hug. She sobbed and sobbed, and the noise of her crying drifted upstairs bringing Jen and Lou down to join them.

'Has she gone?' said Jen 'I didn't think she'd react like that, I'm sorry Alice, I think I overstepped the mark didn't I. What can I do?'

'There's nothing we can do tonight Jen, let's get you upstairs, you look done in, I will stay with you if you want?' said Lou.

Slowly they went upstairs, Holly propping Alice up who's legs didn't seem to want to hold her up again. Going into her bedroom she sat heavily down on the bed, Jen bent down and took off her shoes, and getting her pyjamas out of her bag they helped her get undressed, as she slowly sobbed unconsolably. Once redressed she curled up in bed and Lou covered her with the duvet.

'I'll stay with her' said Holly 'I don't want her to be alone tonight, are you ok with that Jen?'

'I'm sorry I caused this. So very sorry Alice' said Jen leaving the bedroom with Lou and slowly closing the door. Holly quickly went to her room and grabbed her night clothes and changing quickly got into the bed beside Alice and just held her. Knowing neither of them would get much sleep she didn't want to leave her alone.

The night ticked by, Alice was silent, but Holly knew she was awake. They just lay quietly, the sorrow from the other side of the bed could be felt in the air as the hours passed by.

As the sun came up there was a knock at the door and Jen came in with two cups of tea which she put down at the side of the bed. Holly sat up and she passed one of the cups to her. Alice was laid with her eyes open, not reacting to her friend's presence at all.

'Would you like some tea Alice?' asked Holly 'Can we get you anything?'

Alice shook her head.

'What can we do to help, what do you need?' asked Holly

'I don't know anymore. What happened? What can I do to make it all better?' asked Alice quietly.

'I just think she needed some time out, it has been one hell of a rollercoaster since we got back, she's still in recovery and it was all too much maybe' said Holly soothingly.

'I'm so sorry Alice, maybe I should go and talk to her and apologise' said Jen 'If I hadn't been so mean to her last night she wouldn't have gone. Should I ring her?'

'I just want it all to stop, I can't bear these silences, her cutting me off as soon as there is something that crops up. It all feels so cruel. I've only ever shown her kindness despite everything. What do I do now?' appealed Alice but no one had the answer that she needed. Only Charlie could give her that and they all knew it.

'Let's get you up and have something to drink, and then we can have a think of what to do next, she'll probably ring you soon' said Lou reassuringly, passing the cup of tea to Alice who had sat up on the side of the bed. 'Can I get you some toast?'

'No I couldn't face anything, my stomach hurts, my head hurts, in fact I don't feel well at all,' said Alice.

Holly touched her forehead and sure enough she was burning up. 'Jen, can you get me my bag from our room, I think I need to check Alice over, everyone out please' she said firmly. Once she'd her bag she took her temp and did a covid test which almost immediately threw up two thick red lines.

'Well that explains why you're feeling unwell lovely, it's positive. I'm afraid you aren't going anywhere,' said Holly.

'God no. Damn it. I need to ring Charlie,' said Alice. 'Do you think she'll answer?'

'I'm sure she will, just ring her, she needs to talk to you, and she needs to know to test for covid' said Holly passing Alice her phone.

Alice dialled Charlie's number which rang a couple of times then was answered.

'Charlie? Are you ok? I'm ever so worried about you. I've just tested positive for covid, so you need to do a test too. Charlie?' repeated Alice as there was silence down the phone.

'Hi Alice, it's Di. Charlie's just on the landline, she won't be long. Are you ok?' she asked.

'Not really, is she ok?' asked Alice. 'I'm really worried about her'.

'I don't think she is but she's not talking much. Sorry you've got covid, guess we'll need to test now then?' asked Di.

'Sorry but yes I think you will' said Alice apologetically. 'I'd no idea until this morning'

Di shouted out into the void of the house. 'Charlie, it's Alice. She's got covid. Catch you later Alice' said Di audibly passing the phone over.

'Are you ok? I'm ever so worried about you' said Alice longing to hear her voice.

'You've got covid?' said Charlie coldly, ignoring what Alice said.

'Yes but that isn't why I'm ringing, I'm so sorry about last night, it all got out of hand. Are you ok?' said Alice hurriedly.

'Not really no, how could I be?' replied Charlie.

'Jen's so sorry for accusing you, as am I. Please forgive me, what can I do?' asked Alice emotionally.

'I'm sure you're all very sorry but what was said hurt me so much Alice. I've been trying so hard, and it all feels for nothing' she explained. 'I just need some time out. I'm going up to the lakes this afternoon for a few days then I'm in Leeds on Friday, that's if I haven't got covid. Oh crap that will fuck things right up if I'm positive'.

'I'm sorry, I didn't know until this morning when I tested positive. I was fine yesterday' said Alice 'I'd no idea'.

'You can't help it, I'm not cross about that, it's the rest of the shit show. Look let me have a few days away and we can talk when I get back. If you're positive and I'm not, then we can't see each other anyway. Hang on Di has got me a test, let me just do it while I'm on the phone,' said Charlie. There was then the noise of wrappers being opened and gagging as she heard her swabbing her throat.

'I hope you're negative; I don't want you to miss your adoption appointment. Sorry I can't go with you. I miss you, Charlie. I'm so very sorry,' said Alice. 'If I could take back the past few days I would'.

'I know you would, but you can't. All this crap with Sally, then having to go to Lou's and Jen being vile and then you thinking I'd let you down with drinking, I just need a break to think. I love you Alice, but it shouldn't be this hard so early on' Charlie said.

'No it shouldn't, I'm sorry. I didn't know Sally would ever come back, I've no feelings for her at all, I just want her to go away. I don't want her back. I never would. You're all that I want. ALL that I need. Nobody else. It's just you' cried Alice 'Please forgive me'.

'Let's just have a few days apart, just let me do this Alice if you love me. I'm sorry to stress you out but I just need to keep healthy, and this is making me not want to be,' said Charlie. 'The test is negative'.

'That's a relief that it's negative. I'm glad about that. Ok you go and do what you need to do. Will you message to let me know you're, ok?' asked Alice.

'I will, but I need to have some head space. I will message you tomorrow to let you know I've got there ok. Will take a bunch of tests with me but think I'll be ok. Take care Alice' and with that Charlie hung up.

Alice sat with her head bowed, staring at the phone screen, longing for Charlie to ring back, but she knew in her heart that she wouldn't.

'What did she say?' asked Holly coming back into the bedroom with toast and a packet of paracetamol.

'That she needs a break and is going back up to the lakes. I should've asked her if she was going to the centre again or to the restaurant. She's tested negative. I hope that she stays that way as she has an appointment at the adoption place on Friday. I hope I haven't messed it up for her,' said Alice.

'She might not get it; some people just seem to avoid it despite being surrounded by it. But don't be worrying yourself about that, have some toast and then take two of these. Lou and Henry have said that they'll look after you, but Jen and I are going home today. I need to get into the office tomorrow and Jen is much better. Sorry to abandon you lovely but I really have to go back into work and Jen just wants to be in her own bed. Is that ok?' asked Holly taking two tablets out of the strip.

'Of course. Should I just go home too? If Charlie isn't going to be there? Will stop Lou and Henry getting it maybe?' asked Alice.

'It's up to you, Henry has said he'll take us home in his convertible with the roof down in an hour or so. Will you be ok to take care of yourself if it gets worse? I think you'd be better off here lovely,' said Holly.

'No I think I want to go home. I don't care if Sally comes round again. I need to be around all my things, and I've a ton of food in the fridge and freezer I got for when you all came back from the lakes. I want to go home' Alice said firmly.

Alice took a couple of bites of toast then swallowed the two paracetamols, doing as instructed, then putting on the clothes from the previous day began packing her bag.

Holly came into the bedroom with a mask on and gave one to Alice. 'Thanks, I'm packed so ready when you are'.

'Ok will shout when all's set, here's some gloves too' she said handing her some latex gloves 'Put them on just before you come down'.

'Could do with a hazmat suit' smiled Alice 'Sorry for all the hassle I'm causing'.

'You can't help getting ill, you've done well to avoid it so far, I'm just going to finish packing and then we can get off' said Holly heading down the corridor.

Alice sat on the bed with her bags next to her. She didn't care if Sally came back and threw bricks at her at that point. She'd lost the woman she loved again, and the pain was just too much to bear.

Hearing her name called she put on the gloves, grabbed her bags and headed downstairs making sure not to touch anything on the way down. Lou and Henry were stood outside the French doors as they all left both wearing masks too.

'I'm sorry about all this, I hope that you don't get it. Thank you for letting me stay, I really appreciate it' said Alice 'I'll ring you later, thanks for taking us back.

'I've put your coats and some scarves to wear to wrap up and a blanket on the back seat because you'll get cold with the top down. God what a mess eh. Call me later. It was nice to meet you Holly and Jen, sorry it was under such peculiar circumstances'.

'Thanks Lou, you've been so kind' said Alice 'Bye for now. I'll return the favour one day'.

It was a bit of a squeeze in Henry's car, but they managed to pack themselves and their luggage into the space. It was a very cold journey back but thankfully there wasn't much traffic so in no time at all he was dropping Alice off at her house, waiting to see her safely inside before he set off again to take Jen and Holly home too. Charlie's house was in darkness and her car was gone; Alice's heart sank. In her slightly feverish state she hoped she'd still be there.

Alice's house was cold, and she put on the heating and put a match to the already laid wood burner. Putting her dirty clothes straight into the washer she set up her laptop on the coffee table and opened her emails. She knew she was really letting work down lately and knew with her promotion she really needed to knuckle down. So just as she'd thrown herself into work after Sally left, she did the same now. She felt shocking and the chills had set in and body aches, but she just went head on into work mode.

A rising temperature and further aches reminded her that she needed more pain relief and food, so raiding the fridge and getting more water she threw a ready meal into the microwave. Tonight was definitely a pierce and ping day.

Suddenly Alice heard her phone ringing from the living room so rushing through she got there just before it went to the answerphone.

It was Charlie.

'Hi, I've got to Bowness alright. How are you feeling?' she asked, her voice had a cold edge to it, not the soft kind tone that she usually spoke to her like.

'A bit shaky, I'm back home as just wanted to be here, just making some food then going to bed to try and sleep it off' replied Alice 'Are you staying at the centre?'

'No, why would I?' snapped Charlie.

'Sorry it's just with you saying you'd been struggling, thought you might have gone back there' Alice said, her heart heavy, it was as though Charlie was taking offence at every word that came out of her mouth.

'I'm at the West Lodge whilst I sort things at the café, I don't need any more therapy Alice, I just need people to believe in me, especially someone who says they love me,' said Charlie.

'I do love you, I honestly do, I'm so very sorry' said Alice terrified what she would say to her next.

'I'll let you know when I'm back home, hope you feel better soon' and with that Charlie hung up the phone.

Alice couldn't believe that everything could turn badly so quickly. What the hell was going on? She knew that accusing her of drinking and all the Sally stuff must have tapped into her fears of being abandoned, but why couldn't she stay and at least talk. Why did she keep running away? Looking at her left hand, her engagement ring still shining bright in the light from the fire, yet the spark had gone from her life with Charlie being so distant.

Forcing herself to eat what the label said was a lasagne, Alice took two more pills then switching off the lights headed to bed feeling utterly shocking. Before turning off the light she texted Lou and Holly to say all was well, then retreating under the duvet she laid down and prayed for oblivion.

28

Volcano of the Heart

Arriving in Windermere should have brought Charlie joy. The calming views, the fresh air and the lovely welcome she got from the owners of the café should have warmed her heart, instead everything felt sour and dulled.

Her two days there were busy, being shown how the restaurant was run, talking through design ideas and having minor disagreements when the elder family members pushed back at the thought of change. It was frustrating and the pain of the loss of Alice ate into her every single day. On Friday morning she checked out of the West Lodge and then headed to Leeds, opting to go on the country roads rather than the motorway, she wasn't sure she had the concentration for that. She missed the main of the rush hour traffic as she pulled into the forecourt where the adoption agency had a small car park.

Going into reception she said her name and was directed to a seated area where there were pamphlets about adoption and the walls had pictures of happy parents and smiling babies. If only it had been a happy ending for me thought Charlie.

She hadn't been waiting long before Ms Pearson came through and took her into her office, and once they'd exchanged pleasantries, and they both had a drink in front of them, the very efficient looking Judith got out Charlie's file.

'Ok so you need to know that your mum is very keen to meet you, very keen. She's written you a letter which you can read now or later which we haven't read of course, but I wanted to give you the full facts before you do. Is that ok?'.

Charlie nodded, she was so nervous, her mouth was dry, so she sipped the water that Judith had given her and tried to steady her shaking hands.

'Ok, your mums full name is Madeline Lejoune, she was born in Lyon, France but came here to be an au pair in the mid-1960s. Your father was Christopher Harrison who she worked for in their house in Chapel Allerton. We don't have any further details about him at present. After she gave you up for adoption she met and married Gerald Smith and had one further child Genevieve. She lives in York but is retired. She never ever forgot you Charlie and she is desperate to build a relationship with you. You were always wanted, but she didn't have any way to support you as she obviously lost her job when the family found out she was pregnant. Have you any questions?' asked Judith.

'I have a half-sister. That's amazing, so I have a mum and a sister. Does the sister know about me?' asked Charlie shakily.

'I don't know at this stage who knows what, but I think that she will either be talking to her soon or will have done so. That is something you can work through with her when you get in touch. She's left you her number and her address so you can get in touch' said Judith passing her a typed piece of paper with her mother's name, address and phone number.

Staring at the paper she realised she knew the street already; she'd looked at buying a house down there when she first moved to York.

'Should I ring her now or later? What's best to do? Does she know I'm here today?' asked Charlie.

'Yes she knows you're here. It's up to you to take your time to ring her, or you can ring her whilst I'm here, whichever suits you' said Judith gently.

'I think I want to ring her now, is that ok?' asked Charlie.

Judith nodded.

Charlie dialled the number on the paper, her fingers shaking on the phone screen she had to delete it once and try again.

The phone rang and within two rings had been picked up. A woman with a light French accent answered.

'Hi, can I speak to Madeline please' said Charlie softly.

'Charlie, is that you? Yes it's me, Madeline. I'm so happy you've called, I'm sorry it's taken so long to find you, I've been trying for years' she explained, her voice soft and calm with a hint of a French accent.

'It's ok, you've found me now. Are you well? I can't believe that you live in York, so do I. Have you lived there a long time?' asked Charlie.

'Yes around 20 years, I worked at Rowntrees for many years before I retired, but I now work in a shop in the Shambles' said Madeline 'If only I'd known you were there too. What is it that you do Charlie?'

'I own a bar down Stonegate, Valentine's, if you've heard of it?' asked Charlie.

'Yes of course, it's very lovely in there. What a small world. I'd really like to meet you if you wanted to arrange something. If you wanted to take your time that's fine, but wherever and whenever suited you Charlie' said Madeline gently. 'Where do you live?'

'I live on St Stephen's Road off Bootham. I'd really like that, shall I come to you tomorrow? Judith has given me your address, I'm happy to come there over the weekend or you could come to mine. Or is that too soon?' asked Charlie keenly.

'That would be perfect. Let me come to yours tomorrow, I go to town on a Saturday so I could come there afterwards. How does 11 o'clock sound?' she asked calmly.

'That'd be perfect Madeline. I can't wait to meet you' said Charlie shakily. 'I'll text you my address'.

'Thank you. I can't wait either Charlie. See you tomorrow, drive home safely' said Madeline and she hung up.

Charlie smiled at Judith, the joy within her emitted rays around the room as the sun came out and streamed through the windows. 'I'm going to meet my mum'.

'Yes you are, I can't tell you how happy I am for you, as are the whole team who have been working on your case for the past few years. I'm so glad that it went well. If you need any further help, you know where we are. Good luck tomorrow and let me know how it went on Monday?' asked Judith.

'Of course. Wow, I'm blown away and I have a half-sister too. It couldn't have gone any better at all. Thank you so much for all you've done' said Charlie shaking Judith's hand and leaving the office.

Getting back into her car she knew the only person she wanted to talk to about it was Alice. She hadn't called her at all since she left earlier in the week. Her finger hovered over her contact number then flicking it quickly she dialled it. It rang and rang for some time, and just when Charlie was thinking of hanging up it was answered.

'Charlie, are you ok? How was your appointment?' asked Alice breathlessly.

'It went really well, and I've arranged to meet up with my birth mum who's called Madeline. She's really pleased to hear from me. It's such a relief,' said Charlie.

'That's amazing I'm so happy for you. Are you coming home now?' asked Alice, Charlie noticing the anxiety in her voice.

'Yes I am. I should be back in about an hour. Do you want to come round? I think we need to talk,' said Charlie.

'I tested negative today so I'm just on campus, but I can come over about 2 if that's ok, yes we do need to talk in person rather than over the phone,' said Alice.

'Ok come round when you get back, will have the kettle on' said Charlie hanging up.

Her satnav told her that the A64 was heaving, so rather than battle her way through the traffic she opted to go back via Harewood and then called in at Tescos to stock up on food for her empty fridge and cupboards. Arriving home just before lunch she threw a ready meal in the oven and went up and showered before returning to the kitchen to eat and prepare for Alice's arrival. She'd no idea what she was going to say to her when she got there though.

The clock ticked on and just when she thought that time had stood still, she heard the awaited knock at the door.

Letting Alice in her heart that had been frozen for the past week melted when she saw her stood on the doorstep. Her blonde hair blowing gently in the wind and her complexion peaches and cream as she smiled at her in greeting.

'Come in, can I get you something?' said Charlie walking through the jungle into the kitchen.

'Just a tea for me please, I couldn't get a drink in the library so I'm gasping,' said Alice.

Charlie made them both tea and they then sat at the bench and table in the corner. At first it was very quiet except for the sipping of tea, neither of them daring to begin that difficult conversation.

Alice broke the ice.

'Do you want to finish? Is that why you wanted to see me? I know I've hurt you and I'm so very sorry' said Alice gently. Her hands gripping her mug to stop her hands shaking.

'Do you?' asked Charlie the sick feeling rising in her throat.

'No of course not, it was just a blip, but I don't know how to come back from it. I don't know how to make it right. Tell me what I need to do' begged Alice.

'I don't know. I think we've both hurt each other a lot and I don't know how to come back from it either. Maybe we should just stop now before we hurt each other more?' said Charlie.

'Is that what you really want?' said Alice, her voice breaking with emotion.

'I really don't know Alice. I love you. That I do know. But maybe it's all just too much too soon' said Charlie apologetically.

'I agree things have gone fast, but I don't want to stop seeing you. I love you so much Charlie, I truly love you' her voice breaking totally.

'I know. I do know that. How about if we just go back a bit. Start dating like we should have from the beginning?' suggested Charlie 'Just take our time'.

'Yes, I'll do anything at all, I just don't want to lose you' said Alice 'Please hold me, I can't bear not being close to you'.

Charlie put her arm around Alice, and they hugged for a while in silence, there were no words needed, the bond between them was so obvious. They both relaxed and let themselves just feel. It was the most relaxed either of them had felt that whole week.

'Do I dare ask what has happened with Sally?' asked Charlie bracing herself.

'She was arrested for criminal damage and charged, and I've taken out an injunction out against her, so she isn't allowed near the house nor to contact me. She's gone back down to Emily again, so I hope that's all over with. She'll probably lose her legal licence' Alice explained, the relief in her voice was noticeable.

'Wow, I wasn't expecting that. I'm glad you sorted an injunction. You must be so relieved,' said Charlie.

'I am. I don't understand why she came back, and I don't want to know. I'm just glad it's all over,' said Alice. 'I'm sorry but I will need to go soon, I'm staying over at Lou and Henry's tonight as they're going away for the night so I said I would look after the horses, do you want me to ask if you can come too? Jen and Holly are coming too'.

'No it's ok, I've a few things to do here if that's ok, Madeline is coming here in the morning, and I need to do some serious housework as not been here properly for a while' said Charlie really hoping that Alice wouldn't be upset.

'No that's fine, can I ring you tonight?' asked Alice.

'Of course, that'd be lovely' said Charlie, standing up and walking with Alice to the front door giving her another hug and a gentle kiss. It was enough for her to know that the affection and love was still there within her.

The day of cleaning kept her busy, along with a brief chat with Alice until bedtime. The house was sparkling as she ascended up through the jungle to bed where she slept more soundly than she had that whole week.

29

Mother Love

The morning dawned with Charlie's stomach doing cartwheels. Madeline was her first thought as she opened her eyes. She was going to meet her birth mother. The dream she'd held for so many decades was coming true. She could barely contain herself. After showering she heard her phone ping with a message from Alice wishing her luck which made her smile, and then seeing the time she realised she'd 4 hours before Madeline arrived.

Deciding what to wear took care of a considerable amount of time, she'd so many clothes, but opted to for a smart shirt and her black trousers. Her hair had gone a bit wild having not had time to go to the hairdressers lately, so she spent a while trying to arrange it into something decent, deciding that it was more of a messy undercut now, but it looked ok once she threw a ton of product at it. She wondered if she'd inherited unruly hair from her mother or her father. Hopefully she'd find out in an hour. An hour! God where had the time gone?

Soon enough it was almost 11 and she window watched waiting to see if Madeline could be spotted before she got to the door. She saw a short dark-haired lady walking down the street looking at house numbers and she knew immediately that this was her mother. She felt it in her bones, and a sensation of total relief washed over her. She couldn't wait any longer, so she went and stood at her gate watching her approach, raising her hand in welcome.

'Hi Charlie' came a voice from behind her. Turning her head round she saw Alice, Jen and Holly getting out of the car. 'Is she here yet?'

'Yes, I think this is her now' said Charlie smiling from ear to ear.

Charlie turned and waved at Madeline who returned with a shake of her hand also, a big smile spread across her face. A smile that was very familiar strangely.

'Er Mum?' came another voice from behind her 'What are you doing here?'

Madeline's face had gone from broad smile to one of shock 'Genevieve?'

Everyone stared at Jen puzzled.

30

Is it a Beginning or an End?

The five women stood in silence, mouths agape. Looking at one another hoping that someone would say something.

Madeline, who looked the most shocked leant heavily on Charlie's wall. 'I'd hoped to talk to you Genevieve after I met with Charlie. Can we all go sit somewhere and talk?'

'Er yes, come in' said Charlie stuttering, she was confused and looked at Jen, then at Madeline, the resemblance between them all was huge. The same mop of dark hair, not dissimilar to her own, the eye colour, and the big cheeky smile. Why had she not seen it before?

They all went into the house and into the living room.

'Genevieve, this is your half-sister, Charlie. I always wanted to tell you, but I didn't want you to judge me for giving her away. We've had such a fractured relationship; I didn't want to break it further' she explained.

'Charlie's my sister? No. What?' frowned Jen.

'Yes she is. I gave her up for adoption but always longed to have her back in my life' said Madeline quietly, looking at Charlie, then at Jen.

Holly, who'd sat next to Jen stroking her back could feel the tension building within her.

'I don't know what to say mum, how could you not tell me?' asked Jen.

Madeline knelt down in front of Jen and looking deep into her eyes began to explain.

'Because your father never wanted me to tell anyone. You know what he was like? You couldn't tell him anything. He bullied and pushed me around for years, I did my best to protect you from it. Telling you about Charlie would have been just putting myself and you in further harm's way. I'm so sorry'.

'But why didn't you tell me after he died? You've had years to tell me,' said Jen avoiding eye contact with anyone.

'Because we weren't getting on, I felt so distant from you, we hardly saw each other. I know we didn't react well to your coming out, and for that I can't apologise enough. I was blinkered and stuck in the past. Please forgive me. And Charlie, this isn't how I wanted our first meeting to go, but I hope you aren't too disappointed finding out Genevieve is your sister?' asked Madeline looking at Charlie. 'You look so alike'.

Charlie, who was sat in an armchair in stunned silence kept looking between Madeline and Jen. The more she looked, the more she saw herself in them both. Seeing Alice doing the same, and from the expression on her face, equally stunned as she was.

'I don't know what to say Madeline. Jen and I don't see eye to eye at all for reasons I don't want to go into right now. This isn't how I pictured meeting you. How do you feel that you've two daughters who are lesbians? I was a disappointment to my adopted parents. I don't want to be a disappointment to you too'.

'I'm not explaining myself well. I don't want you to feel you're a disappointment, neither of you are. I'm sorry that I didn't try and make an effort after your dad died Jen, I just wanted to let you live your life and not have to deal with me. I've made so many mistakes Genevieve, I'm sorry' said Madeline with tears streaming down her face.

'Mum, don't cry, it's ok' said Jen 'I don't want you to be upset, we can work it out. Can't we. Can't we Charlie?'

Jen was sending an invisible olive branch across the living room to Charlie who gave a brief smile.

'It'll take time, but I think it's good to start from here. How didn't I know your name is Genevieve?' asked Holly 'We've been together ten years!'

'Sorry love, because the name is part of my past that I wanted to leave behind. I never took you home, so it never seemed relevant. Mum, this is my girlfriend Holly' said Jen realising that her mother didn't know who was who in the room 'And this is Alice, Charlie's girlfriend. Hope that's ok to say, Sis'.

Charlie smiled at Jen and then at Alice. The relief on Alice's face to see Charlie not balk at being called her girlfriend gave her some reassurance that maybe it was all going to be ok.

'Would anyone like something to drink? Tea, coffee, water?' asked Charlie as everyone gave her their orders and she headed to the kitchen with Alice leaving Jen, Madeline and Holly to get acquainted.

'Bloody hell,' said Charlie. 'How sodding freaky is this. How can Jen be my sister? This is a total head fuck'.

'I've no words, this is just bonkers. I'd no idea her mother was French, or her real name. Bloody hell. How are you feeling besides freaked out?' asked Alice helping Charlie set out cups and what everyone wanted.

'I'm just stunned. How didn't we see how familiar we are? We even have the same eyes. Mind you she's been scowling at me for most of the time she's known me, so it's been hard to tell' laughed Charlie nervously.

'It's nuts. I'm so happy for you though, you've a family Charlie, what you've always wanted, the chance to have a family with a sister too. That makes me feel so happy for you' said Alice hugging her.

'I'm sorry we've had such a rough few weeks, well a rough few months if we're totally honest. Do you think she likes me? Or too soon to say?' asked Charlie anxiously.

'Of course she does, how could she not, you're lovely. She didn't run away when she could have done on the doorstep, it's all going well. Let's take these through and you can have a proper chat' said Alice taking two cups and Charlie took the others.

Whilst they sipped their tea they chatted amicably, Jen and Madeline were more relaxed and Charlie listened intently as she was told more about her mother's upbringing in France, about her birth father and his family and what had happened to her once she'd been born.

'It must have been torturous having to look after me for six weeks and then having to let me go, I'm so sorry. Do you've any photos of me from back then?' asked Charlie.

'I do, I've kept it safe all these years in the family bible as no one ever looked there' smiled Madeline. She took out the small black and white photograph and passed it to Charlie, she then gave her another one with Genevieve written on the back, they were almost identical. A thick mop of black hair, big cheeks and rosebud lips.

'Wow that's just amazing, how alike we are Jen, look at these' as she passed them over to her.

'Bloody hell mum, no wonder you had to write my name on the back' said Jen smiling.

'I've always known the difference, you were a quiet baby Charlie, so placid and you'd look at me for hours and hours with your big hazel eyes. Genevieve was different in temperament, she cried a lot and had colic, but I think that's my fault. Her father was cruel from the beginning, and I think you picked up on that. I loved you both equally, you need to know that' Madeline said smiling at both her daughters. 'What kind of childhood did you have Charlie?'

Charlie relayed her growing up story and what she went through with her adoptive parents. Madeline smiled when she said that she'd been a tomboy, but that soon turned to sadness hearing that she felt she'd been a disappointment to them.

'I'm so very sorry Charlie, you deserved more than that, a better upbringing. I hope that we can get to know each other, you and Jen are both my daughters and I want to spend what time I have left making sure you both know how loved you are. If you'll both let me?' she asked, looking at them both, willing them to agree.

They both smiled and nodded, there were tears in their eyes and Charlie swore she saw Jen's bottom lip wobbling a little. Madeline stood up and opened her arms to them both, so they went forward and hugged each other.

Alice's heart felt warm at the sight before her, Charlie needed this so much and she hoped that it would go some way to healing the hurt within her. She didn't know what the future held for them both but perhaps the healing from her mother would somehow help her to trust herself in a proper relationship.

After some time, Madeline said she needed to get back home but refused a lift back saying she fancied a walk and some fresh air. As they all waved her goodbye from the gate Jen linked arms with Charlie, the ice wall between them was thawed and the future looked brighter.

Taking hold of Alice's hand, Charlie looked deep into her eyes, closing in on the most delicious, soft and beautiful kiss either of them had ever shared, their link rekindled, their love strong and the healing had begun.

'I love you Alice, thank you for being you' said Charlie as they walked hand in hand back into the jungle, and into their future.

Authors Social Media

Facebook – Carol Leyland Author

TikTok - @carolleyland5

Website:- **https://carolleylandauthor.uk**

Printed in Great Britain
by Amazon